When the Sky Comes Looking For You

Also Available

The Thunder Road Trilogy
By Chadwick Ginther

Thunder Road

Tombstone Blues

Too Far Gone

WHEN THE SKY COMES LOOKING FOR YOU

By Chadwick Ginther

Published by Ravenstone, an imprint of Turnstone Press
Artspace Building, 206-100 Arthur Street
Winnipeg, MB. R3B 1H3 Canada
www.TurnstonePress.com

Turnstone Press gratefully acknowledges the assistance of the Canada Council for the Arts, the Manitoba Arts Council, the Government of Canada through the Canada Book Fund, and the Province of Manitoba through the Book Publishing Tax Credit and the Book Publisher Marketing Assistance Program.

This book is a work of fiction. Names, characters, places and incidents are either the product of the author's imagination or are used fictitiously, and any resemblance to actual persons living or dead, events or locales, is entirely coincidental.

Printed and bound in Canada.

Library and Archives Canada Cataloguing in Publication

Title: When the sky comes looking for you : short trips down the
    Thunder Road / Chadwick Ginther.
Names: Ginther, Chadwick, 1975- author.
Description: Short stories.
Identifiers: Canadiana (print) 20220272247 | Canadiana (ebook)
    20220272417 | ISBN 9780888017659 (softcover) |
    ISBN 9780888017666 (EPUB) | ISBN 9780888017673 (PDF)
Classification: LCC PS8613.I59 W54 2022 | DDC C813/.6—dc23

Contents

To my Uncles Ben

Benjamin Franklin Cox "Uncle Sandy"
and Benjamin Franklin Cherpaw "Uncle Ben."

Two great (or great-great- and great-great-great-) uncles.
Thanks for the stories, the card games,
and the memories.

Introduction

Ten years. TEN YEARS. TEN. Years. Ten years. As I sat down to write this introduction, the scene in *Grosse Pointe Blank* where Martin Blank reconnects with his high school friend Paul kept running through my mind. Paul's repetition of two words in seemingly every inflection, emphasis, and volume: ten years.

How has it been ten years?

Ten years since *Thunder Road* released. For me, I've been living in the Nine Worlds even longer. The bones of the Thunder Road trilogy formed in some of my earliest memories when I was first exposed to tales of high adventure. I came to storytelling through my great-great- and great-great-great-uncles, who shared with me a mixture of tales of their growing up on the prairies, and pulpy Lone Ranger and Tarzan stories they'd enjoyed in their youth. My great-great-uncle was more of a raconteur than a reader; one day, he told me he was out of stories, and maybe I should tell *him* one for a change. And I did—and I haven't been able to keep the stories out of my head since. Those early shared stories inculcated my love of adventure, which led, naturally, to comic books. Comics forged my love of reading early, and then that love grew into a love of science fiction, and horror, but most of all, fantasy novels.

While I'd always loved books and stories, being a writer didn't always seem like a realistic goal. Authors came from somewhere else. Somewhere glamourous. I didn't really know of any Canadian authors when I was growing up—I definitely couldn't name any from Manitoba, let alone Morden. All that changed when I started working in a Winnipeg bookstore in my mid-twenties. In hindsight, I realized they'd always been there: Guy Gavriel Kay, Tanya Huff—two great Canadian fantasists—and the first book I read by a Manitoba author, Armin Wiebe's *The Salvation of Yasch Siemens* (from Ravenstone's parent publisher, Turnstone Press, and for which I needed family to translate and explain some of the Low German jokes). I saw authors, many of them local, launching books seemingly every day, and I realized it was a path that could be walked. And so I walked it the only way I could, by sitting my butt in front of a keyboard and typing until something was actually done.

Thunder Road wasn't the first novel I'd written or submitted, but it was another first: the first one to get published. I started writing *Thunder Road* in September 2008 and wrote the first fifty pages while house-sitting for my parents. I'd recently finished my first (unpublished) novel and wanted to try something different than a multiple-point-of-view epic fantasy. I didn't have much of a plan when I sat down to write *Thunder Road,* and there was no thought to a series yet. All I had was a vague idea about a blue-collar guy getting thrown into a world of weird and terrible things. I also knew generally that I wanted that world to be our world, and specifically set in my home province of Manitoba.

I wanted it to be set in our world, not just because of wanting to write something different. I'd encountered the urban fantasy genre for the first time not long before I started writing *Thunder Road*. Authors like Kelley Armstrong, Carrie Vaughn, Patricia Briggs, Tanya Huff, and Jim Butcher (among many, many others) showed me the types of stories I really wanted to write, and read. Urban fantasy also gave me the opportunity to talk about some of the things I loved: movies, music, and folklore, while still keeping the other things I loved: swords and monsters.

It was perfect.

How to get the fantasy into the mundane? For me, the answer came in mythology. I've been reading mythology in general, and specifically the Norse myths, almost as long as I've been reading. That mythological education started with *D'Aulaires' Book of Norse Myths*. No, back up, it started a bit before that. My first exposure to mythology was *The Mighty Hercules* cartoon. Maybe you remember it? He had a ring, there was an annoying centaur, and the Mask of Vulcan. I loved it, so I did what any normal bookish kid in a hockey town would do: I checked out every Greek mythology book I could find until right there, next to *D'Aulaires' Book of Greek Myths*, was *D'Aulaires' Book of Norse Myths*. I checked those two books out of my hometown library one after the other, again and again. Eventually the librarian suggested that perhaps another boy would want to learn about mythology. She must have realized how unlikely her proposition was, as she never did stop me. And I never stopped. Those two D'Aulaires titles are two of the most treasured books in my own library now.

While I enjoyed Greek mythology, there was something about the Norse stories that stuck with me more deeply. Odin and Thor and Loki and all characters in Norse mythology felt more human to me than the Greek gods. They not only could die, but they knew when, where, and how they were going to die. It was fascinating. And, as a young Dungeons & Dragons player, I felt they definitely had the better magic items.

I decided to lean into those influences and give the nascent series a Norse mythology flavour. I've been reading about Thor, Odin, and Loki for so long that even when I'm not writing specifically Norse-inspired tales, elements of their myths and sagas tend to creep in from the sidelines.

Most people don't think of Manitoba when they think of fantasy, but I do. We still have wilderness. And in all that wilderness why couldn't there also be monsters? Manitoba has lake serpent sightings, Sasquatch sightings, and everyone in Winnipeg knows of at least one haunted building. The monsters and magic were already here, I just had to put them on the page.

And as the monsters were already here, so were the Norse myths. They were right there on the map. Manitoba has a rural municipality named Bifrost, Bifröst being the name of the rainbow bridge that connected Midgard—Earth—to Asgard, the home of the gods. Even the name Gimli, which is probably more familiar to you as the name of a dwarf in *The Lord of the Rings*, is right out of Norse mythology (and a lakeside town in Manitoba where some of *Thunder Road*'s action happens): it's the place where the survivors of Ragnarök, "the fate of the gods," are foretold to settle.

So I knew generally what I wanted to write, while also not knowing at all what I wanted to write. *Thunder Road* continued to grow out of two abandoned short story concepts from the earliest days of my decision to write seriously. (And this is why you never, ever, throw anything away. Eventually that story that doesn't work will click into place, or that character you cut out will find the story that does.) The abandoned concepts I used as my springboard were both Norse mythology influenced. In the first, the gods Thor and Sif lived in Winnipeg's St. Vital neighbourhood and were deciding to divorce; in the second, I considered that Jormungandur, the serpent that surrounds the world, was actually every instance of a lake serpent sighting. The Loch Ness monster in Scotland, Ogopogo in the Okanagan, and Manipogo in Lake Manitoba.

Nothing ever happened with these stories—only a few pages of each were ever written—but some of these early words exist pretty much unchanged in *Thunder Road*; specifically, some of Jormungandur's dialogue with Ted, Tilda, and Loki, and his description in Lake Winnipeg, and Ted taking a piss in the Osborne Village Inn, which happened in his condo bathroom, before he was Ted.

So I had those ideas in the back of my head as I started writing, but I didn't expect to use them, necessarily. They were a feeling of how I wanted to mix the magic and the mundane, the Nine Worlds and our world. More insistent was imagining a blue-collar guy facing off with magic and monsters. I grew up around mechanics and farmers. Something about that voice appealed to me as a writer, and it was one I knew I could capture. As these ideas jumbled together, possible plot points revealed themselves: a meeting with Jormungandur; a hitchhiking Norn; if it's set in Winnipeg, I have to take the characters to Gimli; *giants, there had to be giants* (because in Norse mythology, if it's not Loki to blame, it's the giants); post-Ragnarök. I wanted it to be post-Ragnarök for a couple of reasons. First: this way all of the stories that people might remember would have unfolded largely as they had read or heard them (or at least as I had read and heard them); I was taking nothing away from the mythology I'd loved as child. Secondly, in the many (many) times Thor had faced Ragnarök in Marvel Comics' *The Mighty Thor* series, what came after was always more interesting to me than the lead-up to a story I already knew the grand steps of.

The first scenes of *Thunder Road* I ended up writing were Ted's fight with the giant outside of The Pas, and his being forcibly tattooed in a grungy hotel room by a trio of dwarves. A scene of power and scene of powerlessness, a juxtaposition that would continue through the series. After I wrote that tattooing scene, I was hooked. I knew I had a book. I went back to the beginning to figure out who that nameless guy in the hotel room was, how he ended up there, and why he got those fantastic gifts. Loki wasn't even supposed to show up at all! Loki had died during Ragnarök. And then a stranger showed up in a bar to offer Ted a mistletoe boutonniere, and I immediately knew who that stranger was.

While I may not have had much of a plan when I sat down to write *Thunder Road* (I rarely do. I discover my novels as I write them and tend not to outline), I love music. The closest I come to outlining is making a soundtrack for my stories, picking songs that evoke the book's tone. An audio outline. I always write to music, so I noted any song that felt right, and skipped any song that didn't. In those heady early days of drafting *Thunder Road,* I started a playlist for Ted Callan, an unemployed Alberta oil worker, recently divorced and trying to start a new life in Manitoba. Because this novel was to be set in then-present-day-2008, I started to think about what Ted's musical taste would tell me about him.

When the list became too long and unwieldy, I whittled it down to my favourites and arranged them as if they were my chapter titles. Twenty also seemed like a good number of chapters, neither too short nor too long, and it was also about the average number of songs I could fit on a mix CD. I still make mix CDs (yes, I'm old).

If you've read (or watched) *High Fidelity* (last John Cusack reference, I promise), you'll know that there are "rules" about how to start off a good mix, and they don't differ much from outlining a tightly paced novel. Kick it off with a bang, up the ante with the next song and then change up the tone with the third. Songs in a good mix should flow from one track to the next—just like chapters in a novel—whether that be a smooth transition, or an abrupt switch to shake you up, there should be intent in the placement. Whenever I got stuck I'd go back to that soundtrack, take a listen and find a clue about where to write myself next. I usually found that even if a scene didn't work, the mood evoked by the song I'd used for my chapter title usually did.

I sometimes wonder how things would be different if I'd heard another song at a different time instead of "If You Want Blood (You've Got It)." Would Ted have tried to negotiate in that moment outside of Flin Flon? Would Loki have talked their way out of Rungnir's Hall? Or was the thunder-and-lightning-laced punch-'em-up always inevitable? All I know is I listened to that song on repeat until I finished *that* chapter, even though I'd just *finished* the chapter prior and I really should've been getting ready for work. (I've learned a lot of my writing problems can be solved by judiciously applying AC/DC.)

Here is the playlist for *Thunder Road* if you ever feel like listening along:

"When the Levee Breaks"—Led Zeppelin

"There She Goes, My Beautiful World"—Nick Cave & the Bad Seeds

"Riders on the Storm"—The Doors

"Things Ain't What They Used to Be"—The Black Keys

"Great Expectations"—The Gaslight Anthem

"Little Miss Fortune"—The Now Time Delegation

"Town Called Malice"—The Jam

"Welcome to My Nightmare"—Alice Cooper

"Until Morale Improves, The Beatings Will Continue"—Murder By Death

"Gimme Shelter"—The Rolling Stones (or The Sisters of Mercy cover version)

"Too Tough to Die"—Ramones

"Misery Loves Company"—Mike Ness (with Bruce Springsteen)

"Scary Monsters (and Super Creeps)"—David Bowie

"Big Mouth Strikes Again"—The Smiths

"Where Evil Grows"—The Poppy Family

"Beautiful Future"—Primal Scream

"This World"—The Staple Singers

"Fire and Brimstone"—Link Wray

"If You Want Blood (You've Got It)"—AC/DC

"Red Headed Stranger"—Willie Nelson

Observant readers will notice those initial twenty songs didn't necessarily end up as my chapter titles (sometimes the song itself suited the narrative though its title did not); but years later, that CD is still in regular rotation in my home and car. The playlists for *Tombstone Blues* and *Too Far Gone* do follow the chapter titles, and were what I used as my audio outline for these books.

Because I'm a pantser—as in, I write by the seat of my pants instead of plotting everything out—I tend to liken my writing a lot like driving at night with the headlights on. I'm not sure where I first heard that metaphor, but it's paraphrased from E. L. Doctorow, who I've never read, and it's apt for me and my writing. When I'm working, I can see far enough to keep going, but I can't see everything, and don't even often know the destination, or if I do, what it will look like when I get there. Other than the scenes of Ted being tattooed, and the giant fight outside of The Pas, I wrote the book pretty much chronologically from beginning to end. In about nine months I had my first draft. But a first draft is not a book. After I discovered where the book needed to go, I went there too. I drove to Gimli and Flin Flon, following the routes my characters took, absorbing that flavour, and then revising and polishing the text.

I quickly realized at the end of the first draft that *Thunder Road* could become an ongoing series. I had some ideas as I was writing about other kinds of trouble Loki and Ted could get into with some standalone adventures. These future novels didn't have much substance behind them other than notes of "a werewolf book," "a heist novel," "a ghost and undead book," "the Surtur Book." I thought nine books, given the subject matter, would be pretty nice, maybe each third book having some major development toward the larger series. A trilogy of trilogies. But not having a plan while writing the first book totally changed that plan. Near the end of *Thunder Road*, I wrote the line, "Hel is jealous and strong" and I knew that she wasn't going to wait around to get her revenge on Ted, for summoning the Honoured Dead, and on her father Loki for, well, being Loki. Suddenly those side adventures seemed like a delay of the book I needed to write next, that "ghost and undead book" that became *Tombstone Blues*. My high school D&D group had a running joke whenever I took a turn as Dungeon Master: "Welcome to Chadland, population zero. They're all undead." Maybe I just wanted to flood Winnipeg with ghouls.

After *Tombstone Blues* ended with my heroic trio fractured, again, I felt that simple standalone adventures would take away from the series' building tension. So both Hel, and then Surtur, showed up sooner than I'd initially expected, and the "trilogy of trilogies" collapsed into a trilogy, singular. A still-unnamed trilogy, led by a book with only a working title.

I *hate* coming up with titles. Maybe that's why I like grabbing song titles for my work. In my first round of submissions to publishing houses, *Thunder Road*'s working title was "Ink and Thunder" and it got across what I wanted it to, but I also knew that it was temporary. Prior to submitting the book to Ravenstone, hearing Springsteen on one of my extended playlists gave me the epiphany that the book had to be called *Thunder Road*.

There weren't any Winnipeg publishers interested in fantasy novels when I started writing. Fortunately for me, another local author, my friend Karen Dudley, who'd already had her mysteries published by Ravenstone, was working on what would become the Greek-myth-inspired fantasy novel *Food for the Gods,* and she told me that Ravenstone was considering expanding to include speculative fiction. I submitted *Thunder Road* along with the note that I had a first draft of *Tombstone Blues* completed as well, and before long, I heard back. Ravenstone wanted to launch their foray into fantasy with *Thunder Road* (and for the eventual *Thunder Road* edition of Trivial Pursuit, in a strange bit of serendipity I was offered my contract on Bruce Springsteen's birthday)! My writing group hosted a party for me, complete with a congratulatory apple pie and a bottle of what I've come to call my Victory Bourbon (Booker's, if you're curious), which I only crack out for finishing big drafts, publication days, or special award-winning occasions.

Just as the book needed a name change, so did my protagonist. When it came to naming Ted, I knew I wanted a surname of Irish origins to honour that great-great-uncle who gave me a love of stories, but I also didn't necessarily want a reader to immediately recognize it as such. I found Cullen and I loved it. It had a hard "c" sound and felt sharp to my ears. My great-grandfather was named Edward, so that seemed like a good way to honour him, too, even though Ted as a shorthand was there from the beginning. Maybe you see where this is going. Despite being a bookseller at the time, it totally didn't register that I'd just essentially named my protagonist Edward Cullen, one of the vampires in Stephanie Meyer's YA romance *Twilight*. Ravenstone was like, "You can't. You. Just. Can't." I wanted to fight the decision because I'd never read those books, but I was a bookseller and *knew* the name would be a shadow over the work. Whatever your thoughts toward the series, since I'd never read it, it wasn't something I wanted to reference, or pay homage to, or disparage. So it was back to square one. I kept Ted. No stopping me there. The character was already too firmly named Ted in my brain to accept any changes there, but Ted became short for Theodore instead of Edward. Theodore contained all the elements of "Thor," and since Ted was going to my giant-slayer, that worked for me. Cullen became Callan, because it was of similar derivation, it had the same hard "c" sound at the beginning, and was close enough that I could trick my brain into believing it'd been there all along.

With a contract in hand, I blazed along the Thunder Road in earnest with Ted, Tilda, and Loki as my co-pilots, discovering their story as they did. I grew as a writer as Ted grew as a character: I'd drafted novels before writing *Thunder Road*, but they were, like *Thunder Road,* first novels in what might have been series, and as they didn't sell, I didn't follow up on them. Once *Thunder Road* was done, and on submission, and then accepted for publication, I needed to learn how to follow it up. I'd never written a book two before, let alone finished a series. But now I was committed. (A contract will do that.)

Thunder Road wasn't my first experience with editorial. I'd published a couple of stories by the time my first substantive edit letter came in, and had revised reviews and articles according to editorial feedback in the past. But this was my first real novel revision, and it felt huge. A larger task, somehow, than actually writing the book. The thing I remember most strongly was my editor Wayne Tefs' note about the rune-reading chapter of the book. "You need to cut 3000 words here." To which I thought, "*That's the whole chapter!*" But once I got over the initial shock, and dug more deeply into Wayne's suggestions, I saw the framework he'd left me explaining exactly how to do it. I still didn't end up cutting 3000 words, it was more like 1200, but that'd probably been what he'd wanted from me in the first place. Had Wayne said 1200 words, I wouldn't have been as ruthless as I needed to tighten that chapter's pacing.

I probably have the least to say about writing *Tombstone Blues*. Sorry, but it's not to give it a case of middle-book syndrome. Despite never having written a second book in a series, *Tombstone Blues* was the easiest book I've ever drafted (which is probably why I joke it's my favourite). Start to finish, *Tombstone Blues*' first draft took barely two months. The story arrived whole in my brain, and my typing fingers raced my brain trying to transcribe it before I lost it. I drafted *Tombstone Blues* when *Thunder Road*'s first draft was barely cold; the book was that insistent.

My song-title outline had worked so well that when I started writing *Tombstone Blues*, I did it again. Songs that had fit Ted but not the narrative of *Thunder Road* bubbled to the top of *Tombstone Blues*' playlist with their own story to tell.

Whereas I'd struggled to find the right title for *Thunder Road*, *Tombstone Blues,* by contrast, always felt like the right title for book two. Oh, I briefly entertained "Hell's Bells" (but kickass paranormal romance and YA author Jackie Kessler beat me to using that song) and "Highway to Hell," but neither song felt quite right. Maybe because for accuracy I'd wanted to drop an "l" and turn Hell into Hel, and I'm not a fan of pun titles.

But while *Tombstone Blues* had been easy to name and easy to draft, it required more substantial changes structurally and narratively before I was willing to submit it. After I finished work on *Thunder Road* edits, *Tombstone Blues* changed substantially, to better match where I'd left the characters' relationships in *Thunder Road*. I pulled apart swaths of that easy first draft to fix it, and sadly—but necessarily—downplayed Jenny Hildebrandt's role in the series; but in the long run, I think it made things stronger for my big three, and especially for Ted. Since I'd never written a book two before, I went and read a bunch of second books in series, some I'd already read, some I hadn't, to try and consciously absorb how the book needed to proceed, and how to backfill information from a previous book. I even revisited Wayne's first substantive edit letter for *Thunder Road* to ensure I didn't make any of the same errors in *Tombstone Blues*. I was pretty chuffed at how he'd noticed I hadn't revisited those flaws, then he promptly told me what new errors I'd made. But that's writing, isn't it? Every book and every story is its own challenge; you never learn how to write *novels* or *stories*. You learn how to write *that* novel, or *that* story.

Too Far Gone was probably the hardest thing I've ever written, and it's definitely the work I'm most proud of. Why? It wasn't just the writing. Everything seemed to be going against me (yes, even the title). *Too Far Gone* coincided with an arm injury that kept me from typing just when I'd been about to start drafting. My injury was followed by a change in day job and complete upending of the writing schedule that'd served me quite well for years. But the book needed to come out, and for that to happen apparently I needed to write it, so I muddled through as best I could. I wrote the entire first draft on the bus, slowly, by hand, about 100-500 words at a time, in no particular order, and then, after transcribing it, had to stitch it together and make it cohesive.

I was really struggling with making the book work, and not only with physically writing it. The means I'd envisioned to get to the end of the series wasn't working. I felt pulled in the wrong directions. And, as *Thunder Road* and *Tombstone Blues* had been drafted so long prior to working on *Too Far Gone,* it was the longest I'd been away from Ted's voice—from any character's voice—and then tried to return and reclaim it. I'd also drafted a couple other novels and numerous short stories, all with other characters, in between *Tombstone Blues* and *Too Far Gone.* I was complaining about how it was going to my friend Samantha Beiko, who also happens to be a kickass editor and author, and she gave me the advice that carried me through the finale in her typically bombastic way: "Kill everyone. Burn it all down. *Scorched earth, motherfucker.* It's *your* series. End it however you want."

Obviously, I didn't kill everyone. But her words were so freeing in the moment, and they got that first draft done. I found Ted's voice again in the vulgar. You could actually see in the first draft when I'd been writing Ted for a while, as Ted's profanity would settle back down to what was normal for the series, and then you'd come to the start of a new writing session, and be greeted with a shotgun blast of "fucks" indicating when I'd been away from writing for a while. (That first draft also received my favourite editorial note of all time, Ravenstone told me, "This book contains a staggering amount of profanity." I *really* wanted to use that as a pull quote.)

Because of the fractured nature of how I drafted the book, it took me the longest to write, and then the longest to revise of any novel I'd written. I called my first draft complete once I reached 100,000 words of scenes. I had three major timeframes of reference. Before Ted reached Edmonton, before Surtur attacked Edmonton, and the big battle. Once I had everything shuffled and ordered into those categories, I stitched all the words together. Many ideas I'd held about the book for a long time didn't make the final cut. A prologue set on the Icelandic volcanic island of Surtsey was cut during the first editorial pass to trim the book's length. As was my take on a *Lord-of-the-Rings*-inspired "Council of Elrond" chapter where Ted tried to get his allies in order before leaving for Edmonton which I'd jokingly called "The Council of Humpty's." There was even a time travel element at one point! But in the end, it was better to just get Ted on the road to his doom.

Since *Too Far Gone* was set in Edmonton, not Winnipeg, I also needed to get on the road. I'd previously visited Edmonton a few times, and knew it well enough to block out some of the scenes I needed, but it was no substitute for an official research trip.

While I was in Edmonton, I kept a detailed journal of everything I did, saw, and especially what was happening with the weather (relevant when your hero can control the weather but is trying to remain incognito). Would I have thought of including the Fringe Festival as background, or the Perseid meteor shower otherwise? Probably not. Having the hero's fight with a fire giant looming when the city was under the grips of a heat wave may have been out of my control, but it also really worked. Not all of this background made it into the text, of course, but it definitely informed my writing.

I took tons of photos for reference, and used them as a slideshow while I wrote. Once I was done with locations, and back home polishing my next draft, an old familiar problem reared its head. What to title the book? I'd been calling the work-in-progress "Play With Fire" for almost as long as I've been writing about Ted Callan, adding occasional notes and scenes for the future as I wrote the first two books, but I also knew I wanted to change that title.

Ravenstone wasn't keen on "Play With Fire" either, and not just because it broke the "T" portion of the established title pattern. *Thunder Road. Tombstone Blues.* Both song titles starting with "T," both three beats, and an alphabetical progression. As I was writing a trilogy, and I wanted the titles to all feel of a piece, I found myself a bit stuck.

Or, to steal a phrase from Ted: "Well, shit."

I powered through the dictionary looking for a word to kick off the title. I haunted song lyrics search sites. "Songs about weather." "Songs about fire." "Songs about fate." Any titles I found that might've worked weren't songs that I liked. I searched the discographies of musicians I liked. Most proved unhelpful, or teased me with a title that would hit all of the elements of the pattern but wouldn't work thematically for the story I wanted to tell. "Tumbling Dice," I'm looking at you.

Eventually, between myself, Ravenstone, and Neil Young, we finally thought we had it. More importantly, when I said it aloud for the first time, and in the context of being the title of book three, it rolled off my tongue. We all knew it was right.

Wayne Tefs passed away in September 2014. He never got to read *Too Far Gone*. His death was hard. I felt like he really understood what I was trying to do with the series, and I'd enjoyed working with him so damn much. Michael Matheson took over on editorial and they helped me hone the 135,000-word *Too Far Gone* monster down to a sleek, yet hefty 115,000—to date, still my longest work. I read from Wayne's story collection *Meteor Storm* (the story was "The Ringer") and then a short bit from *Too Far Gone* at Wayne's memorial during the Winnipeg International Writers Festival. I hope I did Wayne's piece justice.

Despite all the struggles with that book, the trilogy reached the end, even if it was a bear right up to the launch (I got food poisoning *and* had to rebuild my backyard fence following a storm the week before launch day) *Too Far Gone* was the end. Thunder Road was done. I'd known *how* I wanted the series to end for a long time—long before I ever sat down to start writing *Too Far Gone.* Long before I decided to make *Thunder Road* a trilogy, and not an open-ended series, or the nine-book trilogy of trilogies. I even knew years before I typed them what the final words of the trilogy would be. I'm not going to lie: it was a bittersweet, and somewhat melancholy affair for me to wrap things up. Odd, considering I write about a foul-mouthed thug who professionally punches giants, but it was. Which is probably why I kept writing stories set in this world.

What do you do after you've saved the world? I contended with this question both before and after I finished the trilogy. If *Star Wars* and D&D have taught me anything, it's that worlds don't stay saved for very long. It's a constant struggle to keep moving forward to something better.

And because "The End" is never really the end, here we are with another book in the series, something a little different. *When the Sky Comes Looking for You: Short Trips Down the Thunder Road.*

Short stories gave me an excuse to try some new characters and some new things with the series. One thing I've never liked is mixing first- and third-person perspectives in the same story, so short fiction allowed me to tell different types of stories with different characters that mightn't have fit in the Thunder Road novels proper. Sometimes when you write the way I do, you build up something to understand it better, but it doesn't fit into the story you're working on at the time. So it gets cut. Even material that didn't make it into the novels was important in shaping the trilogy, and in the cases of the stories in this collection, so important to me, I felt compelled to give that material a story of its own. I used those bones to shape something new, and collected those pieces here. I'm not saying my partially-envisioned Thunder Road werewolf book would've looked exactly like "Runt of the Litter," but the concept of using shapeshifting descendants of Fenrir as my "werewolves" was definitely the plan. Maybe someday I'll get to that heist novel too …

This collection doesn't have a playlist, per se. But "Far Gone and Out," "Golden Goose," and "Ballroom Blitz" are all song titles, as is this collection's title, "When the Sky Comes Looking for You," and yes, I listened to those songs a whole bunch. While I can't recall what else I was listening to at the time of drafting each individual story, I'm glad this book doesn't fit neatly in the same mould as the trilogy. Because it is different, and not only informed by Ted's voice.

Rather than just putting everything Thunder Road into one book, we curated all my materials into a collection we felt best added to the series. My hope is this will give you new insight into some old favourite characters and find some new ones to love.

Because, while the Thunder Road *trilogy* may be finished, I'm not sure the Thunder Road *series* ever will be. I've published several Thunder Road short stories. "Runt of the Litter," reprinted in this collection, was the first of them, but there were more, and there will be more. There are dozens of other tales from different corners of Thunder Road waiting to be finished. With or without Ted Callan, I doubt I'll ever tire of these misfits, or the world they helped create, this world I keep returning to. Ted Callan may not be the *star* of this book, because, for the moment, his larger story is done; and I think he got the ending he deserved, even if he's still out there, being a troublemaker, and having adventures. Nevertheless, the big guy does keep yelling in my ear to get back to him. And maybe I will.

Whenever Loki gets him into enough trouble to justify a full-length book, anyway.

The Thunder Road series has been good to me. From invitations to festivals and conferences, to speaking at schools and universities, to artists gifting me work inspired by my words—none of that might have happened if I hadn't written that first book in this series. Going on book tours and appearing at conferences meant more to me than just selling books. It also became an excuse for reconnecting with old friends, and reinforcing new friendships won at conventions. Some folks I hadn't seen in years welcomed me into their homes, as did some folks I'd just met.

So much has happened in my life because of these books—and because of readers like you, because a book or a story hasn't done its job until it has been read. So my work is done. I'm going to crack out the Victory Bourbon. Your job is just beginning.

When the Sky Comes Looking for You is a collection of stories from magazines, anthologies, convention exclusives, and some new material. Just for you.

Happy reading.
Chadwick Ginther

When the Sky Comes Looking For You

All Cats Go to Valhalla

"Well, we're fucked," Kills-the-Sky muttered at the far-off storm. If only his name meant he had the power to rule a storm, like Thor, instead of being a noted bird hunter.

A soft mew from behind him, and Kills-the-Sky turned to see a ginger cat named Sunchaser. "When will we make landfall?" she asked.

"Soon," he lied. His tail entwined with hers, his green eyes met her golden ones. "Land is on the other side of those clouds."

Satisfied with the lie, Sunchaser wandered off, their tails clinging a moment before she was gone. "I'll tell the others."

Kills-the-Sky looked back to the seething clouds. "So totally fucked." They were a long way from home, and further from safety. Once that dark bank of clouds reached the ship it would capsize, and then they'd all drown.

That is, if the nightmare didn't get them first. After the nightmare had killed the cats' human servants, it had seemed unconcerned with them—perhaps cats didn't dream the way humans did?—but there was no telling how long that would continue.

While the hold had normally been filled with trade goods or war gear, this time there was only their servants' provisions and the box that had imprisoned their nightmares. Kills-the-Sky and the cats guarded the hold from rats. The hold was their purview, and, as the leader of the ship's cats, *his* purview. And he had failed. Failed so mightily. He stared into the hold at the opened chest and hissed his annoyance into the wind.

Kills-the-Sky didn't know how the nightmare had escaped her imprisonment and it didn't matter. A number of cats had begged Kills-the-Sky to open the box during the voyage, so they could sleep in it, or play with whatever was inside, but he'd held to his duty. They protected the stores from rats and he'd done the same for this prison. For all the good it had done.

With their servants dead, Kills-the-Sky and his cats would die, too. No cat could tow the oars, or cut into the wind with the sail. Even if the cats knew how to sail the ship, it'd be no help. Great rends marred the square woolen cloth from the top to the bottom, as if Jólakötturinn, the Yule Cat, had shredded it in a fit of pique. Cats were as adept with a needle and thread as they were at manning the oars. Frayed fabric was a toy, not something to mend.

Kills-the-Sky licked sea salt from his fur, feigning nonchalance to the other cats roaming on their listing vessel. They looked up to him. They needed him.

But they were fucked.

Kills-the-Sky's ear twitched. The barest whisper of a padded foot over wood from behind him.

"Quite the pickle," said a tortiseshell named Fairweather, watching the sky from the oarsman's seat beside Kills-the-Sky.

Kills-the-Sky didn't catch the reference, but he gathered the cat's context. "One could say that."

"So stoic." She patted Kills-the-Sky. "We both know we're fucked."

Kills-the-Sky hissed and clawed at Fairweather. She dodged the swipe and didn't retaliate. Her back was up, fur on end, and her tail swished warily, teeth bared in an incongruous smug smile. She was the most recent cat to join them on the ship, and a bit odd, which, among this crew, was saying something.

"Do cats go to Valhalla?" asked Fairweather, her mismatched eyes glittering, and her anger gone like a summer squall. "Inquiring for a friend."

"*You* won't," said Kills-the-Sky. "Since you're so afraid to fight."

"There are some fights one can't win," Fairweather said. "Even you."

Kills-the-Sky didn't answer. Still, Fairweather's question prickled Kills-the-Sky's whiskers. A question he couldn't answer. A question he wasn't certain he *wanted* answered. Valhalla didn't sound like the place for a cat to him. Odin was more of a dog man anyway, and the less said of Thor and his goats, the better, but there *were* ways into the Hall of the Great Servants, if one dared. At least Kills-the-Sky had been told so by his grandsire, Sleeps-with-Swords. Better, the old cat had said, were the ways into Fólkvangr, the realm of Freyja. Freyja loved cats. To the skogkatts, those felines with the divine in them, *she* was the first among the Great Servants, for she paid them their due. To laze in the bright sun of her hall, being doted upon, was far superior in Kills-the-Sky's opinion to dodging the spit and kicks of Odin's *einherjar*.

"You're not going to bring up your bloody grandsire again, are you?" Fairweather's playful teasing took on an edge of waiting violence. "*My grandsire* was Sleeps-with-Swords. *My grandsire* climbed to Asgard. *My grandsire* was a skogkatt. *My grandsire* fucked Freyja."

Kills-the-Sky's muzzle twitched. He'd never said that last one. Maybe his grandsire had, but never to him. Fairweather had a surprising amount of disdain for a cat who was dead long before she was born. Stranger, she had even more disdain for Freyja and the other Great Servants.

Fairweather must've been satisfied to have had the last word. She'd disappeared from the deck while Kills-the-Sky hunted a retort.

A cloud glided over the sun and an old woman appeared on the deck beside him in the passing shadow. Kills-the-Sky blinked and the membranes flicked over his eyes, showing the woman for what she was, a nightmare. A mara. Her dirty, cracked nails dripped blood. Lank grey hair hung to her waist, covering a distended belly full of the fears of dead sailors. The rest of her body gaunt, yet corded with ropey muscle. Flashing wild eyes, a sweaty sheen over her skin, moist beads tracing the cavernous lines of her face, as if she'd been running all night. She reeked of horse, lathered beyond endurance.

That sheen of sweat was a salty wave, waiting to break over Kills-the-Sky. He saw their doom in her face. Since his youth, he'd suffered dreams of being dragged down under a tide of rats that wouldn't stop coming. Drowning under a wave of teeth and fur, choking on his own blood instead of water. Maybe the dream was why he'd preferred hunting birds to rats.

The mara's gliding steps, toenails barely touching the wood, were as loud to Kills-the-Sky as the clacking of shod hooves over stone. She stopped and squatted on the chest of a dead servant, his face frozen in a scream; the filed runes in his ochre-stained teeth had been no protection. Kills-the-Sky had never learned that one's name—he hadn't liked cats. Had threatened to feed Kills-the-Sky to his hounds back home, kicked at him when he thought no other sailors were looking and threatened to take his pelt for a fur collar. He would be the first to be eaten, if the mara and storm left him alive long enough. And good riddance.

Their sailors—most of them—had been good

servants. Kills-the-Sky missed the captain. He, for all his violent bluster, had known how to treat a cat. Offering scritches under the chin or pats when desired, treats when demanded, and otherwise left them to hunt and bask in the sun when they chose.

Kills-the-Sky hopped from the rower's bench, soundlessly landing on the deck. The mara turned a baleful eye to him and glided away to another body, the sound of hoofbeats following in her wake, until she squatted on its chest, kneading her clawed fingers into it and staring into its clouded eyes, looking for something. But what?

Slowly, Kills-the-Sky stepped onto the first servant's chest, keeping a wary eye toward the mara. He prodded the corpse with a paw. The sailor's rictus, terror-filled face stared unblinkingly at the sky. Kills-the-Sky found no answers in the dead face. It wouldn't be much longer before the ship cats took to feeding on their dead servants.

They'd already killed all the rats.

Their servants had found a new land across the ocean. Their tales of the hunting, the danger, the sheer expanse … Kills-the-Sky couldn't wait to see it. And now he never would. It was there the servants had been taking the nightmare, to keep it far from home and hearth, as far as wind and sea would take it. Hoping it would never find its way back.

A great yowl rose from the far end of the longship. Kills-the-Sky ran toward the clamour, darting from stem to stern. One of the other cats was dead: Sunchaser. Murdered. Not just murdered—left for Kills-the-Sky like a prize. His eyes narrowed. Or a taunt. If not for the trickle of blood from Sunchaser's mouth, it looked as if she were sleeping in the sun one last time, splayed out to absorb the heat. Except her head was turned around the wrong direction.

She'd been a good hunter. Stealthy. Perceptive. What on the ship could've done this to her? This was no cat's kill. Sunchaser hadn't died like the servants. She hadn't seen death coming and feared it. She'd been ambushed. Or betrayed. It seemed as if she'd been killed by a man's hand and presented as a trophy here. But by whom? And where were they?

As he dragged the body over the side, three other cats, Wintermute, Ghostkill, and Blacklock, helped him. They said nothing as they pushed Sunchaser over the edge into the sea. She'd always had a way of finding a sliver of sun on a cloudy day, never at peace otherwise. Pacing endlessly, mewing her annoyance until the rest of the ship shared her displeasure. No sun for her final rest today. None ever again. Still, it was more ceremony than they usually received from the servants. Maybe the currents would take her home.

Kills-the-Sky didn't know what could have killed Sunchaser. That wasn't good.

He didn't like things he didn't know. But the mystery gave him purpose. Something more than waiting for the sea or the nightmare to claim them. Kills-the-Sky stared at the advancing line of black clouds and the sea that'd swallowed Sunchaser.

The storm might be better.

Another cat, Treespeaker, a ginger with a bent tail and green eyes, had taken to playing with his dead servant's bag of runes, batting the carved bits of antler across the deck and pouncing on them. The servants believed the future could be revealed, the past unveiled, and the present exposed by the position and symbols of the cast runes, playing at understanding the secrets of the Great Servants. Treespeaker had always been fascinated with the runes. Maybe he'd seen something, or heard something, of their fate in those tales Kills-the-Sky could use. He padded to Treespeaker's side. "What do the bones tell you?"

"The bones," Treespeaker said gravely, pushing one

with two crossed lines upon it toward Kills-the-Sky, "tell me nothing. They are only bones."

Kills-the-Sky let out an exasperated sigh. Time wasted. Time they didn't have. Sunchaser's killer, whoever they were, could've found another victim. Who would they target next? The ship was large—to a cat—but not so large one could hide forever.

The only creature still walking the ship with hands that could strangle was the mara. It'd only been a matter of time before the mara turned their nightmares on them. And yet, something about that didn't feel right. So far she'd shown no real interest in them.

Wind ruffled his fur and Kills-the-Sky turned, glancing back. The clouds were closer, the gusts more prevalent. With Sunchaser gone, it seemed the sun itself had gone with her. Kills-the-Sky knew that wasn't true, and yet … and yet … the mara would only be walking more as the storm grew closer, and then, the *real* nightmare would begin.

The last nightmare.

Nightmares could be found anywhere, in anything, and any place, but in Kills-the-Sky's experience, they liked the deepest darkness best. The shadows. Solitude. *That*

was where the mara could best dig their claws into you. She appeared on the deck only in the shadows cast by the mast and sail, and disappeared when the sun crept past them. Kills-the-Sky preferred the sun, but he was well accustomed to hunting in the shadows.

All Kills-the-Sky wanted was to solve this mystery before the sea claimed him. Before it claimed them all.

"I will go below to hunt her," he said. "And I will end this."

He padded to the ladder to the hold, and measured the jump just as Fairweather swiped at him, swatting his tail. The surprise almost drove him over the edge and into the hold. He hissed and swiped back. Fairweather rolled on her back and made a purring sound—an almost human laugh. Kills-the-Sky wrinkled his whiskers. They'd all have been better off if Fairweather had stayed at home with those servants too afraid to take the voyage.

We'd all be better off if we'd stayed there, too.

Kills-the-Sky snuck into darkness while Fairweather waited under a rower's bench, swiping at any cat passing by. She made him so *tired*.

Kills-the-Sky leapt into the hold, and felt a chill when he landed on the box that'd held the nightmare. He kept a wary eye to the shadows. The sealed box had been left open to the elements where any and all could spot the prison and reassure themselves the nightmare had been contained. Not that their placement or concern had saved them.

Two pinpricks of light, a dull glow from the mara's eyes, presaged her stepping into Kills-the-Sky's sight. Cat and hag circled the rune-etched prison box. Each taking the other's measure. The nightmare returned to the chest where the servants had locked her away, drifting in the air, talons dragging over the wood, perched like a vulture.

"Why did you kill them?" Kills-the-Sky demanded.

"Who?" The single word dropped like a turd in the sand. "Your 'servants'?"

"No, not them. We expected that. They expected that. Sunchaser."

The nightmare blinked. "The cat?"

"Yes."

A dismissive snort. "Not my work."

Kills-the Sky choked back a rising yowl of frustration. Her eyes bored into him. "You're not hunting us?"

"Not yet."

"When?"

"Dreams become nightmares," she smiled, cackling, then snapped her fingers, "like that."

Kills-the-Sky looked from the mara to her useless prison. The rune wards had been scratched away. The nightmare's own talons, perhaps? Or a servant's knife? The gouges were too deep and broad to be a cat's work. The sliver of sun was obscured. Fairweather peered in from the tops of the steps, a halo of sunlight ringing her head. The nightmare's eyes shot up, and she glided away in a rush. Galloping hooves rang in Kills-the-Sky's ears as her stink washed over him like a wave, flattening him to the floor.

With another cat's life in the balance—even Fairweather's—Kills-the-Sky grew bolder. He padded closer. He swiped at the mara, but his paw passed through her like she was shadow.

She laughed.

She *laughed.*

The nightmare locked eyes with Kills-the-Sky, and he heard the dying screams of the first man she took and then the next and the next, so hungry, a feast she could've stretched for months was gone in a night. When she chuckled, he heard those pained shrieks in the pause between every guttural laugh. The mara turned back to the ladder.

The nightmare stretched a taloned finger toward Fairweather, coming just shy of broaching the threshold into the light. Then the ship rolled on a wave, pitching Fairweather into shadow. The mara's hands clutched her ruff until the ship rolled back and the grasping hand evaporated and Fairweather fled.

Other than Kills-the-Sky, only Fairweather paid any attention to the nightmare, and she kept a nervous distance from her.

What do you see that others do not, Fairweather?

Kills-the-Sky's ears twitched, and his eyes narrowed as he watched the young cat bolt under a rower's bench.

Now he had a second target.

Fairweather proved harder to stalk than the nightmare. And Kills-the-Sky's failure had cost.

Another cat dead.

Treespeaker, this time. Same method as Sunchaser. His runes scattered around his body in some deliberate pattern that meant nothing to Kills-the-Sky. Lightning flashed in the coming clouds. No time for another funeral. Not if they wanted to find the killer before they all died.

The nightmare came back on deck when the sun went behind a cloud. Whether they saw her or not, all the cats kept their distance. Smart. But for now, she was not Kills-the-Sky's problem. Cats may dream of the sun, but they're not afraid of the dark.

Kills-the-Sky watched, silently, from beneath the rower's bench. The nightmare turned back and looked at him. She licked her lips. He knew—*knew*—he'd be first when her hunger returned. It was his ship. The dreams of cats may be small to her, but his were the biggest among them. A world where his family had spread across the world. Where they no longer had to pretend to be pets, where they walked the heavens mighty as the Great Servants claimed to be, in the days when they hunted men, not for them. Their proper place once more.

Too late, he was pulled from his thoughts to realize it wasn't the shadow of a cloud that'd fallen over him, but the mara.

Kills-the-Sky's breath caught and he felt the hag's full weight pressed on his chest—but when he strained to look, it wasn't the mara on him, it was a wave breaking against the longship. A wave with teeth, and it pulled him under until he couldn't see. Couldn't breathe. Couldn't feel anything but pain.

A dream turned to nightmare. The mara's work. He knew this, and yet, for all the knowing, couldn't make it end. Couldn't rise. Couldn't wake. Couldn't scream.

Something bright seared Kills-the-Sky's eyes. One last patch of sun had burned through the clouds before the storm fell.

The biting wave receded, leaving a dark-haired shadow looming in its place. Its servant-like shape had hair sent curving over its head by the wind, like horns, and broad feet that could crush the swiftest cat and a tongue that whispered faster than Kills-the-Sky could understand. Cat after cat fell under the shadow's hands.

Kills-the-Sky's grandsire, Sleeps-with-Swords, was full of tales like this. He'd boasted he'd climbed to Asgard, and from there, to Freyja's hall, Sessrúmnir, to pilfer from the tables of the Great Servants and their dead believers. That he'd grown to the size of a bear to wrestle Thor, stolen fish from Heimdall, and bested Loki in a flyting. Or how he'd flown to the stars to harass the wolves Hati and Skoll, where he'd lost an eye to Hati and an ear to Skoll.

He'd been a liar and a braggart, but to Kills-the-Sky, Sleeps-with-Swords had been a hero. A skogkatt—a forest cat, or to *him* tell it, an elf-cat, a dwarf-cat, a god-cat. Perhaps there'd been truth to the old cat's tales. Kills-the-Sky had believed the stories as a kitten, but as his years rolled on, and Sleeps-with-Swords was now long dead, it seemed a milk-tale.

Now he wished it *was* true. That he could follow his grandsire and climb the mast until he reached the World Tree and the Great Servants. He wished his grandsire would show him a way out of this nightmare. He wished he could *be* his grandsire. But a ray of sunshine had banished the nightmare and dream both.

"I'd hoped she would finish you," said a familiar, yet strange, voice from behind him. He sprang to his feet.

Fairweather regarded him with her mismatched eyes smouldering; a servant's shadow stretched from her cat's body.

"You are the last," she said. "The last of his seed. I told him he would pay. To the last kitten. To the last "servant" who'd cared for his scions. That what he stole would be replaced in blood. *His* blood.

"I'd have tried to get *you* to open the nightmare's prison, that would've been more pleasing to me, but you're as stubborn as Odin, and harder to kill than Baldur."

There was something half-remembered, from a curse, in Fairweather's eyes. Especially when they looked back at him—as if belonging to a serpent, or a bird, but no cat.

"*Loki.*"

Hate filled Kills-the-Sky. An ancestral grudge he didn't know he bore. A connection to his grandsire. To the forest. To *power*. He shuddered as the hate swelled within and grew until the hold around him felt very small, and Fairweather—Loki—even smaller. Kills-the-Sky put his paw forward and saw it was large enough to crush a cat. Or kill a Great Servant.

The trickster's eyes widened, and he bolted. Kills-the-Sky knew then who had released the mara to kill their sailors. Whether the god of mischief had released the nightmare, or had seen the deed done for them, it didn't matter. Only the result mattered.

If Loki had trapped the cats on this ship to die, Kills-the-Sky would ensure the trickster remained trapped alongside them. It would be small comfort to eat the trickster before he drowned, but when one faced death, small comforts mattered most.

Kills-the-Sky gave chase. He knew every nook of the vessel. Still, he didn't want to lose sight of his target. Loki ran well, the body of a cat as natural to the trickster as if he were born to it. Kills-the-Sky's new form was fast. Faster than Loki, and he gained ground on the trickster.

Another cat—Bugeater—sought to stop Loki. Whether Bugeater sensed the danger, or wrongly assumed Fairweather wanted to play, he pounced. Kills-the-Sky roared in warning. Too late. Contorting his body at the last moment, Loki rolled onto his back and lashed out with his hind legs.

With a startled *mew*, Bugeater was launched off the longship. Kills-the-Sky didn't hear the splash, but he knew Bugeater was lost. Kills-the-Sky couldn't stop the ship without the servants, and they had no means to rescue Bugeater even if he could. Another cat lost because of him.

No. Because of Loki.

Another score to settle.

Fortunately, Bugeater's sacrifice wasn't in vain. The ambush and response had slowed Loki. Kills-the-Sky closed. The rest of the cats joined the chase, harrying and slowing the trickster, wordlessly following Kills-the-Sky's lead.

When he thought they had Loki cornered, the trickster laughed—a very servant-like sound from his cat's mouth—and sprouted broad wings the colour of dried blood, taking to the sky.

Kills-the-Sky bounded to the mast, climbed up it, and sprang backward into the air, colliding with the bird. He sank his teeth into the nape of the trickster's neck and rode him to the deck. The blood tasted thin, not rich, as he'd expected. Cool, like a body left out in winter, but not yet frozen. Fishy and foul, and yet clear and crisp all at once. Loki thrashed and shifted from shape to shape, but Kills-the-Sky kept his teeth deep in Loki's flesh, and his claws deeper. The trickster's attempt to save himself was going to hurt.

"Let me go," Loki wailed.

Kills-the-Sky wanted to retort but kept his teeth stuck in the trickster's neck. Instead he raked the trickster's flanks with his hind legs.

"I see it in you," Loki said through gritted teeth. "You're like your grandsire. You can travel to Asgard. Suckle at the teat of Heiðrún. Leave me go, and I'll show you the way."

Kills-the-Sky cared not for mead, nor goats, nor goats with mead for milk. He *did* care for the Lie-Father's insistence that his grandsire's stories had been true.

"Leave your cats behind. Save yourself."

The trickster's words had a strange sibilance to them, a call from port on a foggy night, offering a path home. A path Kills-the-Sky wanted to take, but couldn't. Port wasn't home. The *ship* was home. And Loki was a fucking liar. Any salvation Loki sought would always be his own.

"I think you'll die with us," Kills-the-Sky said.

The rest of the ship's cats surrounded them. Eyes glittering like gemstones, tongues dancing over whiskered muzzles. They hissed and yowled, scratching the trickster, nipping gobbets of flesh, feasting.

Clouds swallowed the last spear of sun that'd freed Kills-the-Sky from the mara's clutches. Rain peppered the deck, a harbinger of the storm to come. His breath misted like they'd sailed straight into winter, and rime crusted his fur.

The mara.

"Such delicious fears you have. Almost as savoury as Loki's," said the nightmare. She licked her cracked lips. "You *know* doom. And you seek to dodge it. One of you may today, but not forever."

Loki shuddered, looking at the mara. *So that's who she'd been looking for.* The ship cats saw her for certain now, and backed away.

"Trade my fears for yours," Loki pleaded to Kills-the-Sky. "My fate for yours. You'll want no part of what she's planned for me. And at least the storm won't kill you."

"I'll still be dead."

"It's a chance. A chance is better than nothing."

Kills-the-Sky thought on Loki's words. And the mara's. *One may dodge fate.* A chance. Loki was right. Kills-the-Sky didn't want to admit it, especially since he'd placed the cats in this forked stick to begin with when he'd gotten caught in his own trap.

Kills-the-Sky released Loki's neck and repeated, "*We* will take his place. My fears for his."

"You intrigue me," the mara said.

Kills-the-Sky patted his bleeding flank where Loki had scratched him, and laid a bloody paw on the deck at the mara's feet. "He came for my blood. It's yours. *If you can take it.*"

Loki stood smirking, victorious.

"One day, trickster, you *will* see your doom," the mara said, voice a growl. "I *will* bring your nightmares to truth."

The trickster, in servant form now, with a crooked grin and icy eyes, flashed two fingers, the middle on each hand. The gesture meant nothing to Kills-the-Sky. Nothing other than: Loki had won. Kills-the-Sky's cats were beaten. *He* was beaten. Loki changed his shape again as he dived off the boat, taking the form of a salmon. "Good luck getting into Valhalla."

"We'll find you from Freyja's hall, from Asgard, or from Hel, and you'll never sleep true again."

The mara nodded along with Kills-the-Sky's words. "Hel will have you home one day, trickster."

Loki's fishy grin grew wider. "But not today."

The hag disappeared, and, breaking from the storm, another ship, a husk with broken masts and tattered sails, appeared; outrunning the wind, moving faster than any oars could propel it. Kills-the-Sky's nose wrinkled. The oncoming ship stank of Hel. The wind carried it: corruption. Decay. *Wrong.* Kills-the-Sky heard the rustle of serpents writhing and the skitter of rat paws over wooden planks. It was teeming with them. His ears twitched. The wind carried squeaking and the sounds of a seething river of vermin.

"Naglfar?" Kills-the-Sky whispered. He'd heard the name fearfully mentioned whenever the servants had been stuck in fog. The nail-ship. The end-ship. The last voyage for man or giant who had fallen into Hel's clutches. Had Ragnarök come? Had they missed the End of All Hunts while they drifted at sea?

"Nothing so grand." The mara's whispered words tickled Kills-the-Sky's ears. He looked for her but could not see her. "Now there's nothing left but death. The price for trusting Loki."

Kills-the-Sky refused to accept the trickster's victory. The rain fell in earnest. The cats understood their peril now, mewling at the sky in protest, as if to change the weather with the sheer force of their displeasure.

His low rumbling roar carried over the water like thunder. "If this will be our end, it will be such an end. One the Great Servants cannot dispute!"

The cats formed a wedge with Kills-the-Sky at its tip, a feline spear aimed at the rats. They took the high ground of the rower's benches and waited for the press to come to them. The Hel-ship was woven serpents still snapping where their heads protruded from the weave. Kills-the-Sky tried to push the boat away, but the serpents had sunk their fangs fast into the wood of the longship, creating a bridge for the rats.

The whole vessel rattled in warning and although Kills-the-Sky had never seen snakes with the pattern of these scales, he knew—somehow, he knew—their bite meant death. Those fangs weren't the only ones promising death. A rat army, gaunt fur-shrouded skeletons, surged onto the longship as the ships collided. The river of rats flowed below them, covering the bodies of the servants and devouring them. Their bloated bellies distended, they turned from the skeletons to the cats.

For all they looked like starved and desiccated corpses, they had to be alive because they still hungered. Their eyes burned with it.

There'd be no easy victory. It was cat against rat to the end and the odds were against them. Kills-the-Sky swatted a swath of vermin to the side and off the ship. They squeaked as they sailed, their cries growing louder after they splashed. Kills-the-Sky couldn't gut them fast enough and, gaunt as they were, the rats were still near as big as each of his fellow cats. They'd never kill them all. Each rat was but a drop in a sea.

But they kept killing anyway.

He lost himself in the killing. In the work. The job. It was his purpose. His reason for being. He killed until not even the entire ocean could wash the blood from his fur.

He'd been outnumbered before, but never so greatly.

Seen storms, but never like this one.

At least the pounding rain and waves slapping against the hull drowned out the dying cries of his companions.

A rolling wave washed the deck clean of rats, but there were more on the Hel-ship. Always more on the Hel-ship. An entire Hel's worth, and the serpent gang-planks still clutched the longship, giving them a bridge to launch another assault. Only two other cats lived. Wintermute and Blacklock

Maybe he could spare them the worst.

Kills-the-Sky launched himself across the gap between the vessels, breaking the gathering rats, and slashed at the serpents clutching his ship. Some, severed, were lost to the sea. Others detached, snapping at him, striking flanks, and back, and throat. A few, quivering against the pull of the longship, held fast. Rats scurried over their serpent bodies, still trying to swamp the cats under their numbers.

Kills-the-Sky ignored the sharp needle pains of the serpent's fangs and the burning fire they spat into his body as he slashed at the final moorings holding the ships together. His limbs felt heavy as stones.

Maybe it was the wind, but it seemed the Hel-ship screamed as a wave pushed the two vessels apart, sending the longship adrift again. There was a sound, like thunder, and the Hel-ship rolled over, dumping Kills-the-Sky into the ocean. The shock of the cold water was almost enough to drive the poison-induced lethargy from his body. Almost.

As water entered his lungs, a golden hand reached down and grabbed his scruff to pull him up. He stared into a smiling face. Freyja's face. Blacklock, Bugeater, Treespeaker, and Sunchaser—all of the ship's cats—were at her side. The rats floated atop the water until a wave slapped them under, and they didn't surface. Kills-the-Sky smiled a hunter's smile.

They had done it.

He had done it.

Wintermute and Blacklock boarded Freyja's chariot after him. Towing the Great Servant's chariot in a shimmering harness, Kills-the-Sky saw his grandsire, leading the way to take them home above the clouds and into the sun. And when they got to the halls of the Great Servants, after Freyja doted on them for a time, Kills-the-Sky would find Loki. He would tree the trickster and bring him to ground. But for now, the sun felt good on his face, and a scratch under his chin, and Kills-the-Sky purred himself to sleep.

A Door in the Rock

There had been an "accident" with a troll from the mine.

It was the talk of Svarta Mining, that troll, and how it wouldn't return to any dwarf's call. Brunna Sindradóttir volunteered to try one last time, before it was destroyed, because her parents had crafted more rock trolls for the Company than all other *dvergar* together—and this rogue troll happened to be one of theirs. She'd been promised right of travel if she succeeded. She'd make the troll recognize her blood.

So far the Company had kept the Flin Flon RCMP out of their business. Locals listened to the Company. Veiled by the illusion of jack-knifed tanker trailer was a maimed and angry rock troll, wailing over its dead handler and not allowing anyone near the body.

Brunna didn't know why they'd bothered with a cover story at all. Let the *Northern Miner* put the troll on its front page. Invite the damned CBC. Her uncle Andvari *wanted* the *dvergar* to return to the days of old, crafting legends. How could that happen when mortals turned a blind eye to what happened around them? If humans never saw magic, how would they know to seek out dwarves for weapons to fight monsters? How would they forge new legends?

How would they even know there *were* dwarves?

Andvari had seen to that, carving legend *into* a man with ink, and blood, and releasing him to be noticed. To cause the sort of trouble that could not go *unnoticed.*

On the road leading to the troll, she could see the smokestack from the Company's smelter—taller than the Eiffel Tower—standing out from the rock like a giant's middle finger directed at her. There was nowhere in town that she *couldn't* see that stack, or its trail of smoke, venting waste from the Company's mortal and magical labours.

Flin Flon, dubbed "The City Built on Rock," was about 800 kilometres north of the provincial capital of Winnipeg. It was a border town, straddling the provinces of Manitoba and Saskatchewan in the same way it bordered the magic and mundane. Not large as cities go—six thousand souls, give or take. But it had been a perfect place for the *dvergar* to settle, carved out of the Canadian Shield as it was. And the ancient volcanic belt had been a shield indeed, in the days after Ragnarök.

They say that happened. God fought god. Monsters ate the sun and moon. Winter never ended. The dead walked. The very sky shattered. Brunna hadn't seen it, but it was recorded in Sögusalur, the History Hall, that the Nine Worlds had ended. *But here we are. Still living.*

If one could call being in this tiny town living.

Her wayward troll was likely near a path leading to the lake; she hoped it hadn't rambled. If it had, she'd hunt it through the residential streets, where magic was myth and dwarves were naught but a story.

Which would complicate things.

But that story was changing. Magic was returning to Midgard.

Which meant, soon, humans would come to the *dvergar* again. For weapons. For charms. For jewels. And they would pay, in gold or favours. Humans would always pay for glory.

Brunna wanted the time of legends to return as much as any dwarf, if not more. Her parents had talked of nothing else since she was a squalling youth. She also wanted to be long away from the tunnels, seeking adventures of her own, when that happened. Once the glory-seekers came, a life of crafting supplies for the stories of others would be her doom.

Brunna wanted stories of her own, not to be an afterthought in others'.

"Soon enough," she whispered, slapping the dash of her pickup.

It was an old truck, big, and ugly, but it could hold the rock troll, and the truck's covered box would help to hide it and its dead handler from prying eyes.

Brunna stopped at the roadblock, pulling alongside a steep rise of rock. She could see the overturned truck; workers in white suits and respirators. Her stomach trembled, filling her with an overwhelming desire to turn away.

She knew the feeling was false, but it was hard to convince the mind that what the eyes saw was not there. Brunna didn't like the idea of entering blindly, either. The troll would see past the illusion. It would know she was coming. She patted the trumpet case she used to transport her sword: Skeri—The Sever—could cut magic as surely as flesh. The blade had been her mother Valdi's—before she had settled on the forge and given up the fighting life. With Skeri she'd carved truth from giants' lies and fought in other campaigns she'd never shared the tales of. Comforting to have along, but if she drew Skeri now, it would destroy the illusion of the wreck utterly, and with the troll still rampaging about, that would not end well for her or the Company, troll, or town.

A grue crept up Brunna's spine as she inched her truck over the line of blood she knew painted the pavement—all *dvergar* workings required blood. It was afternoon, the autumn sun high overhead, but here, now, in this singular moment, it was twilight. The sun was muted, pale, glowing like a full moon, a mere reflection of its usual intensity.

Her shoulders tightened, waiting for the troll to crush

the hood of her truck. For a windshield to spray glass and slice her face.

She needn't have worried.

The troll was gone. So was the dead dwarf.

There was nothing on the road but a rocky arm and rusty bloodstains.

A raven pecked at the blood, lifting and then discarding a spherical pebble. A second raven landed and the two scavengers croaked imprecations and threats at one another. The birds were everywhere around town. Brunna wondered who they told their secrets to, now that Odin was dead.

She hopped out of the truck. Brunna was tall for a dwarf woman, but it was still a drop. In the chunky soles of her steel-toed boots she topped five feet, if you measured to the top of her curly red hair. And you didn't push down too hard. She straightened her maroon hoodie, the local hockey team's exploding "B" logo emblazoned in white, and tugged it down to hide the shining mail shirt she wore beneath.

The ravens hopped aside as she approached, eyeing her warily. They could fly away. *Unlike me.* They didn't stay rooted to the earth. *Just like me.*

If Brunna had possessed wings, she'd have been gone from Flin Flon already. "But that's not going to happen, is it?" she asked the ravens as she eyed the pebbles scattered from the rock troll's shattered joint.

The pebbles were spherical, like ball bearings.

Thousands of them allowed the giant creature to move and shift its stones. Brunna set her trumpet case down on the road. Her boots crunched over the asphalt. She didn't call to the pebbles. Not yet. Instead, she listened. She'd wanted a rock troll of her own once, but hadn't earned the right to make one.

Binding spirit into rock with blood was serious business. Brunna hadn't taken this task because she'd wanted her freedom, or because her parents had made the troll, but because this was their *last* creation together. Her father Sindri had been a master of crafting them, his trolls were larger and stronger than any other's. Her mother Valdi's gift was instilling instinct and a semblance of thought.

Brunna hoped she could fix this broken troll—assuming she could find him. She felt another rock-caller's pull; a long-spent song, its last note lingering. She was glad she hadn't released a call of her own; it would have alerted whomever had sung this song, letting that unknown voice know to expect her.

Strange, she couldn't place the song. She'd heard all of the voices of the Company's rock-callers. All, it seemed, but this one. She would not have forgotten this wet, gurgling command. She wrinkled her nose and spat, as if that act could get the song's vile taste from her mouth. Instead of singing, she put her hand, palm up, on the asphalt, beckoning to the stony spheres. The pebbles rolled up into her palm as if following a track.

She felt their shrill keening. The troll was in pain. She hadn't known they *could* feel pain. Holding the pebbles, though, she felt its wound, as if one tectonic plate were being ground under another, a shuddering tremor of hurt. The spheres circled in her palm, pulling her toward the broken arm upon the street.

Brunna put a pebble in her mouth, tasting the rock troll's trail. She felt where the troll had gone; its trajectory ran from here into the centre of town. She knew the place it was going. She knew where it had been called. She opened her trumpet case and nicked her thumb on Skeri's edge. Brunna squeezed the drops of blood over the pebbles, coating them; the stones drank the liquid like sponges.

It could come in handy, tying my blood to the troll's mortar.

She stuffed the troll's arm in a beat-up hockey equipment bag and then drew Skeri from its case, slashing it through the air. The illusion had served its purpose. It wavered, like a heat mirage, and collapsed.

In Flin Flon there was a door in the rock.

Beyond a ragged bit of orange mesh netting, and to the right of a billboard proclaiming the pleasures of McDonald's coffee, it lurked between two triangular wedges of cement and beneath wooden scaffolding bearing steps up a huge slab of granite. Graffiti stained the rock, the stairs, and the wooden boxes hiding the city's above-ground water and sewage lines.

The square wooden door had existed as long as Brunna had been alive. There were stories told by locals, and then there were the stories told by the dwarves. It was a bomb shelter left over from the Second World War. It was the abandoned early mines from when the dwarves alone worked this rock. It was a work station for Manitoba Hydro. It led to the last remnants of Niðavellir, ancestral home of the *dvergar*. The only thing dwarves and miners loved more than telling stories was embellishing them.

Dropping the hockey bag holding the troll's arm to the ground, Brunna squinted at the door. It was padlocked on the left and had a bolt that went up and into the rock. Rusted hinges, almost the length of her forearm, were on the right. The door mocked her with a spray-painted profanity.

Fuck, indeed.

Brunna tried to pop the padlock, but it held fast. Unwritten on the door, but just as apparent, was the "off."

The last time Brunna had walked by, there'd been a two-by-four nailed across the door as an additional security measure. Brunna saw it, snapped in two and tangled in the orange mesh. Otherwise, the door didn't appear to be damaged, although some of the scaffolding supporting the stairs above it was.

The door might be locked, but that lock was made of metal and she spoke its language. Brunna didn't hear or see anyone. Feeling safely alone, she spoke to the metal.

"Open," she said, coaxing it. Nothing. It was stubborn. She commanded it, and it dug in like a deer tick. She whispered, using a lover's tongue. It remained shut up tight.

She puckered her lips, ready to spit. *How had the troll even gotten in there?* The lock wouldn't budge. *It should have opened.* She remembered that strange rock-caller's song. Her rock troll wasn't missing. It'd been stolen.

More than one way to crack a lock, Brunna knew.

She spoke stone as well as steel. And she was tired of illusions and subtleties. Brunna laid her palm flat against the granite; the rocks shuddered, cracking the door jamb and splintering the door. The metal bar screeched as it was pushed out of the stone. Brunna slid the broken padlock out of its bar and opened the door.

She hefted her bag over one arm, carrying Skeri's case in the other. Beyond the door was a room of rough-hewn stone so heavily clad by pipes and conduits it seemed the stones were dressed in serpents—as if Brunna had walked into Hel's hall itself.

Boxes and crates littered the floor. They'd been pried open and long since emptied, now guardians to broken beer and whisky bottles, spent cigarette butts, and discarded homemade water pipes.

Some local party boys must have a key. Or someone had locked up behind the troll. Who?

She shut the door behind her and grimaced when it wouldn't close flush. There was no troll, and even to Brunna's sight, there was no other way out of the room.

There was a squeak, followed by a burring rumble. The troll *was* here. It had blended into the rock seamlessly. She called it, trying to drown out that other, more insistent voice, the one she didn't know. Now that she was here, and had the troll in her grasp, she didn't care who heard her. Brunna drew the pebbles out of her pocket: they rolled up her body and into her palm. She sought the tie in her blood, her parents' blood, that would allow her to wrest command of the troll.

It limped toward her, head cocked like a curious hound's, revealing a tunnel its bulk had obscured. Brunna hadn't remembered hearing its leg had been damaged, too. She stared, trying to sense any other hurts, rocking a little unsteadily, her head buzzing from the sharp throb of effort and the thrill of conflict, of testing her voice against another's. The troll rocked along with her, its joints sounding like car tires on a gravel road. With a booming thud, it dropped to its knees and looked her in the eye.

Kneeling, the troll was taller than Brunna. It must've topped ten feet standing. Her parents' work was reflected in its polished quartz eyes as much as it was in her. She felt a kinship with this troll. Even in the dim light, dwarf eyes saw much. The dried, rusty stain along the troll's damaged side. A spring still weeping blood. She pocketed the pebbles and knelt to unzip her bag. With a grunt, she hefted the troll's arm to its broken, ragged socket.

The troll let out a rumbling growl before it loosed a landslide roar. Brunna cut her left palm on her sword, hoping the mixture of blood and Skeri's magical steel might cut through whatever was agitating the troll. It pointed at itself, then Brunna, and back to itself; rocky fist cracking against slate chest. Imploring for aid. Comfort.

Rock trolls were neither once-living souls bound into stone, nor stone given life. They weren't *living* at all. Fossilized bones and a jumble of mismatched stone all mortared together with blood, given a semblance of human form, and sung awake by the will and voice of a rock-caller. Tireless. Near-invulnerable hunters. Unfathomably strong. Smart as a truck full of rocks. When they slept they looked like a pile of stones to the magic-blind eyes of Midgard. This was what Brunna had always been told. But facing this one, feeling its pain and sadness, she felt what she'd been told was wrong. They *could* possess a semblance of life.

The living deserved names. Names were important. If her sword could have a name, so should the troll.

You are alive, aren't you, Rocky?

She wanted to know for certain. Focusing her will on the troll, Brunna sang to its stones; a ballad of stitching Loki's lying mouth shut. It flinched and rumbled backwards, circling as if it were trying to roll into a fetal ball. She reached out a calming hand with her whispered song.

Rocky brushed her cheek with its rough, stony finger. Even that gesture, meant to be gentle, hurt. She ignored the throb in her cheek where a bruise would surely form. She held the arm to the broken joint, keeping her voice steady and she sang. She could see where it should fit together. But it wouldn't.

She felt sorry for him. And then realized with a start that she was no longer thinking of Rocky as a pile of stones, as just a *thing*. She called to the spherical pebbles, and they rolled out of her pocket, up the rock troll's body, and settled into grooves in his wounded arm. He roared, trying to backpedal when stone touched stone.

"I'm trying to fix you, you clod!"

He didn't react to the insult—but someone else did.

In the troll's moment of shock, that foreign rock-caller resumed their song. The voice sounded like the wet gurgle of blood-filled lungs.

"Brunna Sindradóttir. Maggoty child of cowards and thieves."

It sang to Rocky. The vileness of the song was overwhelming, pushing Brunna to her knees. The song didn't stop, but the singer spoke, "Kill her!"

The troll shot up like a geyser and Brunna jumped back with a started yelp. Rocky's good arm slammed into her, hurling her into the wall. She heard a grunting pained cry from behind her before she was enveloped in a darkness too deep for even dwarven eyes.

Brunna awoke, amazed at the simple fact of her survival, head pounding and ribs throbbing. The troll was gone. A sound like an avalanche rumbled off in the distance. Rocky had run off. Again. So had the other caller. She could feel them, moving down, ever down.

She smiled though it made her wince. *You can't lose a dwarf under the earth.*

Rocky was bound to that other call, its drowned voice echoing in her ears, fouling her mind. She grimaced. But she'd found her troll, and she'd return him intact. *Alive.*

She found Skeri. A man's running shoe lay next to its case. Perhaps it belonged to whomever she'd crashed into. With the force the troll had struck Brunna, she half-expected to find a foot inside it. She hefted it cautiously, happy to be proven wrong.

Rubbing at her ribs, she winced; her chain shirt hadn't dissipated the force of the troll's blow. It was good that dwarves were as sturdy as the stone and metal they crafted.

Why would the caller leave her? How was she not dead? Had Rocky stopped him? The troll must have resisted. Both caller and troll had had every possible chance to finish her, but had not. She'd heard the voice's words: *Kill her.* If she was alive, it was the troll's doing, not that caller's. Brunna wasn't out of this fight yet.

The entrance, obvious now with Rocky gone, gaped and waited. She had to delve deeper to get out.

Down, down, down, following the call.

The pull of the earthen darkness emboldened Brunna as she felt the massive weight of the rock above her. If she'd been born among mortals, the dark underground would be overpowering. A tomb of stone, enough to drive a timid person mad. But rock was home to her, even if she wished to part ways with it for a time. She trailed her hands over the tunnel, admiring the work. A dwarf had made this place. The work was too fine for human hands.

It was strange she didn't know it. In her desire to get away from this town, she'd walked every tunnel carved by dwarves and men. At least, she'd thought she had. Listening to the rock, it was as old as any tunnels she'd ever been in. Older. Brunna felt like she could have delved into Niðavellir itself—if only that first home of the dwarves had survived Ragnarök.

Down, down, down, following the call.

This tunnel wasn't mentioned in Sögusalur. Brunna had walked the History Hall with her family, and she had read much. *Dvergur* did not keep secrets from *dvergur*. She'd always been told this.

But carved into the walls of tunnel in runic script were entries detailing new lore. Families. Histories. Names. None of which Brunna knew. But they were here, and had been sunk into the stone without the use of tools, in the *dvergur* fashion.

She looked at these and thought of the stories she'd been told were "lost" in the early days after Ragnarök. Stories don't get lost. They're hidden, buried, forgotten. But stories are truth, and the truth will out.

Of days when a great schism fractured the *dvergar*. There were those who wanted to subjugate and kill humanity, those who wanted to share the toil (if not the wealth) with them, and those who, having been found, wanted to abandon the mines and start over somewhere else, somewhere even more remote, where they would be done with all of Odin's creations.

Her uncle Andvari had risen to power when men had come to the Flin Flon region before it had been given an English name. His faction wanted to use the humans, not harm them. What happened to the dissenters was never spoken of. Their names, and in some cases, their entire lines, had been gouged from Sögusalur during the conflict, and they were to be forgotten.

Odd to find their story here, and when she had Rocky in hand, she'd commit it to memory, but it was not the story she was interested in. More relevant to the moment: revenge fantasies. Scrawled more recently, the stones told her, and descriptions of prospectors' tortured ends in the city's early wilder days.

Her parents' names were on those walls. That was troubling. Uncle Andvari's name was inscribed there, too. Seeing how often Andvari's name was repeated, and the varying ways in which it had been defaced, changing its meaning, was more troubling. As was the repetition of the name Bláinn.

Brunna didn't know a dwarf by that name. But she had heard stories about such a dwarf. They still told stories of his death in hushed whispers in the beer halls, and how it was *ages* before the stones took him.

When she'd asked her parents, they'd said, "We do not speak of him. He is dead. And each of the Nine Worlds is better for that."

The light was faint at first, the dying glow of a distant star, but with every step, more and more fire was poured into that light.

With every step, the caller's gurgling song grew louder, madder. The light grew brighter, and warmth flooded the tunnel. Brunna broached the room where the caller waited, his back to her. A great burning oven filled the chamber with light. The caller sang, and two bladders on his back inflated and deflated like forge bellows with every wheezing word. Sweat poured down Brunna's brow. The smell of hot metal and burning coal filled her nostrils. Despite those comforting sensations, what she saw made Brunna want to retch. Those bladders were lungs, carved out of his body, and left to flap against his back. A "blood eagle" the torture was named, and it was invariably fatal; but somehow, this dwarf had survived.

This had to be Rocky's unseen caller. He appeared bent and broken at first glance, the rest of his body as ravaged as his back. More a spider crushed underfoot than a sturdy dwarf. But when he moved, it was with a speed that pained Brunna to watch: undulating, a boneless sack of flesh. She shivered to witness his tortured limbs scurrying about his workshop from one arcane item to another.

Snapping her gaze from the rock-caller, she scanned the chamber for her true quarry. Rocky stood impassive, arm reattached, on the other side of the work table. On the table itself a young human male—barely an adult—was bound.

"You thought you'd killed me," said the rock-caller. "All of you. Bláinn the Bold did not die, even when you made him Bláinn the Bloody, Bláinn Blood-Eagle. Bláinn will not die. His hate keeps him alive."

Brunna buried a gasp in her hand. The stories were true. She begged the rocks not to reveal her, and found stillness in their touch, and strength in their enveloping presence.

"Please, mister. I didn't—" the boy stopped, as if trying to fathom what the creature was implying. "I didn't do anything."

"Your ancestors, then. And the ancestors of your woman."

"What woman? Oh, Jesus, I stole the key. I just wanted to smoke up. This isn't fair."

The creature gestured at its ruined body. "*Fair*? Is this fair? What you did to me?"

"I didn't—I'm sorry."

"Sorry? I will teach you sorry. Order your lackeys give me the blood eagle and then wait for me to die? And as I welcomed Hel's release, even as Sword-Sleep came for me, you healed me, so more of your puppets could do the same? Have you *any* concept what I have suffered?"

"N-no."

"You will." The creature's voice went from dark to light. Growl to sing-song. "You *will*."

The dead handler of the rock troll was here also. His body, already going to rot, leaned against a table in the centre of the room; the corpse's face was turned to look at her, a neat hole in its forehead staring like a third eye. But another body had more of her attention, and given his constant sobbing, Bláinn Blood-Eagle's as well.

Brunna may have only known Bláinn's name from stories—and those tales were but tin to the steel of this horror—but she'd seen the boy strapped to the table. She knew him from around town. He'd smiled as brightly as Freyr's golden boar when he asked to buy her a beer. Now his wide eyes hunted for escape, not romance. His must have been the cry she'd heard before Rocky had knocked her out.

There were oddities in jars, and the walls were engraved with charts of creatures' anatomy. Brunna saw locals the newspaper had reported dead in a recent wildfire: not burned, but still very, very dead.

The boy's gaze locked on where Brunna hid, and he wailed, "Help me!"

Brunna ducked down as Bláinn spun, following the boy's eyeline, and hoped she hadn't been seen.

"Please," the boy cried, and that single pleading word seemed to echo for an eternity.

"Enough of that," Bláinn wheezed.

When the wails finally stopped, Brunna worried the boy had been silenced by death. She chanced a furtive peek and saw an iron bit crammed into the boy's mouth. It stuck out like a railroad spike waiting to be hammered.

Light reflected in the boy's tears, which ran freely from red-rimmed eyes down cheeks to spatter on the table.

Oozing around the boy, the once-dwarf inserted needles into his prisoner's arteries. The rubber tubing attached to the ends began dripping blood pitter pat, pitter pat, into a large flat vessel positioned underneath the table.

Rocky stood, impassive as the scene unfolded, restrained by bloody runes drawn upon his every stone. Brunna wasn't certain she could free him, or that she could command him now, even if she won the troll his freedom.

But she called anyway.

STILL ALIVE, he answered, using words, which surprised her. *STILL HURT.*

"You would try to take my work from me?" Bláinn asked, lungs puffing up in indignation.

Brunna froze.

"You weren't supposed to be here. You shouldn't have followed."

Brunna didn't answer, but did wonder to herself: *Why not?*

"I expected you to bring them down to me. Summon

the Company. Oh, I would have loved to do to them what they did to me."

The Company did this to him? He had to be wrong.

Wrong, wrong, wrong, her thought echoed, picked up by the caller's song, mocking her.

"I felt you wandering my halls. You thought you could hide your song from me? I know everything, living or dead, under the earth."

She hadn't been sure at first whether Bláinn had been bluffing, but when he'd named her …

Brunna stepped out to face him, Skeri drawn. "*You don't know me.*"

"Yessssss," he whispered, drawing out the word, like a cartoon serpent. Scuttling over the table, and the boy, the once-dwarf said, "Oh yes, I do, Brunna Sindradóttir. I know your entire cursed family."

"Uncle Andvari wouldn't have given that order."

"Such a bright girl you are. Like a ruby in the sun." He paused. And in the waiting, Brunna saw the truth.

Bláinn charged her. Brunna raised her sword and winced. There was no time for pain. Only the craft.

She hacked at him, but his boneless body had no resistance, nothing to cut into. When she slashed, his flesh folded around her blade. She tried stabbing, but his boneless movements were hard to predict. Brunna hit nothing but air.

"Your uncle, your *Company*—" he spat out that last word "—you think they know better? Crafting weapons?

Making humans into weapons? Humanity is *wood*. Coal. Fuel to be spent in the forge. I will craft my own weapon. When I need blood for a working, *I will take it.* I will make the mortals fear the night again. Only when they know fear, terror—monsters. Then they will pay for the tools to triumph. And if the world needs monsters to be great—*I* will forge those monsters. Once-Dwarf. Bláinn Blood-Eagle. Not Bláinn the Bold. Never again, Bláinn the Bold. I will show them *bold*. I will show them *monsters.*"

She kicked at him. His leg wrapped around her ankle. Brunna grabbed at Bláinn's wrist with her free hand and looped the boneless appendage around her arm, dragging him closer and closer.

Close enough to stab.

"That's a damned cart full of slag," said Brunna, sliding Skeri into the once-dwarf. His rubbery skin was hard to pierce. "I read your twisted History Hall. *You* were a monster before this happened to you."

He hissed, as if a forge spark had landed upon his arm, and nothing more.

Through clenched teeth, Brunna said, "And if my uncle hurt you, you *deserved* it."

Bláinn choked out a wet laugh and wriggled free of her, biting and scratching. "We all deserve it."

Brunna reached out to Rocky, hoping the troll could help her. Stone scratched over stone as his head turned to regard her. Bláinn had Rocky penned with a ring of blood. Bláinn recognized her plan, and his lungs pumped against his back as he resumed his song, holding the troll still. Brunna needed to get closer so Skeri could cut through Bláinn's wards, through his call, and release Rocky.

She stabbed at Bláinn—a feint—and when he shifted away, she dove, her blade crossing the plane of the protective ward, severing the enchantment. Rocky's eyes enveloped his head as the runes painted on his stones flared and burned away. Rocky rumbled forward and Bláinn howled. Rocky was free. Free to choose whom to serve. To help. To hurt. Or to run. She called to the troll, reached out to her blood and the connection that bound them. Her blood was in his very bones now, just like that of her parents.

Rocky's newly repaired arm grabbed Brunna by the throat, his other snatched a wriggling Bláinn. Bláinn's command, "Kill," burned, hot and loud. By comparison, Brunna's request, "Please," seemed almost silent.

Bláinn's touch, and toxic blood, coursed through Rocky's repaired arm, as it strangled Brunna, as rock-caller duelled rock-caller to see whose song was superior. Her eyes dimmed as she rooted out Bláinn's influence.

Crafters put something of themselves into their work when they created. A bit of heart, a bit of soul—whatever, *however*, a skald might describe it. And Brunna's parents' souls were there in Rocky. Her mother and father had made this rock troll as surely as they'd made

Brunna. Brunna rooted it out. Blood leaked from his mortar and the arm fell away from the socket, its grasp still tight on Brunna's throat.

Brunna couldn't hear Bláinn's surprised cry, through the pounding of her ears, but she felt the air rush from the room, as if his flapping lungs had blown it away.

Brunna pried Rocky's arm free of her throat and sang the same song her mother had sung to her in nights past, and Bláinn's blood poured from Rocky's arm. It went still.

The rock troll turned to Bláinn, head tilting as he held the dwarf tightly.

Bláinn rasped out, "No."

Brunna shook her head. "Goodbye, Bláinn Blood-Eagle."

Rocky made the only choice he could.

Bláinn resisted, his legs wrapping around Brunna's, hugging tightly even as his fingers pried at Rocky's hands. She sawed at his rubbery body until he let go of her.

Bláinn may have looked boneless, but judging from the cracking as the rock troll wrung him out, there were still some hard points in his eel-like body. His lungs inflated rapidly, filling until they burst, spilling what seemed to be every drop of blood in his body. The rock-caller's final song was a wheezing gurgle as Rocky dropped him to the stone, and then ground him underfoot.

Brunna turned aside, not needing to see Bláinn's end.

There was nothing she could do for the troll's dead handler, but at the least she could get the boy out of here before he woke to a different nightmare.

She cooed at the troll to pick up the dead dwarf.

Gently, gently, now.

Rocky hefted the corpse as if he were holding delicately blown glass.

Brunna freed the boy from his restraints and Bláinn's instruments, and considerably less carefully, hoisted him over her shoulder. His fingers and toes practically dragged on the stone while she walked back to Rocky's side.

She held out her hand to the rock troll, who took it, enveloping her palm in his giant stone mitt. "Let's get you home," she said, flashing the rock troll a broad smile and wiping away a sooty rune image. "You look terrible."

Rocky made a pleased little trill, a sound like shale snapping between her fingers, and fell in behind her.

Whether anyone in the Company would believe her story, Brunna didn't know, and she didn't care. There was nothing left of Bláinn Blood-Eagle to show. His story was over.

Hers had begun.

Murder Mystery

"Heckle. Jeckle. Hit the fucking road."

Despite my irritation at being called by that ridiculous nickname—I was a raven, not some cartoon crow—I almost sighed with pleasure. To be cooped up inside a mortal's skull—and especially *this* mortal—tried my patience more than Muninn's constant reminders of days gone by.

The two of us drifted out from under the man's skin like a dusty cloud, no longer trapped in his tattoos. Our ink coalesced first into a ghostly image of our raven selves and then flesh and feathers formed.

He only set us free when he wanted to know something. And he'd been using us hard lately. In that regard, Ted Callan was no different than our old master, Odin.

"What would you have us search for?" I asked. "Loki? The *álfar*? Hidden threats to your city?"

Ted appeared thoughtful—a trick for him, admittedly—before saying, "I don't give a shit, Huginn. Do whatever you want—you've earned a day off to look for shiny things."

We spoke in croaking ravens' voices, but our words

could be understood in the man's mind—such as it was—most of the time.

"Truly?" Muninn asked.

I had to agree with my brother bird. Even Muninn's memory couldn't hold a hint of a time when we might be only ravens—only birds on the wing, rather than Odin's harbingers. It was an embarrassment, serving an oil worker, rather than the Most High. It smacked of punishment for a failure not our own, but this small gift would go far toward redress.

He waved us away. "I care about goddamned peace and quiet more than any fucking thing you have to tell me."

I croaked an involuntary protest. If the man were more like Odin, he would see the connections from the seemingly disparate threads and morsels we retrieved, and understand the larger nest of information we crafted for him. Today, I was glad this man was *not* like Odin.

The All-Father had never given me a day off. Relentlessly driven by his doom (and towards it), that one.

"Then let us fly, so you may enjoy the silence," I said.

"Didn't know you were a Depeche Mode fan," Ted said.

Muninn chuckled. I should know what that meant, too, but Muninn was more in tune with the man's memories. It had to be some musician or group. Music was the only thing that roosted for any length of time in Ted's brain, besides football or sex.

A pity he could not sing.

We drifted through the simple glass as inky clouds, regaining our flesh on the other side. He didn't like when we did this; he claimed it took forever to get the glass clean again. When he wasn't wondering "where the fuck our bodies even came from."

I snickered to myself. Sometimes the simple pleasures were the best.

Outside, with the last sun of summer overhead, Muninn and I flew to roost among the lesser birds populating Winnipeg. We landed on a branch. A red squirrel chittered angrily, as if we cared to steal the nuts he'd hidden away for winter. I flapped my wings and hopped closer, not about to be cowed by this lesser beast. It turned and fled down the tree's trunk. I enjoyed its fear.

"Was that necessary?" Muninn asked.

"Perhaps not," I admitted. "But it was pleasant. Surely you remember the sensation."

Muninn preened himself with his beak rather than answering immediately. He listed many pleasures we had once enjoyed, and he was right: it had been ages since we hunted, or scavenged, or cached anything but thought and memory.

"You have no imagination," I said. "Only contented by what you have done before. We should do something new."

"New," Muninn muttered.

I had thought he would protest more fervently.

"New memories," he said. **"I think I would like that."**

I was surprised. I had not expected Muninn to acquiesce so easily or so quickly..

"What would you suggest?" he asked.

I'm not ashamed to admit I hadn't thought much beyond the idea of something new. Ideas—thoughts—came to me swift as a hunting raptor.

"I would like to know where our flesh and feathers come from," I said, spreading my wings wide, as if they were human arms, blurting out the first idea to jolt from brain to beak.

Muninn asked, **"Where shall we start?"**

"With them?" I said, pointing my beak towards crows gathered upon a poorly manicured property, shrouding the weedy grass in black.

The lesser corvids had surrounded a corpse—one of their own. From the solemnity they displayed, it appeared we'd stumbled on a funeral.

"They loved her, their dead sister. Taken too soon," I said.

As one, the crows' heads swivelled to stare at us.

"I do not think they like us," Muninn said.

"I will not be bullied by *them*."

"They are angry, full of loss."

"So?"

A small group hopped along the ground to cover the corpse with their wings. The others took to the air.

Toward us.

They swarmed our branch, cawing, shrieking. We buffeted them aside with our wings. Snapped with our beaks. They tried to snatch our feathers. Steal our eyes. We could prevail. We were larger. Smarter. But if we failed, if we died, we'd have to return to our host. Something neither I, nor Muninn, would be ready to admit.

The crows pecked and fought with us, their sheer numbers growing, murder on their minds. We chose to take wing and leave their brainless chatter behind us. Muninn would have a different recollection of events. He can be fussy about such matters.

"They were no help," I complained.

"Yes," Muninn agreed. "Perhaps if we'd not intruded upon their mourning."

"Dead is dead, and our silence would not have brought the fellow bird back to wing."

"No, but it may have earned us their respect."

"Feh. They should respect us as a matter of course. We are greater than they."

"And yet we flee from them."

"We do not flee," I said, turning away. "I merely had no desire to hear what they had to say."

"Indeed," Muninn said. "Perhaps they felt we had stolen the feathers from their fallen sister."

The utter gall.

"We. Do. Not. Steal."

"Are you sure?" Muninn asked. "Because I

remember stealing thoughts and memories for Odin."

He had a point, not that I'd concede it. He'd not let this go without a fight. "Then let's discover the truth."

Muninn made a self-satisfied *quork*. "Where shall we try next, if you are so full of ideas?"

"It was the dvergar who turned us from flesh and feather to ink. We could go to the dwarves for answers."

"With what for payment?" Muninn asked. "The dvergar have ever been harsh bargainers."

He was correct, damn him.

I had no other ideas, so we flew on, the ground a blur beneath our wings. These borrowed bodies were as fast as ours had ever been, back when we lived. Faster.

Muninn caught my reminiscence.

"We live still."

"Not in the same way."

"All things change in time."

"Except our times are always filled with blood and death."

We flew.

Whenever we alighted upon a branch, crows waited. They shrieked defiance, loss, and anger, but had little to say as to *why*. When we found a solitary bird—rare—we bullied answers from them. Muninn felt it wouldn't help our cause. I didn't care. They, like us, are social birds. They would talk.

I wanted answers.

There'd been many deaths in the crows' community—the funeral we'd witnessed was not an isolated incident—and the deaths could not be attributed to the normal sources: predators, age, humanity. They believed *we* were the cause.

Their actions had spoken loud enough, but wrangling confirmation from one of the crows pleased me.

I knew Muninn would know the exact count of times he and I had flown on feathers, and if I believed there was correlation between our appearances and the deaths of our lesser cousins, I might've asked him for the number. I preened my plumage. Crow feathers. *Honestly*.

"It is possible," Muninn said, waiting, surprisingly, until the crows had fled. He didn't usually consider such things. "That we are, in part, responsible, and our borrowed flesh comes at a price to the nearby crows."

"Dressed as a crow?" I asked incredulous. "A crow? Ludicrous. You should stick to the halls of memory, brother."

"It is not ludicrous to them," Muninn said,

gesturing with his beak towards a nearby tree where the last crow we'd interrogated had roosted. He'd summoned friends. They eyed us from their tree, making a cacophonous racket.

"We should continue our hunt," I said.

"Yes," Muninn added, not taking an eye from the crow tree. "Since you are certain we have no part in their tragedy."

I spied another dead crow on a lawn. Several, in fact. They looked small in death's quiet. Looking closer, and now that the body was not being obscured by its brethren, I could see each corpse had no wings. Its blood was fresh, as was the magic that had killed it. Its wings had been sheared away with precision; this was not a predator's work—beast or human. The corpses reeked of dwarf magic.

Fresh dwarf magic.

As did my brother bird and I. "Now we know why our cousins accuse us."

Muninn nodded. "Indeed."

"Who would steal crow wings?" I asked.

"A mystery," Muninn said.

"For us to solve."

Muninn turned from the corpse to regard me. "I thought you cared nothing for our lesser cousins."

"I do not. Not really. However, by finding vengeance for them, we may find answers for ourselves."

"Very well."

We lit out from the tree, following the diminishing remnant of magic through the air, a disintegrating rune here and there, as a way-post.

The trail of runes led us from corpse-crow to corpse-crow—their funerals had all been completed and the bodies left for the cats and worms. There was no discernible pattern. But it was difficult to find such, when we could not relate each location to the others as a whole picture, and not series of caches.

Finally, we lost the trail. The path had diminished too far, hidden in the general air of rising magic that had overtaken Winnipeg since our awakening. Without a fresh corpse, or a new fact, there would be no answers.

"We need a map," I said.

"I know where to find one," Muninn said.

We followed a worm line of cars until one veered from the pack. Even from this height, I could see the rainbow slick of oil in the parking lot.

"How do you wish to proceed?" Muninn asked as we perched atop a sign.

We drew a few stares from pedestrians, who pointed, impressed with our size and appearance. I preened myself in appreciation, while I considered.

"We cannot just fly in and steal what we need," I said.

"And why not?"

"We do not belong in their buildings. And the less we interact with the humans, the better."

Muninn dropped his head. I think my brother looked forward to doing just that—a pity we could not. Or could we?

It would be easy enough to dart in when a patron entered the business.

"You get the map," I said to Muninn.

"So we're thieves again?"

"You are," I shot back, "since you were so keen to take on the mantle earlier."

He shook his head, side to side. "And you?"

"I will chase those inside until they run

screaming and we will fly out the door with them."

"Your task sounds like more fun."

I nodded. "It does, doesn't it?"

I imagined we looked comical, shuffling foot to foot, by the gas station's entrance. I didn't want to chance getting a wing pinched. Nothing would take the sky from me again. Better those watching think us tame, so they would ignore us.

Most patrons gave us a wide berth, but for one, who smiled, and reached into his pockets. I was wary at first, until he removed a plastic-wrapped muffin and broke half off, tossing it to the sidewalk. I lunged for it as the door opened.

Muninn squawked, "The door!"

Muffin abandoned, we hopped inside, following the man, who seemed nonplussed that we had entered the gas station. I nodded at him, he sketched a shallow bow, smiling. I looked back through the glass at the bit of muffin, hoping no one cached it away before we left.

It did not take Muninn long to locate the maps. He flapped into the air, snatching one with his beak. There was a shrill cry from behind the counter. The three patrons in the station, other than the muffin man, joined in the shouts. One pointed, the other darted for the door. The man who'd tossed me the muffin used the distraction to tuck something under his jacket before leaving.

I leapt into the air, flapping my wings in the cashier's face. He swatted at me clumsily with his price scanner. The door opened and Muninn darted outside with the map.

Taunting the cashier was fun, and for that, I indulged a moment too long. As I disengaged from the cashier, the door closed.

There was still one person in the building, other than the cashier, who I felt would be hard pressed to abandon his post. Now he huddled under the desk, cradling a telephone. Perhaps he wanted to summon someone to deal with me.

That wouldn't do.

The woman at the back of the store. She hid behind a rack of potato chips, trying not to be seen. She would do. I only needed to flush her out. I swooped around, angling toward her. She bolted for the door. She hurled a bag of potato chips behind her. As if *that* would slow me.

I caught them in my talons, spinning to hold my direction and momentum. The bag popped under the pressure of my claws, spilling its contents everywhere.

I only had a moment to regret the lost bounty when I heard the chime from the opening door.

I followed the woman out. I circled back to snatch the muffin in my beak before I joined Muninn in a tree across the street.

My brother shook his head, as if disappointed in me, and I vowed I'd not share any of the treat with him.

We laid the pilfered map out upon a patio table in someone's backyard. They were not home, and no dog guarded the premises, so we were unlikely to be disturbed. I pinned the map to the table with gravel from the side of the house. Muninn marked the locations of the dead crows with colourful stones, all south and west of the two rivers that snaked through the city. I would come back for those stones later.

"I see nothing," Muninn said.

The map was an imprecise tool, and worse: incomplete. We couldn't possibly know where every crow had died. But there was something to it. Something scratching at the edges of my thought. A revelation just out of sight.

Our trail had led us south; wherever we needed to go, our answers were in that direction.

I poked at the northernmost stone, near where the rivers met. "This is as far as they've travelled to kill a crow."

"So?"

"If we plot a southern point, we'll have a search range."

"If we had a southern point we could trust as the limit of the thieving murderer's range."

I squawked in frustration. Muninn was correct again, much as I hated to admit. Even worse was the frequency with which his correctness occurred.

"We could keep circling south," Muninn said. "We might get lucky."

"I do not wish to waste our freedom trusting to luck and then spend our days of labour dodging angry crows. We can solve this puzzle. We can find this murderer, and stop them."

"If you say so." Muninn sounded dubious. I didn't blame him.

"You really are trying to help," said a crow from behind us.

Muninn started, squawking, into the air. *I* managed to maintain my sense of decorum.

The crow seemed pleased at the reaction she'd engendered. She wasn't alone. The trees had gone black with murder, and if they turned their ire to us, we wouldn't escape. Not this time.

Several crows lit out from the trees, gathering pebbles

from the flower beds. They lined up to place their stones on the map alongside ours.

Soon we had a much clearer picture, and I saw what was at the centre of the deaths. I knew where we had to go.

We flew.

The sun was setting on our day of freedom, and our flight would be extinguished before long. The murderer's trail had ended at a university near a squarish, squat residence that appeared to be attached to a chapel. More precisely, the trail ended at a second-storey window above a dumpster. A raccoon's eyes glowed yellow in the light from the building's front door. It hissed at us as it pulled a bit of trash from the bin.

A wing.

Or, what was left of one, after the feathers had been plucked.

"Our thief?" Muninn asked.

"They are worse thieves than Loki," I said. "Like you." Muninn buffeted me with a wing, and I laughed. "But this one is merely a scavenger."

Muninn clicked his beak, sulking. "Stealing the map was your idea."

"You stole it. Not me."

He had no answer to that.

"The room is empty. I'm going in," I said as I fluttered towards a window. The glass and screen would not bar me.

Except they did.

My feathers and meat splashed against the window like a thrown egg. I shuddered with shock, smelled the bloody tang—mine and another's—and heard the dissonant bars of something our host would probably call "metal."

I shook my head.

"It's warded," Muninn said. "Any other clever ideas?"

"You tell me," I muttered. "Why didn't you warn me?"

"I didn't think I would need to *remind* you that the one we pursue uses *dvergur* magic. Proof enough they have the power to keep us out. And every other intruder." Muninn turned his head as if feigning innocence. "Besides, would you have listened?"

He had a point; however, it was not one I wished to concede aloud. Especially not with his rude squawking laugh.

"You weakened it," Muninn said.

"Try again?" I asked. "Together?"

Sitting on the ledge, the blood was clearly visible.

Some was dried, brown and crusted, other spatters fresher. Whoever lived in this room had painted blood around the entire window frame. This was definitely *dvergur* work, but what were they doing so far south? Why were they at a university campus? The caster's magic was crude, succeeding with innate power rather than skill.

"**Whoever their teacher might have been, they should be ashamed at the laziness of this work,**" I said.

"**This 'lazy work' is enough to keep us out,**" Muninn reminded.

"**Not forever,**" I said.

I looked down. There were more plucked wings scattered in the trash bin amid the used condoms and junk food wrappers. To the ignorant, they would look like any discarded meat and bone. Not upsetting. Not alarming.

I saw the truth. A charnel pit.

We would stop this killer.

I poked at the window screen, the ward crackling with my touch. I hopped back from the shock and shook my head, trying to hide my discomfort in preening at my wing. Muninn was correct. The effect *had* been less than the first time.

"**We could try the same trick as at the gas station,**" Muninn offered.

I shook my head. "**His room will be locked in a more conventional, but equally vexing, way, and we will find ourselves just as stymied.**"

"True."

"Besides, if this building is anything like our host's memories of his time in university, there will be more than one door to contend with."

If it were anything like Ted's time in university, everyone would be too drunk to be concerned with our presence.

"Sometimes when he thinks he's hungover," Muninn said, "I'm making him relive a rough morning from his past."

"Outstanding," I said. "If not immediately helpful."

"Our target's neighbour is home. He may be helpful."

Without physical contact, it would be difficult for us to glean much from the neighbour's mind. Especially with the blood ward around the window muddying the waters. But it was something.

We hopped into the air, fluttering around to land one windowsill over and probed the thoughts and memories of a young man sitting at a desk, head buried in a book.

"He does not like his neighbour," Muninn said.

"Fears him," I corrected.

"Rightly so, but dislike is stronger in his mind. The murderer always listens to the same song."

"Only one?" I asked, incredulous.

"Yes."

"Sing the song."

Muninn shrugged, sharing the tune and the words with me as best he could. I left my perch and returned to the murderer's window. I tried to sing the song, but raven songs are not the same as rock 'n' roll. I doubted my idea would work.

I poked the screen with my beak. There was no shock.

A pity I couldn't smile. "I've weakened the ward enough for us to enter."

"You first," Muninn said.

"Fine," I said. "Chickenshit."

Muninn laughed. "Our host is rubbing off on you."

I ruffled my feathers in protest. "Were that the case, I'd have called you a chickenshit motherfucker."

Muninn squawked a prissy protest. I shredded the window screen with my beak.

We were in.

It was not a *dvergur* we sought at all, but a human. A glance at the pictures on his desk. A human in a cap and gown. I would call him a child. But if he was in this place, his society had deemed him an adult. Human decisions were so arbitrary. A ticking of minutes and hours and days becoming years, rather than a ritual or achievement.

Assuming this boy was the murderer, he held a scroll proudly. A wizard? We already knew he used dwarf magic. Perhaps he *had* passed some test of human or dwarf. It mattered not to me. How long before he turned his attention from our lesser cousins to ravens? To Muninn or myself?

As our host would say, **"Fuck that noise."**

I chuckled, drawing a sullen glance from my brother bird. He could not see it, but in trying times there was a great pleasure to be taken in profanity.

That tiny digression was all I allowed myself on the topic. The murderer might not be a *dvergur*, but he used their magic. Blood magic was a part of his crafting.

What was he crafting? Other pictures showed the youth staring sour-faced while wearing overalls and a helmet. A mine worker. That explained his connection to the *dvergar* and where he'd learned their blood-magic tricks. There was a woman next to him, dressed the same and wearing a shiny-shiny golden hoop through the centre of her bottom lip. I tore my eyes from the gold. Gold was not what we sought today.

There were books on biology, geology, and chemistry stacked on a cluttered desk. A pile of loose papers mostly obscured a stone slate. I knocked the papers aside. *Dvergur* writing scored the stone. A ritual for stealing power.

I tapped it with my beak to draw Muninn's attention. **"I doubt this was adopted for study by any of his professors."**

"What do you make of these?" Muninn asked, gesturing toward the walls.

Airplanes on glossy posters or in framed pictures filled the rest of the room's spare decoration. I knew his motivation now. So simple.

He wanted to fly.

I told Muninn as much.

Muninn croaked, shrill and angry. "He is stealing the sky from our cousins."

"What if he steals our wings? Our purpose? What will we do then?" I shuddered.

Thinking of our host, and how his gifts had been inked into his body by dwarves, what the boy desired no longer seemed unfathomable. And with the right craft, it would be possible. He would fly.

I understood. Who would not want to?

But the killer would not fly far. We had found his roost.

No one can hide from Thought and Memory.

We waited.

The door swung open as I hid his papers out of spite.

The murderer was shorter than I'd expected, but also more powerfully muscled than the images had implied.

Not a dwarf, though he could've been mistaken for one. He stank of physical effort. Sweat glistened on his forehead and stained his shirt; he held a duffel bag in his hand.

His eyes went wide when he saw us. Fear. Anger. Covetousness. It all flashed across his face as quickly as a lightning strike.

"We will stop you," I said.

He dropped his bag to the floor. "I'm not going back underground. You can't make me."

"We can put you under the ground," said Muninn.

"We will," I added.

"Not now," he said. He laughed a wild laugh. The hair on his arms and head bristled. Each thin hair darkened, and thickened, and became a feather. Each feather, a tiny wing. "Nevermore."

We flew to intercept him, to mete out justice. He bulled through us, diving through his screened window, and into the sky.

He thought he could outfly us. The angles he turned seemed to defy physics. We had only four wings between us. To this brash youth, we must seem foolish for even attempting pursuit. I could see his contempt. A bright cloud around him flashing like blood on snow. He would destroy us in the air to demonstrate his superiority.

We shall see. Correcting our course, we followed.

The murderer's direction was as obvious as his

contempt, body black against the setting sun. I darted to intercept him.

He spun without needing to bank or turn. His magically stolen wings gave him surprising manoeuvrability. I quorked my defiance and dove again.

Muninn hung back, circling wide and watching. If there were a pattern to the creature's dash, my brother bird would find it. The sorcerer didn't know my abilities, either. If he came too close, I could intercept his thoughts more easily than his body, and be where he was going, not where he was.

Our pursuit took us over a broad, murky river the locals referred to as "red." I snatched a feather from a wing on his head, but he dived again. I released the feather, regretfully, and let it drift on the wind like greasy smoke. This was no time to make a nest. Or take trophies.

We stole his wings one by one. For a time, I thought our efforts might work. But it was not enough. He had too many. He was too fast. We were but two. He *would* break away from us. We needed more wings.

We had them.

"Muninn, find the crows!"

"The sun is setting!" he cried, tearing another wing from the murderer's shoulder. "They will be sleeping."

"Then wake them!"

Muninn pulled away as I darted into the sorcerer's

face. I buffeted him with my wings, as if to say, *try and take these*. It was, as my host would say, a "fuck you," to the sorcerer. A challenge. One I hoped he'd feel compelled to accept.

I counted upon his contempt. His belief he could beat me. Toy with me. Leave any time he chose.

The sorcerer grabbed at me, and the hard-edged magical feathers covering his body cut. Before long, he *would* take my wings. I pecked his face in defiance, one of the few places on his body not bristling with feathers, and he jolted back.

I'd missed his eye. Pity. But I'd angered him. I tucked my wings and dived. He followed. Good. It was dark, but my eyes were still sharp, and as I angled away from the university and over the river, I could see Muninn with murder at his tail.

I flew, leading the sorcerer to his fate.

Vengeful crows fell upon him like he was a berry bush, ripe for the plucking. They were a pecking cloud that could not be sated. The murderer knew how high he had flown. His fearful thoughts were simple to pluck from the air. He tried to escape, but for all the wings he had stolen, the crows had more. They stole back what was theirs, one by one by one. He fell. He screamed. And he had a long drop in which to consider what he'd done.

I had witnessed crow funerals, now I saw crow justice.

"Justice is murder," I said as Muninn joined me on the wing.

He groaned at the play on words, but said, "Job well done."

"What shall we do with our next day off?"

"You're assuming we'll get another."

"A precedent has been set. I will demand we get another. You also."

"I like the way you think," Muninn said.

"Do not forget you said that."

"Let's go home," said Muninn, watching the crows swarm and peck, pulling stolen feathers from the sorcerer's flesh as he fell, all the way to the water. "We still haven't learned where our feathers come from."

"Another time," I said. "I look forward to flying again."

Without another look back, we turned for our roost. And we flew.

Runt of the Litter

He arrived like a lightning strike in a dry wood.

Loki. My ultimate ancestor. My father with so many "greats" in between as to render any connection moot. Moot to me, perhaps, but not to him. *He* saw me as family.

The trickster behaved less like a father figure than a shiftless, unemployed cousin: eating my food, smoking my cigarettes, drinking my beer, and abandoning used condoms atop the bathroom garbage. He made my life miserable and my home unlivable.

"You're not much of a wolf, Grim," he said, flipping through channels until he found a hockey game.

I shrugged. "You're not much of a god."

Loki furrowed his brow; white pinprick scars outlined his thin, pursed lips and I wondered if I'd gone too far. The god of mischief may not have had the power he'd once corralled, but he could still make my life uncomfortable.

People think of giants—especially *jötnar*—as big, dumb thugs. They're wrong. Or at least, they're not always right. We're masters of illusion and magic—fine, *I'm* not, but my ancestors often outwitted the Aesir and the Vanir. Not much of a feat if you know Thor, but it sounds impressive.

Loki wasn't the only one of us to slip from shape to shape, either. His son Fenrir—a real son of a witch—had been a terror. Asgard, Jötunheim, Midgard—Earth— you name it, he'd sown a lot of seed there. Any who had a touch of his blood found themselves close to the wolf. That's where me and my clan come from.

I was the runt of the litter. I'd learned a few tricks to compensate for that. Unlike my siblings, I wasn't trapped in my wolf form. Granted, I wasn't much of a giant— stretched out, I barely topped ten feet. Maybe that was why Loki had taken a shine to me. He was always the skinny smart kid to Thor's hulking linebacker. I could relate to that.

If you ignored the soft flesh that had no natural defences or weapons, and that grew cold far too easily, humanity had its advantages. It made picking up beer considerably easier, for one. Even if my family'd had the wherewithal to steal a case, they'd never be able to open up the bottles. The teasing ended when it was time to twist off the caps, that's for damn sure. They could've stolen cans, I suppose. But then they'd be drinking canned beer.

As far as I was aware, I was the only *jötunn* making a home in Winnipeg. My brothers, sister, and cousins much preferred the North, where trees outnumbered people, game was plentiful, and they didn't need to hide what they were. Where they could revel in it, instead.

Loki still hadn't spoken up about what prompted his visit. So I asked him: "Why now?"

"I need a reason to call on my favourite descendant?"

"You have a reason for everything you do. Even if I can't sniff it out."

"Well, I was staying with one of your brothers—"

Thor's fat sack. "Which one did you piss off?"

"The big one."

I groaned, shaking my head. Fen. He'd taken the name of Loki's son, but my brother had none of Fenrir's sunny disposition. No doubt Loki had taken something, said something, or screwed something that had pissed him off.

I couldn't believe I was going to ask, but I did anyway: "What did you do?"

Loki looked up from his hockey game, and, as if he'd read my mind, said, "Let's just say I scored a hat trick."

"Why in Hel would you choose to stay with him? He hates you more than—" I stopped before I could finish the statement. Before I knew for sure what was going to come out next. More than I do. More than he hates me. Was I afraid of Loki? You're damn right I was. He might not look like much now in his rumpled suit and glasses, but he tried to end the entirety of Odin's creation. Out of spite. Pretty much succeeded, too, except for us scattered remnants. "More than the rest," I finished awkwardly.

If Loki had caught on, he let it slide. Or he filed it away for later. He drained his beer and set the bottle down with a clink on my glass-topped coffee table.

"I like you, Grim."

I liked him, too. I just liked him better when he wasn't in my apartment. I asked, "You want to go for a run?"

"With you?" he snorted. "In the middle of the city?"

"Apartment's starting to feel a little cramped."

It was the largest place I could afford. I could take on a human height, but I still had to account for several hundred extra pounds, and it wasn't always pretty. The way the hardwood creaked beneath my every step, I did occasionally worry about the floor taking my weight, but at least the old building's twelve-foot ceilings allowed me to walk around at my full height. It wasn't much, but it *was* home.

If Loki got me kicked out, I doubted I'd be able to sleep without the ting of the radiator. Or the sounds of angry sex from the apartment below that steamed up the pipe along with my heat.

"If you're *afraid*, make sure that no one sees us." Loki had already shucked off his clothes. He didn't need to, his clothes changed with him. I think he just liked being naked.

Clothes aside, his change was different than mine. A difference born of the distance between our blood. One moment he was a man, next he was a wolf. My transformation would take some time. Not long by my reckoning, but long enough for Loki to be bored.

"C'mon, c'mon," he urged.

I pulled off my shirt and started to change.

"Hey, you've been working out?" Loki said. "Looking good."

A pleasant scent caught my nose.

Loki hadn't just changed into a wolf, he'd changed into a *female* wolf. And she was smirking. "Thought we could take the edge off."

His long tongue lolled out the side of his mouth. Some of us retained human speech despite our inhuman forms. Fen could make his wolf's mouth scrape out words in the *jötunn* tongue, but not any human language. If he weren't so much bigger than the rest of us, I might've teased him about it. But while he couldn't speak, he could still understand. Our blood was as unpredictable as Loki's temper, and no one chanced it.

The trickster had other advantages; he could change his shape from rat to *jötunn* and anything in between. When I slid into my wolf skin, it was at my true size. Conservation of mass doesn't exist for the dirty bugger, not like it does for me. But then, I'm no god.

No one would ever mistake me for a dog with a touch of wild. If I got spotted, they were more likely to cry, "bear" than "wolf."

I felt the fur sprouting from my spine and rushed to

my balcony. I didn't have long and I wouldn't fit through the door if I waited. I had to go, now.

I lost sight of Loki for a moment as my eyes shifted from human to wolf, but I could smell him down on the street. I hit the asphalt with a thud. I felt at home here in Winnipeg's downtown, with its old buildings littered with spirits of the uneasy dead.

Winnipeg was a good home. Essentially in the middle of nowhere, surrounded by farmland, it was easy to disappear. The city often challenged for the title of Murder Capital of Canada, so if any came hunting *jötnar*, a couple extra bodies didn't make too much noise. There was also a forest within city limits. Normally, I would've bused to it before making the change. But with Loki as my wingman, I *should* be safe from detection.

Unless he decided to make things … interesting.

It had been a long time since I'd stretched my limbs like this. We ran, heedless, into oncoming traffic. No driver made any attempt to avoid us. To them we were invisible. We'd yip and dance out of the cars' way at the last moment. Loki laughed and howled. I joined him, shaking the windows of an office tower.

Soon, I took the lead. It *was* my city, after all. We followed the river. Despite trusting in Loki's skill at not being seen, I didn't trust *him*. I wanted to minimize our chances of being spotted by the wrong eyes.

Midgard wasn't the gods' playground anymore. Humanity had come into their own sort of power—power that even Ragnarök would pale in comparison to. Loki was tricky, but could he outwit a nuke? Better to hide. To run.

To say my family's views differed would be an understatement.

They *loved* being seen. Once someone had witnessed true magic, it stained their world. Free game. None lasted long. I wish I could say I'd never joined in. I'd like to say I'd had the strength to leave because I refused to hunt men. But if I had, I'd be dead.

A lot of wealthy Winnipeggers made their homes along the river. People who would be missed, if not mourned. We ran just at the edges of their property, setting off motion detectors and dogs, both. I looked at Loki, and he shrugged. Allowing the animals to see us, to wake their masters: this small mischief was a pleasure he could not deny himself.

I have nothing on my brother when it comes to intimidation, but when one of the Fenrisúlfar howls, things shut the fuck up. A purse-dog was no challenge to quiet.

We made it to the park that was gateway to the forest. There was a zoo within that park, and the stink and distress of its prisoners grew sharper as I ran by. I was uncertain what bothered them more—me, or my freedom.

Parkland gave way to bush and I felt my *jötunn* size as I shouldered past trees, uprooting small poplars. There were deer here, I could smell them. I licked my lips—a proper hunt would do me good. Take the edge off of city life. "Let's hunt," I growled.

"A fine idea, little one," a woman's voice boomed—my sister's voice. I whirled. How had she snuck up on us?

Angr was wearing human clothes, loosely stitched together. Mismatched denim made up her skirt and shredded and knotted dresses covered her breasts. Despite my growing fear, I did manage to be impressed: she'd finally learned some modesty.

She wasn't alone. A long, low growl rumbled from behind her.

Fen.

I'd know that growl even if I were deaf. I'd feel his hatred. Looks like he'd finally won the right to court our sister. I wondered if any of my other brothers still lived. I can't say I really gave a shit, but I was curious.

Jötnar are often incestuous. Our women are too rare. Brother marries sister, or father marries daughter when he feels like trading up. I was too far down the family pecking order to compete for Angr's attentions, but I'm not too proud to say that I would've if I'd thought she'd choose me. If I thought I'd had a chance in Hel.

Like me, Angr could change forms. She lived as wolf and *jötunn*. Imagine how terrified you'd be if someone literally twice your size walked up to you in a bar, poked you in the chest and wanted to start some shit. You'd back down if I came calling. Well, despite being ten feet tall, a wolf the size of a damned grizzly, *I'm* still terrified of *her*. And Fen makes her look like a puppy.

"Oh shit," said Loki, actually showing the good sense to sound worried.

"You thought you'd get away with it, trickster?" Angr demanded.

"Well obviously," Loki answered. "Or I wouldn't have done it."

"*Enough.*"

Fen's answering growl made me shudder. In the *jötunn* language the word carried an unspoken "or else." A lot of our words did. And don't ask "or else, what?" It's a question that leads to being eaten.

The instinct to drop my gaze, to cower and beg, was overwhelming. But I stood my ground. He was going to kill me, anyway. And, this was *my* city, damn it. Not his.

If Loki had gotten Fen's blood up enough to make him leave the North and set paw in civilization, my brother'd never let me live. And if Angr had finally chosen him, I was the only threat left for our sister's affection. Such as it was.

Angr ran her fingers through Fen's ruff. His growls eased into a steady rhythm—like a cat's purr.

"One last hunt," Angr said. "*Little* brother."

Loki leaned in close. "I don't think they're talking about the deer."

"No shit," I hissed back at him.

"We want to be like you," Angr said. "But without

your other … handicaps. Our plans are too great to be limited to our birth forms."

"I can't teach you," I said. "You can do it or you can't."

"Not you. When we eat Loki's heart, we can steal his power. There are rituals that will let us lap up his power with his blood."

I shot a glance at the trickster. He shifted from foot to foot, avoiding my gaze.

"You want *me* to join *your* ritual?" I asked. "To hunt Loki?"

I thought of every stolen beer, or five spot. Every time that something the trickster had done had led the cops down on me. His sexual advances. But to hunt him with Angr and Fen?

Loki looked up at me, and damned if he didn't give a fine set of puppy-dog eyes. He'd managed to suck Odin in to making him a blood brother. Odin had been the wisest of the gods, but you could say that was damning someone with faint praise.

Loki had few friends left; lots of offspring, but no real family. He'd always been the runt of the pantheon. He'd saved the gods as many times as he'd betrayed them, but he'd never been one of them. I suppose we had something in common, there.

I let loose a throaty growl, and Loki started running.

"No," I said, bolting after him.

"They were going to kill you, anyway," he said as we ran, by way of thank-you.

I nodded. "I know."

The forest was a great place to run. To hunt. But it wasn't a great place to hide—not from my family.

Loki led the way, trying to keep to smaller paths. They were tight for me. I had to hope they'd be impassable for Fen. His angry roar, not far enough behind us, accompanied by trees snapping to kindling, was not boosting my confidence.

"I can't believe you led them to me." I tried not to whine. I did. It was hard in my wolf shape. Instinct bled into all of my action.

"They were coming for you, regardless. Together we have a chance." Loki ducked under a fallen tree. I pushed off from its trunk and sailed over top of it. "We'll be fine. Trust me," Loki said.

Trust me. A phrase that immediately got my fur ruffled. Trust me. That phrase has seen me captured by dwarves. Hit by a Greyhound bus. Both my hands broken—after I'd opened the beer, mind you. "Trust me" had nearly gotten me killed more times than I could count. But what can you do when the speaker will do whatever they want anyway? Hope, rather than trust.

Hoping I could trust Loki—a thought scarier than Fen, the big bad wolf. "Well, I can't take Angr on my own, let alone Fen, so if she scares you, I don't see why you came to me for help."

If wolves could smile, Loki did as he looked back at

me. "Leave Fen to me. He's dumber than he is mean. You worry about your sister."

I shook my head. I didn't see how he'd pull it off. Fen wanted me dead as much as he wanted Loki's power. He'd come for me first. Not that I had a clue how I'd handle Angr if he didn't.

Loki stopped running and stood up naked in his human shape. With a flourish, he conjured a Zippo and cigarette, seemingly from thin air, but I knew better. He'd reached into some unsuspecting soul's pocket to pilfer them.

"Are you high?" I asked. "Fen'll smell that a mile away."

"I know." Loki exhaled, and then I was looking at my *jötunn* form. The trickster had become an annoying mirror. "Trust me," he said again. "The dumb shit will come for me."

Loki took a power drag from his cigarette, then tossed it, exhaling a plume of smoke through his nostrils. I watched the red ember pinwheel lazily into the night. I snatched it out of the air. If Loki was wearing *my* shape, someone would have to wear his.

Angr had come for Loki.

So I'd give him to her.

I left the wolf behind, standing, straightening. Stretching for a form that wasn't my own, but was a part of me down to my very beginnings. I reached my normal height and tried to push past it. Pain. I pushed harder. I needed to be more. Taller. A ten-foot, squat Loki wouldn't fool Fen, let alone Angr. In the skin of his birth, Loki was also short for a *jötunn*, though taller than me. He was also slighter. I shaved some of my bulk, directing it upwards. More pain, but I could feel it work. Unfortunately, Loki's shape wasn't enough.

His scent also had to be mine. That was easier to mimic. Loki's body knew its own smell, but the scent on me was distracting. I kept looking round, trying to spot the trickster. Sensing the God of Mischief, but being unable to see him, is unsettling. Like waiting for the guillotine blade to drop.

Fen howled behind us. Another tree fell.

"That's a good look for you, Grim," Loki said. He wore my wolf shape now, and sat, bored and licking his balls—my balls, I supposed—waiting for Fen's arrival. "Now, get going."

I nodded and bolted past the trickster.

There were growls and barks from behind me. Fen's deep rumble, and noises that were higher-pitched, frightened. Pained.

I didn't sound like that, did I?

Even without my wolf's nose, I could smell Angr. She hadn't left the clearing. I stopped at its edge, watching her. She was sitting atop a felled tree, still in her *jötunn* form; still beautiful, carving a branch she'd torn from the tree's trunk. Lit by moonlight, her lips moved in song.

Rune magic.

When had she learned *that*?

Angr looked up from her work but didn't stop her song. I strutted into the clearing. I could feel the magic coming off the wood. I concentrated instead on maintaining my "no worries" Loki walk.

I'm no witch, but I can read the Elder Runes. I've carved a few myself, but there was no chance they'd carried anything like the power Angr was feeding that branch.

Her song stopped. "Hello, Loki."

Well, what do you know? My trick had worked. I should have been surprised. I didn't want to do anything to break Loki's disguise, so I shrugged, non-committal.

"You left Grim to Fen's tender mercies?"

"I did," I said, my voice sounding strange to my ears. Not me. Not Loki.

She sighed. "I'll miss him, you know?"

I didn't believe her. I searched her smile for a hint of lies, or triumph. If anything, it seemed sad. Since she thought I was Loki, I decided to run with it.

"Fen?" I asked, mustering my most mocking tone.

Angr frowned, irritated. "I'm not surprised you were left chained to the rock to be tortured."

Okay, I had to admit: I could see why Loki was the way he was. It was *fun*. "Look how well that turned out," I said. "So, why will you miss Little Grim?"

"He was the only one of our father's brood who could rub one thought next to another and come up with two."

"I had no idea you fancied him."

That was truth. I hoped she'd elaborate on those feelings, but instead she only shrugged.

It was often surprising what Loki knew. I could probably bring up any moment from our childhood and Angr would accept that he'd know it.

"How many times did you lead him around by his dick? Promise it a home in that canyon between your legs?"

"Hardly my fault our brothers always caught him before he could seal the deal. I was willing to choose him. Size or no."

I hadn't known that. I could feel the power of her cutting into me like an arctic wind. Her scent, it held no lie. I shook it off. "He's weak. You tortured him."

"He wouldn't have lived long if he'd been weak," Angr said. "And how long do you think he would've lasted if I had shown any favour? Fen would've eaten him alive."

"Grim ran," I said, remembering the last day I'd seen my brother. He'd just killed our father for rulership of our little family tribe. I'd been certain I was next. "Left you to them. He's a coward."

"No more than I." Angr stood, holding her carved branch. She spoke a rune. The branch glowed, and then it was a spear. "A weapon as fine as Gungnir," she said, nodding approval at her work. "And meant for you, trickster."

"They say Odin's spear never missed."

Angr's canines flashed in the moonlight. "Neither will mine."

I heard a loud, pained howl. Familiar, but it hadn't been Fen. I sighed. I'd had hope, for a moment. Hope that cocky little Loki would be able to kill my brother for me. Now I was a snake caught in a fork, fucked no matter which way I wriggled.

We circled each other, two wolves each wanting to rule our tiny pack.

She hurled her spear and I bolted. It jerked in the air to follow me. I knew it was going to strike home. It thudded into my side, sending me spinning to the dirt. I lay there, panting. I felt pain, but not as much as I *should* have. The spear's tip had barely pierced my skin. I didn't feel like I was dying.

So I folded up my body, hiding the wound, and pretended to.

Angr sauntered over, grinning her lupine smile. She jerked the spear from my flank and rolled me over onto my back. I saw her sniff. She wrinkled her nose and sniffed again.

"Grim?"

I groaned. "Hey, sis."

"But … but …" She shook her head. "Your scent … Loki … the spear shouldn't have missed."

"*It* didn't," Loki said from behind us.

Angr looked up and growled.

"*You* didn't know what you were aiming at."

"I don't know how you—"

"Please," said Loki. "If you have to explain a joke, it's just not funny anymore."

"Fen?" I asked.

"He's strong, but … easily distracted." Loki smiled. "I've known you long enough to wear your shape, Angr. Take it as a compliment. You stopped him in his tracks."

I shuddered, sloughing into my natural form. "You fucked my brother?"

Loki pulled an insulted face. "Of course not."

I released a relieved breath. Thankfully, I wouldn't have to picture their coupling.

"*He* did the fucking," Loki said, shattering my peace of mind.

Angr was seething. "You've used my body for the last time, trickster."

"You brought the big, bad wolf down here to kill Loki—and *me*, I might add," I shot back at her. "You don't get to complain about not liking the result."

To me, the trickster said, "You're the man of the family now, so I guess you can take Angr for your wife. Do all that shit you growl about in your sleep."

I started to speak, but Loki waved me off. He smiled at Angr; the grin was a hooked little knife. "Or kill her. Like she still wants to do to me."

The first prospect had its appeal. So did the second. My sister was a fine-looking *jötunn*, but she held grudges. I wasn't sure whether the wish fulfillment was worth having to worry about waking up dead. Every day. For the rest of my life. Still, I didn't want her blood on my hands.

"Or we could grab a beer."

"Done," Loki said.

"You." I pointed a finger at my sister like it was a cocked pistol; firing it with my best mocking wink. A gesture that came easier after wearing Loki's form, somehow. "Don't come back here. Ever."

She sulked. It had been a while since I'd seen Angr not get her way.

"And clean up after yourself," Loki added. "Before Fen starts to stink."

Loki didn't want to wait for the beers. He pulled two tall, cold ones from wherever it is that he pulls things, and passed me one. It tasted good. Better, in fact, than any beer before it.

"Thanks," I said.

"Hey," he said, his smile flashing like a prairie grass fire. "We're family."

Family. For once the word didn't fill me with dread.

Eating of the Tree

That goddamn squirrel left his nuts in my coffee cup. Again.

There are things that don't exist for the daytime world. Things you only see when you work night shift security in Winnipeg. Of all the strangeness Marie Belanger had encountered, the *worst*—the fucking worst—was that squirrel.

"I will get you for this, you furry-tailed, piss-drinking, pack rat!"

Marie scanned the break room. She couldn't see her rodent nemesis. She sighed and dumped the acorns into the trash. She washed her cup in case the squirrel had left her any other surprises.

She'd assembled quite the collection of "gifts" in her cup over the last few months. Beads. Buttons. Feathers. Wingnuts. A weird-looking, dead lizard. Lately it had been Scrabble tiles. So far, she had two each of R, A, and T, and a single O, S, K, and U, respectively. At least she knew the squirrel couldn't spell worth shit. Sometimes Marie believed the squirrel talked to her and she thought she was going crazy. Other times, she thought the squirrel plotted against her.

On those days she *knew* she was going crazy.

An ash tree grew in the centre of Union Station. No one knew who'd planted it, but it'd grown fast since last November when something had blown the roof off the station rotunda. The tree had been a wispy five feet tall then—little more than a broom handle—but in the months since, it had more than doubled in size.

The tree—and the wishing well constructed around it—were the source of most of Marie's problems. They'd become a symbol of hope for some. A sign of resilience and growth in the face of inexplicable tragedy. If anybody knew for sure what'd happened that night, the answer was lost in a blizzard of conspiracy theories and finger-pointing. Some blamed a leak from the infectious diseases lab; others claimed it'd been a trial run of the zombie apocalypse. As if there'd ever be a satisfactory explanation for the days-long impenetrable fog and the bodies in the streets. Marie wouldn't hazard a guess; all she knew was people turned up at all hours to drop coins and wish for … whatever idiots without train tickets asked for. Cleverer, less-scrupulous idiots showed up later to steal those same coins. The thefts had ramped up lately, but Marie had seen no sign of the culprits.

Do we blame the day shift, Marie?

Yes, we do, Marie.

Before the tree, nights had been a great time to do sweet fuck-all. There were the occasional drunks or sightseers who wandered in from The Forks Market, nearby, but those were few and far between. Mostly, Marie's job was peaceful. Quiet. Except now she froze her ass off eight months a year because some idiot had decided to leave the rotunda open-air after the repairs. The decision not to remove the tree was likely a factor. And *best of all*, now it was Marie's duty to keep an eye on it, on top of everything else she had to watch.

She gulped more coffee and headed to the rotunda to make certain it was still clear.

It wasn't.

A crowd encircled the tree, holding hands. They wore embroidered cloaks and chanted in a language Marie didn't understand. Maybe *they* were her thieves.

Marie yelled out, "Security!"

They ignored her. One, a woman, broke the circle, and dropped something in the wishing well. A coin? The circle closed hands behind her while she ladled water from the well onto the tree's trunk with her hands.

Still ignoring Marie, the woman said loudly, in English this time, "Grow powerful and strong."

There was a shimmer, like a heat mirage in summer, and fog rolled off the well, engulfing the tree. *Are they putting dry ice in the well?*

Marie blinked—was the tree taller? Broader? It looked to be. Had to be a trick of the light. Edges of night and caffeine jitters.

She tried again. "What's going on?"

They still ignored her.

"I've got bear spray, and I'm not afraid to use it," Marie said.

That got them. They turned as one and stared at her like she was crazy. Maybe she was, but not because she wanted them out of her building.

Make them think you're crazier than them, Marie. Or they'll never leave.

"Go on, shoo!"

That probably isn't going to do it.

The last wisher addressed Marie with the haughty tone of a River Heights soccer mom. "We are not leaving Yggdrasilsson unprotected."

She couldn't make out the word—presumably their name for the tree. Why would they name it? Did they expect it to answer?

Probably.

Weirdos.

"Your … sick Iggy … dress tree is in good hands," she said, brandishing her bear spray. "It's my job to protect it. Now leave. Before I call the cops."

The woman narrowed her eyes and pursed her lips as if she wanted to ask for a refund without a receipt. "And what can the police do to keep the tree whole? To bring the worlds back together? What can *you* do?"

Worlds? "I've also got handcuffs and a good left hook."

And a stun gun and telescoping baton. Not perfectly legal, so she wasn't about to bring it up with them. Just because they were trespassing didn't mean she had to go down with them.

"Not enough," a cultist said, shaking her head.

Something shrieked from above. Marie flinched and hoped her fear hadn't shown. The last thing she wanted was these weirdos knowing she was frightened.

A squirrel—*the* squirrel—leapt from the roof. The squirrel hit the thin top branches of the ash and the tree swayed so violently, Marie worried its trunk would snap. She didn't want to be the one to explain why, and how, it'd happened. The squirrel scrambled down the ash and bounded through their ranks, darting between Marie's legs. She tried not to squeak. It would diminish the badass pose she'd struck to intimidate the trespassers.

You totally squeaked, Marie.

Quiet, Marie.

The squirrel circled round and came to a stop beside her. Red as a cartoon devil, and *big*. The little prick looked like the offspring of a drunken night between a raccoon and an Irish setter. It *stared* at her.

"I see," the lead weirdo said, inclining her head to the squirrel. She looked ready to bloody bow. "It appears you do have matters well in hand."

Because of the squirrel?

Don't look a gift horse in the mouth, Marie. Move them along.

"Right. Move along," Marie said, giving them a brisk nod—which she hoped conveyed a confidence in her statement she didn't quite feel. "Leave it to me."

They bobbed their hooded heads emphatically in return. The leader passed her a business card for Ashes to Ashes, some holistic health store in the city's Little Italy area. "If you need us," she said, "don't hesitate to call."

"Got it," said Marie, tucking the card into a pocket. She stole another look at the squirrel standing at attention beside her. She didn't like the way it looked at her. Also: she was glad she didn't wear skirts to work. "We see anything, we'll holler."

The cloaked figures spun their finery off their shoulders, rolled up their cloaks, and tucked them into their oversized purses. Absent the renaissance-fair garb, dressed in skinny jeans or yoga pants and blouses or sweaters, they looked strangely normal. Without another word, they filed out, leaving Marie alone with the tree.

And the squirrel.

The tree *seemed* fine. Coins peppered the wishing well, a few shining silver in the moonlight. It was mostly pennies. *What wish do you expect for a cent? Seriously.* She shrugged. Not like there was any other use for pennies since Canada had decommissioned the copper.

"Foolish thing, putting a wishing well near that tree," said a male voice from behind Marie. She jumped in surprise and wheeled around, but no one was there.

Only the squirrel, still standing on its haunches.

Looking at her.

"Worse: not specifying *who* you're wishing to grow powerful and strong."

Marie blinked. The voice … it'd come from the squirrel. It couldn't have come from the squirrel.

"Shitshitshit."

Deep breath—don't show fear. You've talked down meth heads and wrestled bikers, Marie. You can do this.

"Destiny and fate can get … confused where wishes abound," the squirrel said. Then. It. Smiled. "Hello, Marie."

Stay calm.

Must I?

No.

"Ahhhhh!"

That wasn't calm, Marie.

The squirrel picked at an ear, as if in discomfort. "*Must* you?"

"Ahhhhh!"

Apparently, I must.

The squirrel winced. *Can squirrels wince?*

"Please stop," it said.

It said, "please," Marie.

"Ahhhhh!"

The squirrel waited for her to finish yelling. That took a while.

Eventually Marie sputtered, hoarsely, "You … you can talk."

"Obviously," said the squirrel, looking up at her. "Surprisingly, so can *you*."

"Oh, don't be a dick."

Okay, Marie, the squirrel is *talking to you. No avoiding that.*

With a shaking hand, Marie took out her phone and pointed it at the squirrel, fumbling with the camera app, and tried to hold her bear spray steady in her other hand.

"Say something else."

The squirrel raised a tiny paw … *was he? Yup. He's flipping me off.*

"Aww, c'mon. No one will believe me if you don't talk."

The squirrel asked, "Why do you care if they don't?"

"*I* won't believe me if you don't."

It nodded. "Fair."

The squirrel scampered toward the tree, and Marie backpedalled away from him. He tested the water with a paw, dabbing it several times before he raised it to his lips.

"This water tastes like bull piss."

Marie's first thought was, *Really?* Followed by, *You've tasted bull piss?* She said nothing.

The squirrel pulled a bug off the tree and ate it. He chewed noisily before turning around to address Marie.

"I remember when Odin wished for wisdom. And what did that get him? No peripheral vision and a blind spot for Loki to exploit," the squirrel said. "'Grow powerful and strong.' Be careful what you wish for, meat bags."

"Odin? Loki?"

"An Aesir and a *jötunn*, respectively."

"I can make up words too, you grunklefink."

"Vikings and giants. *Norse mythology?* Frigg's taint, go see a movie."

She'd heard the names, but not the titles that followed. She wanted more out of this squirrel. Even if just to prove to herself this was actually happening. Marie eased her stance but didn't put away her bear spray in case the squirrel was rabid or it wanted her wallet. She kept her phone out too. Marie was pretty sure she hadn't drunk a forty before work, or eaten a bag of mushrooms, but in the morning she'd need proof this'd happened. The big red bastard looked at her, cocked his head, *tsked*, and bounded away.

Toward the break room.

Marie turned to the tree. Smoke, or fog, rose from the well. Hoarfrost crusted the tree's trunk. Whatever was happening, Marie hadn't seen it before. Somebody ought to look into that.

Somebody who was paid to care.

That's you, Marie.

She sighed. *It is, isn't it?*

'Fraid so, Marie.

Well, shit.

Marie followed the squirrel. She could use some more coffee. She looked over her shoulder and saw a black shape, like a lizard, peel a strip of bark from the tree. Another held a shining coin in its jaws. A grue ran up Marie's spine and she rubbed at the gooseflesh peppering her arms. The coin thief disappeared into the well in a flash of steam and a splash of water. *There's not enough coffee in the world, Marie.* Bobby always kept a mickey in his locker. Maybe she'd make her coffee Irish.

"The tree is dying," said the squirrel, hopping onto the counter and rummaging through the cupboards.

"Looks fine to me," Marie said. The coffee had helped. The rye had helped more. "Growing, even."

"Looks can be deceiving." The squirrel sipped coffee he hadn't paid for and grimaced at the taste. He rubbed his little chin thoughtfully. "Especially since the tree is being devoured. From below."

"By those lizards?" Marie dropped a quarter into the staff coffee fund and paid for the squirrel's coffee. That meagre gift was the last of her change, but she was unlikely to need caffeine to stay awake with a talking squirrel doing a ride-along.

"They're *dragons*." The squirrel's voice held surprising graveness. Marie still wasn't convinced any of tonight's events were happening. "Children of Níðhöggur, the Root-Eater."

"Of course they are." Marie shrugged. If talking squirrels could exist, why not dragons? She'd call the Church of St. George. Maybe she'd get to ride one! "Why haven't I seen them before?"

"They used to be content to chew the roots, like their mother. The ablutions those weirdos provide, and their wishes for the tree to grow strong and tall, abate the damage. Somewhat.

"Those supplicants call the tree Yggdrasilsson, but they're wrong. It's just Yggdrasill. The World Ash, the World Tree. This tree was made from a cutting of the original. It's the same tree—or will be—given time and protection. They believe in it. In the power it has. The power it *could* have. *If* it grows strong enough. If it lives long enough."

"And what power might that be?"

"To reconnect the remnants of nine broken, shattered worlds. To return your world to an age of legend."

"That might explain some of my Friday night shifts. 'Legendary.'"

The squirrel huffed and jammed its fists into its haunches. "Be serious."

"*You* are telling *me* to be serious?"

The squirrel wrinkled its nose. It looked cute when it scowled. *Don't get distracted, Marie.*

"Unfortunately, the dragons figured out what these would-be wise women are doing, and they're stealing the wishes, and they're growing along with the tree. They hate it. It came to be after their brothers and sisters died."

"And what if the tree dies?"

"Without the World Ash—a World Ash—acting as a conduit and anchor connecting the Nine Worlds, eventually there will only be one world left. Maybe it'll be yours. Maybe it'll be Muspelheim, the world of fire. I hope you brought your sun block."

"That's all well and good, but how did a magic tree end up in *Winnipeg*?"

"This tree was planted by Odin's brother Ve. An attempt to bring order to the world that is dawning." The squirrel gestured at the night sky in the open rotunda. "This place was already connected strongly to another world. That connection to the underworld, to Niflheim, was strengthened when the hordes of Hel were released here."

Underworld. "I *knew* this place was haunted."

Wait. Hordes of Hel? That sounds like zombies. Is he talking about that night, Marie?

I think he is, Marie.

She didn't want to see a repeat of that night. "This Ve? Is he a good-guy god?"

"Are any of them good?"

Marie wasn't sure whether the squirrel meant guys or gods. "Do you trust him?"

"About as far as I can throw you."

Was that a dig, Marie?

I think it was, Marie.

She wasn't sure whether she wanted the squirrel to be right, or wrong. She'd read legends. They didn't work out well for most people. Even heroes had a hard time. It was a rare hero who got a fair shake where gods and magic were concerned. If the squirrel were wrong, she was sharing a coffee with a giant talking squirrel. If she was imagining all this … *Not better.*

"If you can talk—and I'm not crazy—I guess I should know your name."

Yeah, knowing the name of the talking squirrel you're imagining is real *helpful, Marie. Bravo.*

The squirrel scowled. A cute look. She took a picture. It'd make a great animal meme. After she picked a celebrity to compare him to.

But who?

Kevin Costner?

You'd call him *a celebrity? What has he done lately?*

What have you done?

Low, Marie. Real low.

The squirrel's scowl hadn't abated. He really had expected her to know who he was. Marie shrugged, and the squirrel held out his hands as if pleading. "I gave you my name. Thor's nuts, I *spelled* it out for you."

Marie scrunched her brow. Spelled … "The Scrabble tiles?"

"Yes."

Marie tried to make a word—a name—out of the letters the squirrel had left for her. "Rostakraut? What kind of name is that?"

The squirrel let out a peeved sigh. He rubbed at his nose with little paws. Another photo opportunity wasted. "The name is Ratatoskur."

Marie repeated the name in her head. It sounded more like someone clearing their throat than a proper name.

"And that's supposed to mean something to me."

"Gods damn it, woman, haven't you heard of Google?"

"Obviously."

"Well if you'd tried *that* you'd know what's going on."

The squirrel stood on his hind legs and leaned against the counter like an office raconteur. He reminded her of Bobby, whose funny stories always ended in a creepy compliment or request for a date. The squirrel was only missing the polo shirt (and pants).

Don't look there, Marie.

Too late.

The squirrel winked.

Yeah, just like Bobby.

"You're right," Marie said. "I'm sorry."

"I need more coffee," the squirrel said. "*Good* coffee. Where do you keep the espresso?"

She needed to de-escalate this … Ratatoskur. Squirrels were trouble enough. A talking one hopped-up on caffeine …

Marie tried to convince herself she'd dealt with worse. Plenty of times. Especially when she'd worked loss prevention at the Hudson's Bay Company downtown. Something about that place brought out the weirdos. She'd had people come at her with switchblades, drywall saws, whatever they could get their hands on. One guy'd kept a full set of kitchen knives down his pants.

She muttered, "I can't believe I'm talking to a fucking squirrel."

"I'm not *a* fucking squirrel. I'm *the* fucking squirrel, thank you very much."

"But … why are you … why would you? Why are you?"

Bravo, Marie.

I thought we handled that superbly.

The squirrel rubbed at his face and took another sip of coffee. "Okay, here's the deal: I need you to save the tree."

She shrugged. "I'm not sure what *I'm* supposed to do about it. I'm a security guard, not an arborist."

"I used to run insults between Níðhöggur and the know-it-all eagle that lived in the tree's summit. It kept the dragon distracted from eating the tree, and the eagle distracted from eating *me*. I kept the tree alive for as long as possible. I'm getting too old for this shit. I couldn't save the last one, just prolong its end. Maybe you'll have better luck. Ve's offered me a different gig. *This* is your call to adventure."

"This is my call to go to the hospital," Marie said, rubbing at her eyes. *How many hours can you go without sleep before you hallucinate?*

"How about this? You will be visited by three—"

"No."

"Aww, c'mon."

"*No.*"

"Fine," the squirrel said, crossing its arms and sulking.

"Why me?"

The squirrel snorted a laugh. "Why does everyone given a quest ask 'why me?' I know all the secret ways between worlds and they led me to you. Boo-fucking-hoo. Life's unfair. I'm sure you've seen the shoe commercials. Just do it, Marie."

"I'm not complaining, you bushy-tailed dick. I'm curious. Why me? Why does it *have* to be me? What do I bring to the table?"

"You control the tokens," the squirrel said, holding a loonie he'd pilfered from the staff coffee fund. "You control the wishes."

"And you're what—a furry genie?"

"Wrong pantheon. How would you understand it?" The squirrel puffed himself up, straightened his shoulders and loomed. The action looked ridiculous. Marie felt ridiculous. "More like your Gandalf. Or Obi-Wan," he said.

"I don't need either," Marie said, wondering why all the film references, and also where squirrels went to movies. Did they go alone? Or did a bunch of them climb into a trench coat so they only had to pay one admission?

Ratatoskur continued rummaging through the break room cabinets. "What did you do with those nuts I gave you?"

Marie blushed. "I threw them in the trash. I … I didn't know where they'd been."

The squirrel cast some serious shade and maintained his angry stare. He lashed out with a foot, kicking over the garbage bin. He rummaged for a minute, fished one of the nuts from the trash and gave his head a disappointed *tut-tut* shake. He also held up a half-eaten egg salad sandwich.

"You gonna eat this?"

Marie shuddered. "All yours."

Ratatoskur nodded his thanks and crammed the whole thing into his mouth. He pressed the acorn into her hand.

Dealing with after-hours drunks was more adventure than she'd ever had—or needed. She'd pulled a woman from a moving Jeep. The Jeep kept moving and the would-be thief lost control of her bladder while they'd tousled. Marie had been scared before, but she'd never feared for her life until today.

Ratatoskur kept talking, cheeks bursting as he spread garbage *everywhere*. "Here's the thing …"

Marie rolled the acorn around in her fingers. It had scratches that looked like they might be letters, only not in any alphabet she recognized. Had to be a coincidence.

He passed her the other acorns. "Keep these with you."

"I don't want any of this."

"And yet," the squirrel said, now stuffing its cheeks with *her* lunch, "here we are."

The squirrel hadn't helped her clean the break room. Said he needed to check on the tree, since she wasn't doing her job. Marie decided to refute the little red shit by doing the job she was getting paid for.

He'd said his name was Ratatoskur. The name didn't mean anything to Marie—she could barely pronounce it—but on a whim she'd Googled it while making her rounds, looking for dragons and elves and trolls and any and everything she knew and—not quite—believed to be real. Her results were filled with Norse mythology links. In between checking doors and sipping coffee, Marie read on her phone.

Myths being real made less sense than talking squirrels.

The messenger part seemed to check out. And the insults. There was a tree, also an ash—*the* ash, Yggdrasill, Marie supposed. An eagle. A dragon. Some deer that lived in the tree. The illustrations looked like that dead lizard the squirrel had left her. A baby dragon? No more outrageous than anything else that'd been happening lately. It was all there. Well, most of it. There was a bunch of other stuff mentioned too. Fortune tellers and wells of wisdom. Cows. Runes. Other worlds. None of that had shown up yet—unless you counted those weird ladies at the wishing well. Nonsense.

Ratatoskur appeared to be on the level. As on the level as a shape-changing talking squirrel *could* be. And if he was on the level, she was living in a viking fantasyland and not Winnipeg.

What if he's a guy who turns into a squirrel?

Why would he choose a squirrel and not a wolf, Marie? Or a bear?

Exactly.

Can lycanthropes choose what they turn into?

More squirrels in the city than wolves or bears. Easier to hide.

True.

And he could've Googled all this Norse shit as easily as I did. All his "proof" is right there. He might just be fucking with us.

Still doesn't explain the lizards, Marie.

Dragons.

Right. Dragons.

Or the tree. Or the weird cultists …

It could be a long con. Like something out of Ocean's Eleven.

For pocket change? Unlikely.

Maybe myths being real made more sense after all. She didn't know why she was trying to make sense of it instead of drinking until the squirrel was quiet. Marie's phone rang.

Ratatoskur's voice, several octaves higher and a hundred decibels louder than Marie remembered, screamed, "Where *are* you?"

"Doing my job," Marie shot back. "How'd you get this number?"

"Hurry!"

Marie didn't want to believe the squirrel, but she ran anyway.

She fished out the weirdo's business card on the run, hoping she wasn't about to make a fool of herself. Thinking, *backup would be great.* She fumbled her phone, and as it was either phone or card, she dropped the card and kept running.

The Union Station rotunda was centrally located, but she was about as far away as she could get and still be in the building. And on a different floor. It took her longer to make it back than the squirrel—or she—would've liked.

Fog still rolled off the pool. Marie's breath misted as if the temperature had dropped twenty degrees. Something dark and obscured by the fog clawed at the tree. She heard hissing and scratching. The tree was dying. Its branches drooped, leaves wilting and falling into the wishing pool. Tiger-stripes of eaten bark criss-crossed its trunk.

And Marie had thought the talking squirrel and the tree-worshipping cult were weird. Distracted by the fog, and what was inside, it took a moment for her to notice the creature wasn't alone. Lizards circled the rotunda, darting towards the tree and hopping backwards as if afraid of it.

Dragons, Marie.

Yes, of course. Dragons. *Best not forget that.*

They'd grown. Now they were larger than dogs. Big dogs. Almost as big as her.

Too big.

One saw her and scuttled forward, hissing. The others continued to gnaw at the tree. Marie drew her baton, snapping out the telescoping rod from her belt, extending it with a flick of her wrist. She didn't think that would be enough to keep the dragons from destroying the tree.

The dragon came at her in a serpentine undulating dash. She wasn't sure who screamed louder—her, or the squirrel. The dragon's motion made it hard to track. She swung, striking its side. The baton rebounded like she'd struck a wall and almost hit her shoulder on the backstroke.

She had to get to the tree. Get the dragons off it.

She skittered back to get space, prodding the dragon on the snout with her baton to keep it at bay. The dragons had a manic, hopping gait. When their bellies weren't pressed to the floor, they ran atop one another like a stream of snakes. Their hisses sounded like steam escaping a kettle. She yelled and waved her arms. One dragon leapt off the tree, splashing through the pool toward her. The others scuttled around the hind side of the ash, watching as they ate its bark. They grew larger with every nibble.

Now she had a dragon on either side of her. Tonight was going to get worse before it got better.

"Ratatoskur, help me."

"I'm a lover, not a fighter. I run messages. That's it."

"What are you, a *yellow* squirrel? Help me, you fucking coward!"

"That's the spirit! Do that to the dragons."

"Do what?"

"Insult them. They *have* to react."

Marie wasn't sure she wanted the dragons to react to her any more than they already were. She had nothing else to lose. "You suck, dragons!"

"Do better."

"*You* do better. I'm busy."

"It's like a ritual, Marie. It's as important as fighting

them. Their mother's overly proud; she'd have taught them the game of flyting, if only so they wouldn't be bested by a squirrel."

It would be a cold day in hell before Marie would listen to a squirrel again. It should be too cold for reptiles (the snakes wouldn't be out of their dens in Narcisse for another month or two), but these little buggers were rolling in the freezing mist and basking in the moonlight as if it were sun, pleased as piss to be out in the cold.

"Go on," Marie hollered. "*Shoo!* Get!"

As one they turned. Dull yellow eyes staring. Tongues darting. What did reptiles do with their tongues? The memory came back to Marie in a disgusting rush. They tasted the air with their tongues.

Oh, God. They're tasting *me.*

Marie bit back a scream. Acting would help with the fear. There were a lot of them, but she could handle this.

Something landed on her shoulder and Marie did scream.

"Be careful," said the squirrel, smaller now—the size of an actual squirrel. "They're venomous."

Of course they are.

"Thanks for the tip," Marie said through gritted teeth.

"That's why I'm up here. The longer you stay upright, the safer *I'll* be."

Typical.

The cult weirdos had been splashing the trunk with

water from the well. They'd believed it'd helped. First Marie had to get the dragons out of the water and off the tree. Or the cavalry couldn't ride any further.

Marie struck the lizard to her right and dashed for the pool, splashing through the icy water and swinging wildly at the dragons on the tree and in the pool even as she avoided their hissing strikes. Where water hit the tree, Marie saw the bark grow over its scars. She still saw wounds, but the tree *was* on the mend. If only she could get the dragons angry enough to follow *her* and leave the tree behind.

"Your insults aren't strong enough," Ratatoskur said. After a peeved squawk from Marie, the squirrel looked back to the rotunda's open roof and hollered, "They aren't, and you know they aren't."

"Seriously?" Marie shook her head. "*You're* plenty irritating. Why don't you try?"

The squirrel scowled. "I'm the *messenger*. Why don't *you* try, since my entire life offends you so much?"

She shrugged. Couldn't hurt.

Unless you succeed, and they come after you and hurt you.

Thanks, Marie.

"You're … uh … too fat to fly," Marie said.

Ratatoskur rolled his eyes. "Tried that one."

"Try it again."

The squirrel cupped his paws to his mouth and yelled

something at the dragons in a language Marie didn't understand. They didn't even look up.

"Shit," she muttered.

"You're looking pale."

"Shut up, squirrel."

"You'll have to do better than that." The squirrel looked at her. "They say your uniform isn't very flattering."

It wasn't. Marie didn't care. Okay. She *did* care. But not about a lizard's opinion.

"Tell those jerks go fly a kite."

"You'll have to do better than that, too."

"You look like worms with frostbite!" *Nothing.* She turned to the squirrel. "Any advice on how to make them want to fight?"

"Thor would usually call folks cock-gobblers and threaten them with his hammer. Loki accused people of incest and farting during sex."

I'll definitely have to get more creative.

"Imagine they're me," Ratatoskur suggested. "You always had good insults for me."

"You heard those?"

The squirrel nodded, and Marie smiled, turning back to the dragons. "You lamprey-pricked corpse-gobbler!"

As one, the dragons turned away from the tree and stalked out of the wishing well.

"That did it!" Ratatoskur yelled gleefully. "I didn't need to translate that one!"

Great. Careful what you wish for, Marie.

She bolted from the pool and the dragons clipped at her heels as she ran toward the cafeteria. She flipped tables and chairs behind her to slow their pursuit.

Ratatoskur asked, "You still have those nuts I gave you?"

"Yes."

"What are you waiting for?" The squirrel shook his head. "I can't help those who won't help themselves."

A dragon swiped at Ratatoskur.

"Hey," Ratatoskur squeaked, "*I* didn't say it. She did!"

The dragon didn't seem to care.

Marie didn't know what to do. The tree wilted faster, and she couldn't get to it to change that. To say nothing of the fact she and her squirrel mentor were about to be eaten.

Ratatoskur believed the nuts he'd given her mattered. Could she trust a squirrel? He said she'd guarded the wishes people had put in the wishing well. She rummaged in her pocket and drew them out.

The dragons' attention perked up.

Well, that's *interesting, Marie.*

Sure is, Marie.

"*I'm* the guardian of the tree? Like a valkyrie? Or She-Ra or something?"

Ratatoskur nodded.

She took a deep breath. "You can do this, Marie."

Sure, Marie. It's like riding a bike, except you have to

steal the bike first, and its owner is a dragon and the bike is on fire.

She cracked the nut between her teeth and snapped out her telescoping rod, yelling, "I have the power!"

This wasn't *Masters of the Universe* and she wasn't She-Ra, but she felt something change. It'd been a clear sky, fog in the station notwithstanding, the stars were out, and out of nowhere there was a bright flash, and thunder boomed, shaking the station.

She caught her reflection in a glass door.

"Ah!"

She was smoking. The lightning strike had turned her rod into a sword and her bear spray was a round oaken shield. Twin braids contained her hair now, rather than a ponytail. Her uniform had been replaced with boob cups and furry bikini bottoms; her boots with strappy sandals.

Oh, come on.

She tried to cover herself. The squirrel was watching—and a pervert.

"Hey, this is *your* idea of what a lady warrior looks like, not mine. Do some research."

Yeah, his probably only needed the sandals.

Marie muttered, "I clearly should've said, 'I have the power—and the clothes.'"

She liked the braids. They were pretty. She'd have to get her roommate to teach her how to do them. But now wasn't the time for updating her style. She had dragons to fight.

This is a bad idea, Marie.

Tell me about it.

Hurry up or we'll never go through with it.

She gave the sword a test-swing. "Let's do this."

"Little help?" cried Ratatoskur. A dragon had pinned him. Sickly yellow saliva oozed from its jaws.

"I'm coming," Marie yelled, rushing to the squirrel.

The dragon squatted, covering Ratatoskur. It reared up, ready to fight, tail swaying behind it, a whip waiting to snap.

Marie yelled, "Get off him, you fucker!"

The dragon snarled, but other than the motion of its tail, it didn't move.

"Do better!" Ratatoskur yelled.

"Get off, you … you … shite-eating tree-fucker!"

The dragon hissed. Its claws loosened. Marie rushed it. She closed the distance faster than she'd expected. She felt taller, not just stronger. She slashed at the dragon. Its tail lashed out to batter the blade aside and the sword sliced neatly through it. It shrieked, its jaws darted for her, and Marie crammed her shield between its teeth. Its claws were still free. Marie needed space. She kicked against it, pushing it back, its teeth scratching over the shield. She reared back, hoping to free Ratatoskur, so the squirrel could help her.

She kicked again, and this time the dragon soared

into the air, taking Ratatoskur with it. It crashed into the second-floor balcony, rebounded off the stone and plummeted onto the food court tables. Ratatoskur skittered out from under the debris.

"Thanks," he said, dusting himself off.

"You're welcome."

"I was being sarcastic."

"So was I."

The dragons circled Marie, but at least they were leaving Ratatoskur—and the tree—alone.

That's great, Marie. I'm so happy you've made this happen.

Quiet, Marie. We have monsters to fight.

We'll discuss this later.

Of course we will.

She had to keep them away from the tree. She had to keep them from destroying the rotunda. She'd have a hard time explaining what had happened to the dayshift, as it was. They already thought she was crazy.

Crazy like a fox who knows what's really going on in the chicken coop.

That makes no sense, Marie.

Neither does tonight, Marie.

You've got me there.

Damn straight.

She was the guardian of the wishes as well as the tree. The magic acorn had turned her into one of the *Masters of the Universe* characters. If she'd made her own wish, maybe she could get rid of them for good. Only problem: she had no cash. Ratatoskur's coffee had taken her last quarter. Worse: she had nothing to pay for her next cup of coffee.

The coffee money!

"Ratatoskur! Get me the coffee fund!"

The squirrel gave her a quizzical look, but understanding quickly dawned. "On it!"

She needed to hold off the dragons long enough for the squirrel to get back. Assuming her plan would work.

It had to work.

You're the guardian of the wishes, Marie.

I'd better be.

As the squirrel scurried away, Marie yelled imprecations, hoping to keep the dragons' attention on her until Ratatoskur returned with the coins. For the life of her, she couldn't think of an insult. She *needed* an insult. She searched through a pouch on her belt for her phone, hoping it still worked after whatever power had turned her into a monster fighter. Her baton had become a sword, what if her phone was no longer a phone?

It was.

She typed frantically, the dragons rushed forward.

Insult generator.

"Gorbellied full-gorged maggot pie!

"Spongey ill-breeding codpiece.

"Wimpled trash-eating barnacles.

"Loggerheaded treacherous egg!"

The dragons hissed back at her. They weren't charging. It was as if they were answering her, insult for insult. She couldn't understand what they were saying without Rat there to translate. She wasn't sure she *wanted* to know.

Rat was back, and a ring of dragons separated them.

"I'll piss in your chimneys!" Marie didn't know what that meant.

But it worked.

Ratatoskur darted through the line of dragons, coffee can of coins held high. One of the dragon's tails slapped Ratatoskur aside. The can rolled away, its lid popped open, and the coins spilled onto the rotunda floor.

Marie dived for the coins, scooping up as many as she could.

"I wish you couldn't hurt the tree." Marie tossed one coin for each dragon. They looked back and forth between her and the tree, worried. She tossed in more coins. "Or anyone else."

The dragons splashed past Marie and into the pool, lunging for the tree, but they couldn't touch it. The dragons shrieked, scratching, trying to bite, stab. Nothing they did had any effect.

Marie shook her fist. "Nuh-uh," she said. "Scoot!"

The dragons hissed.

Marie shook her fist full of coins. "My next wish'll be a doozy."

The dragons bolted for the train station exit and towards the riverside market. She should let them be

The Forks Market security's problem. That would teach them.

But she was the tree's guardian, and this was *her* problem. "I wish you'd go home."

The fog caught up with the dragons and dragged them into the well. With a muffled *whump* they, and the fog, were gone.

The squirrel beamed at her, puckering up as if awaiting a kiss. "Now about my reward …"

Marie shook her head. Never trust a squirrel.

Or his nuts.

Ballroom Blitz

No one had bothered to show for work tonight. Not even my boss. It was a nightmare.

A bloody nightmare.

A room full of people. Rich people. The kind who could (and would) find fault in anyone or anything, and I was the only server who'd bothered to come in and offer my faults.

At least the bar was stocked. That was something. No bartender, though. Judy usually ran a tighter ship than this. I took a deep breath, plastered on a smile I didn't feel, and headed into the storm. Looking down at Calgary from the Tower, the tail lights and headlights cutting veins and arteries through downtown didn't have their normal flow, they sat, instead, as if at a standstill. As if the entire bloody city was waiting for something to happen. It felt weird. I felt weird.

My whole bloody day had been weird. *I* never should have showed up in the first place.

Something loud.

Annoying.

I pawed at the nightstand. Pulled my pillow over my head. Phone. My phone.

I'd put it on silent. I was *sure* I'd put it on silent.

Why me? Why today?

I squinted. To my sleepy eyes, the display light on my phone blazed brighter than the sun. Normally I dimmed the brightness before bed. Evidently, I'd forgotten to do that, too.

The call was from Toppers, the all-day breakfast joint I waitressed for. I wasn't scheduled for today.

The call went to voicemail. The phone immediately rang again. I answered.

"Kathleen didn't come in."

Manager Barry couldn't be bothered to say "hello" first, I noticed, let alone "good morning." He never did. I didn't point this out. From the background hustle I could tell they were already slammed. I was his go-to relief waitress because I lived in the neighbourhood. A fact he'd promised not to take advantage of when he'd hired me, but always did.

"I closed last night," I said.

"I know."

"You owe me."

"I know."

"Like, you *really* owe me," I said. "I want two days off in a row. I want a real weekend."

"Please, Megara."

The "please" got me. I heard it so rarely. I sighed. "Be there in thirty."

I popped a couple ibuprofen. It ended up being twenty-eight minutes. Pretty much the last thing that went right.

I normally recognized Toppers' morning regulars, but two strangers crowded a four-top, looking out of place for our family breakfast vibe. Although, stealing glances between serving my tables, I wasn't sure *where* they'd fit in.

A slight, shabbily dressed man in an ill-fitting suit sat next to a hulking bruiser. The smaller man looked like a con artist. His eyes twinkled watching the chaos, and he talked endlessly—loudly—in the big man's ear.

The big guy looked hungover. Bloodshot blue eyes, coffee hand trembling as he raised it to his lips and ignored his loud companion. Unkempt red hair and a beard, both streaked with grey, stood out from a trucker hat with a band name I didn't recognize. His U of A hoodie looked too new to have been bought whenever he'd been a student. He was probably from Edmonton.

I tried not to think of Edmonton. If I lingered on it, on the Day, I'd never get through my shift.

Arms tattooed to the knuckles said maybe he was a musician. Or a biker. Hell, he could be a barista. No telling these days what he was, other than trouble.

The big man's tats looked viking-y, and he looked familiar. Maybe I'd seen him in a mug shot. There'd been problems in Alberta with the Spears of Odin, a white supremacist biker gang who'd harassed me, attacked some of my friends, and done much worse to others. The cops had done nothing. I was glad the two strangers weren't my table. Thugs, I could handle. The knife-in-the-back sort he sat with, they were another story. Reminded me of my old boss, Christian. Smiles while they're killing you. That job felt a lifetime ago.

While the odd couple weren't my problem, my eye kept being drawn across the restaurant to them. I was distracted, tired, and my tips said I should've stayed in bed. But they were an island of calm in the chaos of dropped plates, dropped orders, and, thanks to the local colour, dropped pants. And complaints, complaints, complaints. Jeannie said they tipped well.

There was new graffiti on the wall in the alley behind Toppers when I finally had time to grab a smoke. "Smoke" was the wrong word. "Break" was more accurate. What

I missed most about smoking was the excuse to leave a situation and have it be socially acceptable. "Graffiti" was also the wrong word. This wasn't simple tagging, more like a mural. A man, glowing incandescent, fist raised, grasping lightning. Behind him, a volcano swallowed a city. Fiery monsters lay fallen at his feet. I wasn't sure if he was supposed to be saving the city, or trashing it. The wreckage evoked the very real, and surreal condition of Edmonton after last summer—another reminder that what I'd experienced had actually happened—only Calgary Tower was pretty clearly outlined in the mural's background, fire bursting from its top, over a broken skyline. There'd been no mural last night when I'd closed.

Rough, scratchy letters—like a heavy metal font—above him read: The Red Headed Stranger.

I pinched the bridge of my nose. A storm was coming. Years in Alberta, and I'd never adjusted to the weather. It was calm at the moment, but days like these, I knew it'd be wild. I wished I'd bummed a smoke on my way out. It wouldn't have helped my headache and I'd regret lighting up tomorrow, but "never quit quitting" was my roommate's motto. I distracted myself from the nicotine craving by staring at the mural instead.

I was still thinking about it as I drove home after my shift. The Edmonton wedding I'd catered. The fancy club hosting the reception that blew up when flaming monsters attacked. I'd been saved by a bridesmaid with a sword and the scariest woman I'd ever seen. Seriously, it was like looking on the face of death with a feather cloak and better cheekbones. I could've sworn I'd lived through a B-movie. Except the budget for the destruction was way too high. The people who'd listened to them lived, those who'd ignored them, died. I hadn't wanted to believe any of it was real, but I'm still here, so I guess I did.

Now weirdness happened everywhere with greater frequency.

Calgary was as red with fire as the Tower on Flames game days. The violence that'd always been a part of the city had become more inexplicable. People acting like jerks, never novel, had escalated into a rash of arsons. I kept looking over my shoulder for the creatures I'd seen, and even though I hadn't seen them in Calgary, that didn't shake my belief in what I'd witnessed. I knew I was never getting my old normal back.

And I wasn't the only one. These days, directly over the remains of Edmonton's city centre, the sky glowed red, a grim, inverted aurora. Reds and purples were closer to the ground there than the usual greens. While there were plenty of scientific explanations for why the aurora seemed closer to Earth since the Day, few people warranted it had anything to do with monsters attacking the city.

I didn't have that luxury. They'd almost killed me.

I shouldn't have been anywhere near that wedding reception. I'd had a good job in Edmonton, not fun, but a good one as an assistant for an oil executive, and then a plant on the patch had blown up, and fires covered northern Alberta. A small city burned to the ground, and those fires didn't stop for years. Without the oil, my boss had no job; without my boss, *I* had no job. Christian got a golden parachute. Mine was lead, and still threatening to drag me under. My savings kept me afloat for a bit through one bad interview after another. Desperation and my rapidly dwindling bank account brought me back to the catering gig I'd had during undergrad.

I was grateful for my friend Judy, who'd got me in with her Calgary catering company after I'd left Edmonton behind. Judy's help had made it easier to get the Toppers gig, too. But as it was, I was barely able to pay for rent and I'd needed to find a roommate for the first time since university to keep paying my bills. The complex was townhouse-style, a tangle of two- and three-storey buildings, with a bank of garages on the ground floor. I paused at my door. The music I knew my neighbours had already complained about, and were probably now drafting their next letter to the apartment management about, pounded through it.

"Hey," Leslie yelled when I entered.

"Hey," was all I had the energy to respond with.

"You smell like waffles and despair. An unusual combo, DD."

I didn't know who'd told Leslie my old high school nickname. It sure hadn't been me. Megara "DD" McCain.

DD for Deep and Delicious. I used to love those frozen cakes.

Leslie Lola hadn't shown any references. What she had offered was three months down—in cash—and she seemed fun. Probably a dealer, but fun. And I could use a little fun. I still had hope she'd settle in, and settle down.

"It's been a day, and it's only 2 o'clock. I want a shower and nap. So ..."

I let the unspoken request linger, waiting for Leslie to acknowledge it. She didn't.

Leslie was an avid gamer—a professional gamer, according to her claims—and I rarely heard anything other than Rob Zombie's "Dragula" blasting from her room, whether she was saving Azeroth or wherever. It was her personal theme music. I didn't recognize the game she played. She said it was a new massive multiplayer, a mix of modern-day *Warcraft* and *Grand Theft Auto*. Whatever game she played, the song never changed.

"Dragula." Over and over and over.

She'd turn it down when I asked, but I had to ask. Every. Time.

"No 'Dragula,' 'kay?"

"Got it."

She always "got it," and she never *kept* it. Dubious she even had it this time, I headed to the shower. I still had a few hours before I had to head out to my evening gig with Judy and I needed to be fresh. Fresher. There was no chance of fresh, really, but not-destroyed was still on the table. I hadn't even made my bed from the morning. I crawled in, still warm from the shower, wrapped myself up, and tried to will myself to sleep.

Drums. Drums in the deep. And she was back in her game, digging ditches and burning witches, slamming wherever it led her too.

She paid. She paid in cash.

A blessed moment of blackness.

Peace.

Then drums.

The drums were back.

At least "Dragula" didn't sound as loud as usual. Maybe Leslie was coming around. I reached for my phone to check the time. It wasn't on my nightstand. What time was it?

"Nonononono!"

I leapt out of bed, and my headache, more restored by the little sleep than the rest of me, almost dropped me to my knees. I burst out of my bedroom. My phone, abandoned on the kitchen island, was the song's source.

"You're gonna be late," Leslie said from the couch, chomping into an apple. She was wearing an oversized band T-shirt that slumped off one of her shoulders and striped knee-high socks pushed down to her ankles. "That's been going off for ages."

"Why didn't you wake me?"

She shrugged. "You said you wanted to sleep."

"Not past supper!"

"Well, you did." Apple finished, she licked her fingers and rolled a joint. "Stay home. Fuck that catering gig. You said it would be full of rich assholes? Let 'em grab their own food. We'll get blazed and watch a movie."

Her offer was far more tempting than it should've been. "I need the money."

"You'll be fine. You're better than fine. Trust me."

The way she said "better than fine" made me blush, but the way she said "trust me" made me shudder. "You'll need to find a new place to live if I get evicted."

Another maddening shrug. "I'm not worried."

Leslie *never* worried.

Through clenched teeth, "I am."

"How much is this gig paying?"

"Enough."

"Enough you never need to work again?"

I blinked. What a weird expectation of any night's work. "Well, no."

"Then it's not enough to be concerned about. Something else will come up."

"Judy's my friend."

"Seems to me if she was your friend, she'd be offering more than dregs. Doesn't she need an assistant? That's what you used to do, right?"

I sighed long enough that the urge to claw out Leslie's eyes diminished. I'd never wanted a handout. Leslie believed: why have friends, if you can't ask? I wasn't sure my friends *were* friends anymore. We'd been drifting apart since school. They had some idea of what I'd been going through, but by and large, the Day's impact on them had been negligible. Leslie had no idea how hard it had been for me to reach out for this lifeline. How much I'd wanted to right myself despite my entire life exploding—literally. My old Edmonton condo was in the heart of the city's Exclusion Zone—a walled-off, still-burning scar cutting through the entire city and guarded by RCMP and the military. Even if my last home survived the wreckage, there was no way I was getting in to salvage whatever remained. Stubbornness or an inflated sense of my own skills made me want to get back on my feet without needing my friends' help. They'd all offered their condolences, but Judy had been the only one to offer me a *job*. Maybe that wasn't enough for Leslie, but it mattered to *me*. I couldn't disappoint her. Not for movie night with my stoner roommate.

"I'm going," I said.

"Not with your tits out, you're not."

I looked down. My tank top wasn't doing its job. I quickly covered myself but I was too stressed to be embarrassed. It wasn't the first time Leslie had seen me undressed; it wasn't a large apartment, and she was even more casual about her own nudity. "I'm getting dressed and *then* I'm going."

She chuckled and reached for her lighter. "You'd get more tips as is."

"Please don't smoke that in here."

"'Kay."

"'Kay." The most dismissive letter-posing-as-a-word I'd ever heard. Leslie had a way of making dismissing my concerns into an art form. That joint would be lit the moment the door closed.

She pays on time.

She pays in cash.

I wanted another shower to wake up, but settled for splashing cold water on my face and hoping makeup would hide the sleep lines. My catering uniform wasn't where I'd left it. More time wasted. I found it, brushing my teeth on the way out the door.

I swear to God, the entire world was against me today.

My gig was downtown at Calgary Tower. Fourteen minutes from my place. It's an easy drive. Richmond to Crowchild and then the overpass into downtown on 9th Avenue. The tower is right on 9th, and there's lots of street parking and parkades. Calgary's a suburban city and its downtown typically emptied after five, as everyone flees their offices for their backyards, barbecues, and balconies. Despite oversleeping, I wasn't too worried about being late.

But naturally, given the day I was having, traffic was much worse than normal. As I crawled the last few blocks to the Tower, my confidence evaporated. *And* there was no street parking open, so I had nowhere to stop and walk. The sky was hazy—again—and the sun burned red and angry well before sunset. With all the forest fires in recent years, I was used to apocalyptic-looking skies, even before the red aurora showed up, but tonight was something else. You'd think, looking at it, that you were walking into hell. Maybe I was. If I turned around and went home, I'd have to face the same traffic to get out, and I was almost there.

I unclenched my jaw, took a breath. The world didn't give a shit about my plans. I knew that well. Waiting tables had helped me deal with my life's uncertainty, so I imagined the traffic as a busy room, with a short kitchen. Just get into the flow, move what you can as fast as you can. The Type A Office Bitch scheduler in me still screamed the whole time.

Nothing had gone right today. Not one damn thing.

I used a long red light to dig around for my phone. I wanted to get a hold of Judy, let her know I might be late, but it wasn't in my bag. I remembered with a groan that I'd set it down in my rush to find my uniform and left it on the island back home.

Green light. Finally, a break in the traffic.

I peeled out, swerved around the slowpoke in front of me.

A cop's siren wailed. Another ticket.

I was *definitely* going to be late.

The banquet I'd been hired to work was a fundraiser to "reclaim" the Patch. No other servers, no bartender, no musicians, not even the *food* was here. The only thing here—other than *me*—was the booze. And roughly half the guests. A much smaller turnout than was typical for Judy's events. Despite arriving late, I did what I always did at the start of a serving shift: take a moment to try and get a sense of the room before heading out. I'd checked all the boxes on the disaster flowchart, so there was nothing to do except smile and carry on. Without my phone, I couldn't call Judy. My plan was to keep everyone drinking until I got word from her. Also, it was the only service I could provide until food or other staff arrived. This strategy was not without its flaws.

Drunks are mercurial.

Everyone in the banquet room was immaculately dressed. Black tie for men, and little black dresses for women. There were spatters of colour here and there, almost universally red, with the occasional daub of orange or yellow. One striking blue dress. The crowd skewed older than me. In the weird, smoky light from the 360-degree windows, everybody had a grey pallor. Everybody, that is, but one.

The big guy from Toppers took up most of a booth. He was noticeable from across the room. The red hair and beard. A big man in a room full of big men. The others puffed themselves up with money or power to appear larger, but he stood out from them. Hoodie and cap had been replaced by black gangster suit, white shirt, and no tie. His shirt was open at least two buttons too many for Toppers, let alone a black-tie gala, flashing green and black tattoos. He shouldn't fit in among the big-ticket donor crowd typical to Judy's events and yet, he exuded an aura of I *don't give a shit about anything happening here,* which, I supposed, *was* the best way to fit in at these things.

He also wasn't wearing shoes. Odd. The big guy's rumple-suited companion had been replaced with a beautifully handsome or handsomely beautiful androgynous person. They had the same shady aura though, and mischievous eyes. If not for being almost a foot taller, I'd say it was the same person from how they carried themselves. They seemed to be relating a story, and from the look on the man's face, it was one he'd heard before. More than once. He listened better this time, and cracked a smile when it was done.

I headed to their table first. Chaos had surrounded the big guy in the morning, but it'd never touched him. And I figured if he'd stoop to eat at a diner, he and his new companion might treat me better than the rest of the guests here. If I started the shift well, it'd help keep me smiling through the night. When I approached, the big man's smile became grim. "Bourbon and a beer and keep them coming" was the order. He even added a "please."

He seemed as surprised to see me as I him. As I left for my next table. I caught a snippet of their conversation, "This always happens when you say, 'Trust me,' Loki."

"I don't know, Ted, she wasn't supposed to be here. I did my best."

Their exchange filled me with a dread I couldn't quite articulate. Underneath that dread was the same nagging sense of familiarity I'd felt this morning at Toppers. I didn't have time to dwell on it, fortunately. After I'd delivered a first round of drinks, the rest of the room demanded all my attention. I could only cope because everyone wanted beer, shots, or wine. I hadn't needed to make a single cocktail.

The other donors milled around the room, watching the darkening sky in the distance, fake smiles glowing with the setting sun. People used to getting what they wanted. Demands on my time grew more insistent, and yet, they had no regard for the drinks I'd brought them. Stranger yet, no one had complained about the lack of food, or the rising temperature in the banquet room. It felt like a powder keg. Eyes flashed. The temperature rose. I was the only one in the room who seemed to be sweating.

When I thought my night couldn't get worse, the thing I'd dreaded/fantasized about for years slapped me right in the face.

Christian.

He chatted amiably with Blue Dress, his wife Mary nowhere in sight. Normally she hung off his arm at these events. She must've gotten out. Good for her. I hoped it'd cost him. It was a little pleasing to notice he didn't look good. Puffy, and ashen. His eyes weren't their usual cold blue, and they slid over me as if they'd never seen me, as if I were nothing to him.

Which, I supposed, I was, and had been for years.

I managed to avoid talking to him—serving his table, not him directly. I wasn't sure which hurt more, him not recognizing me, or pretending not to. It'd been a couple years since I'd worked for him, and the hurt, the sense of betrayal, was still there. My hand shook as I tried not to meet his gaze. My attention wandered too far, and I overfilled a glass.

Blue Dress stood in a rush as water spilled over the tablecloth. I hadn't seen any of them drinking, but their glasses kept emptying. I *hoped* they were having some water, with all the alcohol I'd been dropping off. For a while. There was *still* no sight of Judy or any of the other staff.

Outside, lightning flashed above the Calgary skyline.

I stole a glance at Christian and was surprised to see him locked in on the big guy's table. So was Blue Dress. Like they were looking for a fight. The big guy and his partner seemed immune to the room's energy. They joked, and laughed, and drank.

When I offered to take Christian's glass he snarled at me, eyes flashing, and I hissed, involuntarily, when he brushed against me. It was as if he'd held a lit zippo to my arm in that brief touch, that moment of contact forced me to drop the water pitcher. Some splashed over Blue Dress.

Anger almost steamed off her, and she clutched her arm as if I'd dumped acid, not tap water. I thought I'd imagined it, at first, but I felt the heat. Her breath was like watching a heat mirage on the highway.

Blue Dress hissed, "Stupid bitch!"

"You'll pay for this," Christian added, interposing, still no recognition on his face, until a shark's smile spread, and he whispered, "Megara."

"I'm so sorry!"

I wanted to flee into the kitchen, but a milling crowd blocked my path. I wanted to steal five minutes to have a good cry. Fix my makeup, and try again to cope with a day growing beyond endurance. But the universe wouldn't even give me that. Being a waitress often means apologizing for something not your fault. Drunk kitchen, cheapskate owners, and grovelling in the face of active trauma. Even when an error wasn't your fault—especially when it wasn't your fault—you were left to deal with it. Instead of crying, I forced a smile and fled to a friendlier table. The big guy, Ted, beckoned, smiling, which was something, but his smile didn't reach his eyes.

"Another bourbon?" I asked him.

He shook his head and stood, cracking his neck from side to side. He rolled his shoulders and had the look of someone gearing for a fight.

"Time's past for that, I think," said his companion, the one he'd called Loki, who drained their beer and somehow still managing to look dainty. They passed me the glass, too, but didn't stand.

A crash of thunder made me turn back to look at the room behind me. A rapidly building storm cut through the apocalyptic sky beyond the windows and the first fat drops of rain hit the glass.

Everyone stared at us.

In the lightning flashes, it was as if I could see their bones burning through their skin. The shadows played tricks with their hair and poses, casting them as horned and devilish. Blue Dress looked half-melted, a black skeleton showing where the water had splashed her.

"You should head home now," Ted said.

His simple remark, and the kindness in his voice made me want to bolt, but the crowd was cutting off the exit. They'd encircled Ted and Loki's booth. The circle tightened. There was nowhere for me to go. My heart pounded in my ears. Ted interposed himself between me and the crowd.

Loki placed a hand on my shoulder. "You might want to get down. Or find a time machine and stay in bed today."

Rain hit the windows like a slap, and the wind screamed at the seams of the glass. From the Tower's vantage point, the storm had already swallowed Calgary. How fast must the wind be travelling that I could hear it across the room? The building creaked and groaned like we were on a ship, shuddering against the waves. Could the wind blow down the tower? The big guy stepped closer. Could—?

Loki yelled, "I said, 'Get down!'"

The windows of the tower buckled, undulating, like the glass was water forming a wave, and shattered, bursting in from every direction. I screamed and ducked as the glass was blown inward. The storm was here. Right here in the restaurant. The storm was Ted. His hair and beard whipped around his face and lightning sparked in his eyes, mirroring the flashes outside.

I had a momentary worry for Ted's bare feet, and then, a much sharper panic for my own life. Funny how you prioritize others in the service industry. How you've been conditioned to worry about others, no matter your own immediate circumstances. Glass crashed and broke as it hit walls, tables, and the bar. The worst was the sick, thuds of it striking flesh, and I wondered if any of those sounds had come from *my* body.

The wind died as suddenly as it had started. A dead calm overtook the room.

I looked over my body. I didn't seem to be bleeding. Ted had shielded me from the glass.

"Sorry," he said, turning to face the room. The back of his jacket had been *shredded*. He wasn't bleeding either. Tattoos covered his entire back, too; a dark tree running over his spine, a void in bright—almost iridescent—green scales. He tore off the ruined jacket and shirt. A hammer shone on his clenched right fist, glowing incandescent.

Loki hadn't moved from the booth. They lit a cigarette, looking remarkably unruffled. Glass and debris littered the bench, but hadn't touched them, as if they were a knife-thrower's assistant.

I looked away from Ted and Loki to see if all those whispered prayers for revenge over the years had done Christian in. I'd feel bad if they had, and worse if they hadn't. He still stood, Blue Dress with him, at the head of a wedge of patrons in shredded clothing. Like Ted, none were bleeding; unlike Ted, they weren't unscathed.

None screamed. Or cried. Flesh smoked and bubbled from their bodies. Flames in their eyes were an echo of the lightning in Ted's. Viscous blobs slopped from their wounds, catching fire to whatever they landed upon and leaving behind rock-like armour. What was left of their skin was cigarette-ash grey, ready to scatter on the wind. Brows twitched and thick horns, tapering to a point, erupted from their foreheads. The lightning had been showing me the truth. They'd found me. The monsters from the wedding. They'd found me. I'd often joked to Leslie about my tables acting monstrously, but tonight they *were* monsters.

When they spoke, they spoke as one voice with many mouths. Their voices hissed and popped and crackled over each other, sounding like a raging bonfire. Smoke billowed from their mouths.

"Give us the flame."

"You took it from us."

"It's ours."

"We need it."

"We'll take it."

Wherever the wind touched their grey bodies, they glowed. Orange flames burned; skin split and smoked, filling the room. Dimly, I noted the screaming beep of the fire alarm over the storm's roar.

"The *flame*."

They looked as if a stiff breeze could blow them apart, and they still made my knees shake. I hurled Ted's empty bourbon glass at Christian. It punched through his body, leaving a hole where his heart should've been. The ashy skin reformed.

"Sit tight," Ted yelled over his shoulder. "Things are about to get fucking weird."

About to? I wasn't sure if I'd screamed the words or thought them. I repeated them aloud to be sure.

"Smoke?" Loki asked, holding out a cigarette as Ted launched himself into the crowd.

"Yes. No. I quit." I'd answered automatically, entranced by the violence that almost, but never quite, touched me.

"Never quit quitting," Loki said.

I blinked at the familiarity of the expression, then asked, "Aren't you going to help him?"

They cocked their head as if measuring the idea. They shrugged and turned back to the fight, lighting their own cigarette. "I should keep you safe. You *weren't* supposed to be here tonight."

"What?"

"I did my best to keep you away from here, but you're a persistent little mint, aren't you? I *never* expected you to forget your phone. I should've pretended to be Judy sooner, but I figured my contingencies would keep you home."

"Contingencies?"

"Your alarm. Hiding your uniform. The traffic."

"You did *what*?"

Only a coy smile in response.

"Who *are* you?"

"I'm Loki," they said, as if that was the only explanation needed.

The fire alarm made me want to crush my teeth to powder. The emergency lights strobing out of time to the lightning flashes made me dizzy. The dissonance made me want to vomit. This *entire day* made me want to vomit.

Loki pressed a finger over my lips. "Put a pin in that, DD."

How did Loki know my nickname? How was any of this happening? Getting wrapped up in "hows" right now was a bad idea. Ted faced *fifty* monsters. And he was the only thing keeping them from getting at us.

"But he's outnumbered."

"He's always outnumbered."

Ted's punches broke their skin easily. Ash trickled from the wounds as if falling from a dangling cigarette. Grey turned orange. The room grew hotter. Fires flared on spilled liquor and tablecloths. Wherever the fires touched the monsters, they swelled, adding flame and heat to their bodies. Rain sloughed the ash from their bones, leaving behind blackened, cracked skeletons, as if they've been in a conflagration. The bones radiated a bonfire's heat. I stepped back.

"Ash giants," Loki muttered. "I hate these guys."

Ash giants. At least now I had a name for them. They didn't seem big enough yet to be called giants. But they were growing into it.

"What do they want?" I screamed at Loki over the wind and thunder and melee.

"The reclamation they want has nothing to do with the Patch. Though it's what birthed them. Humans and monsters alike, trying to save their own skins by making a deal with Surtur—a lot of good it did them. They were dead already, they just didn't realize it. Their power comes from him, and the dead world he used to rule called Muspelheim, a land of primal fire. They want to bring it here. To finish the job Surtur started in Edmonton."

"Surtur." The name seemed to burn my tongue as I said it. Memories came flooding back. Screams. A world on fire. Footfalls that swallowed the thunder. Glowing symbols hanging in the air, holding the monsters at bay.

"They were gonna eat up enough people tonight and burn this building bright and hot enough to cut a way through to their old world. You were the only one who wouldn't stay away."

Wind bent the rain into the Tower through the shattered windows, and it popped and sizzled whenever it touched the ash giants. They hissed and howled. Inexorably, Ted dragged the pile riding him towards the edge of the tower. The ash giants pushed back, trying to drive deeper into the banquet room to escape the rain.

"I just love watching him work," Loki said, lighting another cigarette. "Seriously. Check him out."

Ted was a thunderstorm with a smile. The smile. *That's* where I recognized him from. Why he'd felt so familiar before. Ted had been at the wedding. He'd been in the bloody wedding party! He'd been paired with the hot bridesmaid who had the sword and had spoken to the woman who'd saved my life.

It *was* mesmerizing. Ted threw a monster out the window. Lightning struck the thing the moment it cleared the window frame. It lit up like a negative image, black against the searing brightness. The skeleton was outlined against the sky and burst. I turned away, squinting as spots burned into my eyes. Thunder shook the room, loud enough that I staggered. Three more lightning strokes in quick succession. Ted grabbed another creature, swinging them like a baseball bat to clear room.

Ted was strong, impossibly strong, but so were the monsters. In the scrum, a few creatures grabbed him. And there were more of them. Skeletons wrapped around his legs. Hung off his arms. It was as if human-sized ants had swarmed him. Ted covered his eyes while they scrabbled to find any vulnerable point, drawing every bit of flame to them—into them. Burning bones buried Ted. I lost sight of him.

I smelled the acrid reek of hair on fire, and the greasy smoke of clothing. The sound of fists on flesh, drumming, as if Leslie had queued "Dragula" again, only sped up. The ash giants hit each other in their frenzy, trying to get another punch in on Ted.

The sky filled with lightning, forking and flashing. The bolts *bent*, seeking the tower. Coming to Ted. I didn't have time to turn my back or close my eyes. The ash giants exploded off Ted. My knees buckled from the shockwave. Some blew apart, others blew toward me and Loki. The surviving ash giants made a break for us, growing as their fires spread. Burned materials swirled around them. Becoming them. The rain wasn't enough to completely degrade them. Not inside.

A monster slipped past Loki. Toward me. I ran for the bar, hoping to put its thick wood between us. Loki grew. Towering over Ted, their back brushed the ceiling, and they swatted any advancing monsters away from me and into Ted's path, hissing as the fire touched them. Those ones never lasted long. Ted's every punch was a thunderclap. I scrambled behind the bar and hid, crouching in the shattered glass, trying not to cut myself. I felt sad, and weak, while these two—what? Heroes? Gods?—fought to keep me alive. And I hid. What else could I do?

The bar had a wet setup and I ran the cold water in both sinks to soak some towels. The ash giants had been avoiding the windows and the rain. It wasn't much, but it was all I could control. Another thunderstroke. I clapped my hands over my ears to save them from the din. As it was, my ears would be ringing for days.

A flash of blue caught my eye. Blue Dress had slipped past Loki in a full sprint.

Right.

At.

Me.

I screamed and hurled a sodden towel at her. Hoping again to soak her, this time on purpose.

More of her ash melted away. She snarled.

A giant meaty arm caught her on its backswing, hurling her from the banquet room, through a shattered window, and into the pounding rain.

That *really* pissed off Christian.

Ignoring Ted and Loki, he scrabbled over the bar, bloated with ash and flame. He grabbed my wrists, and I screamed as his grip burned me.

"No, you don't!" Loki yelled, catching the bar with a long-armed backswing. The faucet burst off its moorings and a jet of water blasted over Christian. His grip slackened and I kicked him away. His arms fell off to the side. His torso bubbled to nothing. Blackened bones clattered to the floor and broke to powder.

It *was* satisfying watching my old boss melt. Horrifying and satisfying. Dream and nightmare come true. Which form it would take would depend on whether I survived long enough to process it. But for an instant, nothing was trying to kill me.

One monster—the last—had grown larger than Loki. It grabbed them and swatted Ted. Ted hurtled toward the bar. I ducked, covering myself. He crashed into the mirror, shattering it, and bounced off the oak bar top, splintering the wood. Loki followed Ted's trajectory, in a similar arc, only Loki changed their shape, shrinking. A black-furred fox with a silver-tipped tail bent and twisted in the air, landing nimbly on the shattered bar, before launching back into the fray. Loudly.

Loki ran interference, and Ted wrestled the last giant into the storm.

With the giants gone, the fires died.

Ted stood, smoking. He didn't appear to be bleeding, or burned. Other than his hair and beard being gone, he was unbothered by being hit by a flamethrower, walking on glass, or being repeatedly punched. He looked at me, wide-eyed, and asked, "You okay?"

"You're on fire."

"Motherfucker." He patted at his pants violently and sighed. "It happens. A lot."

He ran his hand over his now bare chin and scalp. The fires had revealed green scale tattoos on his back and top of his head with two curious blank spots behind his ears. "I almost had my beard the way I liked it."

"It'll never grow back if you keep picking fights with pricks from Muspelheim," Loki said. The fox had been replaced by the rat-faced man from the diner.

"*You're* the one who brought me to fucking Calgary," Ted said, flashing a middle finger. "Home of the *Flames*."

Loki laughed, delighted. "Technically, DD brought us here."

News to me. "*I did?*"

Ted nodded. "We knew you'd need help."

"How?"

"Don't say the runes told you," Loki cut in a little too loudly. "She won't like that."

I arched an eyebrow. "Runes. Like fortune-telling?"

"We know someone who's pretty accurate, eh, Ted? Pretty and accurate."

"A friend. A Norn." Ted turned to Loki. "She'll tie your nuts to a goat if you keep talking about her like that."

"I can do that for myself," Loki said proudly.

I barely heard Ted's retort. My thoughts had gone back to the Day. To the grey-haired woman with a too-young face, glowing blue halo of runic symbols circling her head, and an outrageous feathered cloak. Like an angel. An angel of death. Yeah, I could picture her tying someone's testicles to a goat.

"The woman from the wedding," I blurted out.

Ted nodded. "She saved you and it made her aware of your fate. That connection remains. Gave me a heads-up, because she knew that connection would matter to me."

"Why did you think *I* was important enough to save? Why would *you* care?"

"Everyone is important enough to save," Ted said. "But I can't save everyone. I help who I can. It's all I can do. The more people who know what they're up against, the more they can help themselves. And others. You saw Surtur's power first-hand in Edmonton last year, so the Nine Worlds will keep coming for you. And we might not always be around. We tried to keep you out of this. That didn't work out, but I'm glad it didn't go entirely tits-up."

Ted snorted what I took to be a self-deprecating

chuckle, and looked at Loki. "I'm terrible at asking for help, too. So I recognize it in others. I used to work the rigs, I lost my old life to the fires, same as you."

"You found a new life, obviously."

"You will, too."

Ted grabbed a bottle of top-shelf bourbon from the bar's wreckage—miraculously undamaged. He popped the cork and after a glance didn't turn up any tumblers, took a swig from the bottle and passed it to Loki.

"I don't know if I can handle it." I stretched my arms wide gesturing at the destruction. "Handle this."

"You did handle it. You're alive. That's a win."

He called this a win. The Tower was *trashed*. But, I guess, it was still standing. It could be repaired. There was no burning demon world replacing Calgary. Today, at least. That had to count for something. But what would a loss look like? Edmonton? Or worse? I'd have to be ready.

"Drink?" Loki asked.

I shrugged and took a long swallow, bourbon scouring smoke from my throat. "Well, I already reek of booze."

"Beats waffles and despair," Loki said.

My eyes narrowed. I knew that cadence. A few other things they'd said clicked into place. Loki—*Norse god* Loki, because how could they not be—is a shapeshifter. "Leslie!"

Loki didn't bother looking embarrassed as they

became my roommate. I saw no change; one second Loki wore one shape, then the other. I didn't know if the familiar face made me more or less angry.

This was unbelievable. Had the Leslie I'd known ever existed? What a violation. I wanted to be sick.

"You became my roommate just to keep an eye on me and then ruined my life? You creep!" Pent-up frustration with Leslie and new fury with Loki bubbled up and out. I shoved them. Loki looked crestfallen, not embarrassed or angry. Ted's face turned as red as his hair.

Ted mumbled, "Sorry," like a kid caught breaking a window with an errant football.

I turned to Ted. "And *you*. You let it happen!"

"To be fair," Loki began, "we *did* save your life."

I surveyed the carnage. "I guess, thanks?"

"Just tell people about the Red Headed Stranger," Loki said, looking smug again.

Ted sighed the same long-suffering sigh I recognized from rooming with Leslie. "Could you knock off the 'Red Headed Stranger' shtick?"

The thunderstorm still flashed in the distance, but it'd moved beyond Calgary with the fight's end. That I wasn't alone in Loki's trickery … I didn't know if that was better or worse. Was Loki everyone's asshole roommate? Speaking of which … I sighed. "I guess I'm out a roommate again."

The elevator dinged. Its doors opened, revealing Judy.

"You would *not* believe the day I've been having—" Judy stopped short, and stood in shock at the wreckage.

"For your trouble." A whispered voice said. Something heavy dropped into my hand. I looked. It was a fat, multicoloured roll of money. Leslie's voice on the wind carried to my ears only. "You earned it."

Ted and Loki were gone. I was covered in spilled booze and the ashes of my dead boss. Waffles and despair. My breath bourbon-fresh. The banquet room was totalled. And my future job prospects with Judy along with it.

Finally, she spoke. "What the fuck is going on?"

"You wouldn't believe it. There was this Red Headed Stranger …"

Scatter the Foals
to the Wind

My mom always said, "Michelle, never trust a short man. They've always got something to prove."

Most of her advice hadn't stuck, but that tidbit had; one reason most of the guys I'd dated had been the size of vikings. The latest was a bruiser of a redhead named Ted. More tattoos than a biker. Mouth like a sailor. Smoked like a chimney. Mom would've hated him, six-foot-four or not.

We'd had a few dates. I'm sure he'd made the same plans for tonight I had.

He'd come over to my condo and made me dinner. We were having a toke on my balcony. The air was brisk, but warm for a Winnipeg November. He had one arm around me and the other pointed up at the stars, toward the constellation of Orion.

"So there was this giant, name of Veggbyggir," he said. "And he had this horse, big strong bastard went by Svaðilfari. Could tow a fucking mountain."

The story of the myth behind the stars had a practised feel, as if this was something he said to all the girls. It was also wrong. The "horse" constellation he'd pointed to had been Taurus.

"Veggbyggir and Svaðilfari were tasked with building a wall around Asgard—that's the home of the Norse gods—in only three seasons or he won Freyja, the most beautiful goddess in Odin's court, and the sun and moon besides. *And* they'd almost done it. So Loki had to stop them."

Practised or not, wrong or not, it was working. I wanted to hear where his story went. "Wait? Isn't Loki a bad guy?"

Ted's eyes caught the starlight and he laughed. "You know Loki?"

"Not personally," I said. "Who won?"

"Not the giant," Ted said. "And not Loki."

I took a deep toke, held the smoke in my lungs for a three count, and passed the joint back to Ted as I exhaled. "How'd Loki manage to stop them?"

"He turned into a mare and lured the stallion away."

"Classic honey pot," I said.

Ted laughed. "Right?"

"So why'd you say Loki lost? Sounds like he had the last laugh."

Ted shrugged. "He came back pregnant with an eight-legged foal."

"Bummer," I said. "Which constellation is Loki? Where's he hiding?"

He stopped pointing at the stars to pull me close, and I figured he was going to kiss me, so I closed my eyes, leaned in, and over the balcony I went. I was too shocked to scream. It wouldn't save me anyway. I was going to die. As I tumbled ass over tits, his grin flashed; a crescent that glowed bright as the moon.

The last thing I saw before I clenched my eyes shut and waited for the impact was that *smile*. Wind whipped through my hair. I counted the seconds. One. Two. Three. We'd been on the 16th floor, but I definitely should've hit the ground by now.

I opened my eyes. I was only two floors down from my balcony. Ted looked smaller but his smile looked bigger. The cherry of his joint glowed bright orange after a toke. I smelled the pot. His cologne. His … overwhelming pleasure with himself.

I looked down. I didn't want to, but I needed to see. The ground seemed so far away. So did the balcony. How could I get there? How could I get back? How could I be hanging in the air?

This was madness. It made no sense. None.

"I suppose you're wondering what's going on?" Ted called down from the balcony. "I suppose you also want to know why you're a horse?"

"What?"

The word didn't come out. Just an angry whinny.

I craned my neck around, and the fucker was right. I *was* a horse. My hooves rested on air as if it were asphalt. The wind whipped through a mane and tail, not a head of hair.

Ted leapt over the balcony railing, joint still between his lips, and hurtled toward me. I spun, trying to get away, but he landed on my back.

"Didn't think we'd be going bareback tonight," he said, grabbing a handful of my mane and patted my flank.

The jokes.

I used to love his jokes. I used to think he was funny. Now, I just thought he was an asshole, and I wanted him gone.

I spun. Whirled. Bucked. He held on fast. Each leap shot me higher into the air, and I landed as if it were solid ground. He hung on. I tried something else. I tucked my legs tight to my body, and we plummeted like a rock.

"*Woooooo!*" he yelled. From his enthusiasm, I could only assume if he'd owned a cowboy hat, he'd be waving it.

Two storeys from the ground, I untucked my legs, and ran on the air, gradually changing the angle of my descent. My hooves touched the ground and turned back to bare feet. Ted tumbled off my back and onto the grass. I whirled and kicked him right between the legs. My skin prickled with the cold, and I realized my clothes must've torn off when I'd transformed.

Perfect.

I'd loved that dress. And the lingerie beneath it had been *expensive*.

I was torn between trying to cover myself, or kicking the jerk again.

He moaned, and struggled weakly when I pulled off his now ridiculously-baggy T-shirt to cover myself.

"Okay, prick," I said. "Explain yourself."

"I'm not the one who's a horse," he said.

I kicked him again.

When Ted was done cradling his plums and whining, he started talking. And what he said made no sense.

"First off," he said, exhaling a cloud of weed, "my name's not Ted. I'm Loki."

"You're *Loki*?" I asked. "Norse god, Loki?"

"Yup."

I snorted a laugh, before realizing he was serious. "God of lies and trickery and questionable romantic partners?"

"And you're trying to decide whether Loki would lie about his own name?" He raised and lowered his eyebrows like one of the Marx Brothers.

"No, I wonder why he *wouldn't* lie about being a horse-fucker."

He smiled that shit-eating grin and I wanted to turn back into a horse so I could kick him even harder. "Also, don't be so hard on yourself about the 'questionable romantic partners' thing. You're great."

"Loki? You're serious? *Loki*?"

"Why would I lie?"

"It's what you *do*."

He pouted. He actually pouted. "It's not *all* I do."

"So what am I? Your descendant from when you were a lady horse?"

He tapped his nose with his index finger and then pointed it at me. "Right in one."

"That's ridiculous."

"You're the one who's a horse."

"You're the one creeping on their descendant." I shuddered. *Ewww.* I can't believe we were going to … Just … I shuddered again. "*Ewww.*"

"We should go inside," Loki said, glancing at my chest. "It's cold outside."

I crossed my arms. "I don't have my keys. Thanks to you."

"Leave it to me." He gestured toward the door. I didn't move. "Trust me."

Loki didn't pick the lock to my building's front door. He just walked over and opened it. He bowed, gesturing for me to enter first. I did, and grabbed the door, pulling it shut behind me. I don't know how Loki slithered his way in, but when the door slammed shut, he was behind me. I screamed. More in frustration than terror. The elevator door *dinged* open as we walked across the lobby. It was empty. Loki's grin told me he'd done it. Somehow.

I didn't argue. We got in the elevator and headed up to my condo. He hummed a song … might've been "Genie in a Bottle," the whole way up.

"Why?" I asked as Loki opened the door to the condo as easily as he'd gotten us into the building.

"They always ask 'why?'" he said with a chuckle.

I wanted to protest. Ask who "they" were. I was oddly disappointed Loki fucked with other people's lives. I shouldn't be surprised, though. Disappointed, but not surprised. I guess we'd never said we were exclusive.

Nothing should surprise me anymore, since apparently, I was a werehorse.

"You're not a werehorse," Loki said as we went back inside. "If that's what you were thinking."

I closed the door behind me, hoping he wasn't really a mind-reader. Locked it. Latched it. Not that I believed a thin chain would impede Loki if he wanted to leave.

"Why—?"

Loki chuckled again. "Why?" he muttered, shaking his head.

"Let me finish, you interrupting bastard." I sighed. "Not 'Why me?' *Why now?*"

"Oh." He smiled. "That *is* different. I suppose."

"I haven't heard an answer."

"Demanding little filly, aren't you?"

"If my building didn't have a no-pets clause, I'd turn into a horse and give you *such a kicking*."

"Fine," Loki said. "Fine. Magic is coming back into the world. Hard. There's your 'now.' As for the 'why,' you can probably imagine, I have enemies."

"Really?" I said, voice dripping with sarcasm. "You?"

Loki waved off the remark. "So after I saved Asgard from itself, *again*, Odin stole my first kid."

"The eight-legged one?" I asked with a heavy dollop of sarcasm. He struck me as the type who had more than one bastard in his past.

"Yes." Loki's lips twitched in irritation. "Sleipnir could run on the air and water as well as over land."

"Useful trick, that," I said.

Loki nodded. "Odin thought so. Used my son as his mount. That wasn't enough for the one-eyed prick. Then he bred Sleipnir to make flying horses for his valkyries."

There was something in the way he'd spoken, a hurt still raw, genuine, which made me want to believe him. I'd almost certainly regret it.

"Valkyries are real, too?" I asked.

"Everything's real, hon. Except the stuff that isn't."

That was *no* help. "They're coming for me, aren't they?"

He nodded. "To them, you're nothing but a beast of burden, something to be ridden. Not a person. A *thing*."

"*Hmph.*" That was not an attitude to which I was unaccustomed. "What if I don't want to be their ride?"

"They'll either bind you in your other form, or they'll kill you."

I rubbed at my eyes. "Jesus."

"Yeah, *he's* not going to help you with this. Sorry."

The wine bottle was still half-full. I grabbed it and slugged back a couple swallows. I could've used something stronger. "I'm going to change."

"Not sure there's room in there for a horse," Loki said, smirking.

"Clothes." *Ass.*

Loki snatched the wine and had a pull. "I'll be waiting."

I closed the door behind me, even though Loki had already seen me in my all-together. This wasn't how I saw tonight going. Okay. It was sort of how I'd thought the date would go. Nudity? Hell, yes. Horse transformation, shapeshifting date, and surprise family reunion? Hell, no.

I pulled on a fresh pair of underwear, yoga pants and a sports bra and hoodie. I packed a bag with a few spare undies and shirts and sweats too, just in case.

Loki seemed disappointed with my practical attire.

I didn't care.

I tucked my phone into my bag. "I'm ready."

"Now you sound like my great-great-great—" he kept going, I lost track of how many greats he actually spoke, but I presumed he was being accurate and not snarky, because accuracy in this instance, would irritate me more. "—Granddaughter," he finished.

"I'll take that as a compliment, I guess."

"Oh, it is."

I asked, "Are we running or fighting?"

"We run," Loki said. "You're not ready to fight them."

I looked over my shoulder as we left the condo building. I'd forgotten to turn my lights off. I hated having to leave my home behind. Especially without knowing where we were going, or when I'd be home. I had tenderloin thawing in the fridge. What would I tell work? Would they believe me?

Of course they won't believe you're a magic horse. Don't be fucking ridiculous.

I sighed. It'd been a good job while it'd lasted. If Loki went on making my life "interesting" too long, I'd be sure to lose it. And default on my condo mortgage. I did *not* want to move back in with my parents. They already thought I was weird.

"Since we're running, where do we run to?"

Loki smiled. There was that Cheshire-cat grin again. "I know the perfect place."

That did not make me feel better.

Loki led me toward the river, and not my car.

He watched the sky nervously. "The sooner you master your body, the better."

That made sense. I just … *hated* agreeing with him. "Fine," I muttered. "Whatever you say."

He raised an eyebrow as if he were a cartoon character. "You should probably be more careful with your phrasing in the future."

I scowled, and Loki turned into a falcon, screeching with delight.

I wondered how he did it. The falcon's eyes glittered, as if he was reading my mind. I considered my carefully chosen clothes. They wouldn't survive the transformation—assuming I *could* make myself change. I stripped, stuffing the clothes into my side bag as I hopped, foot to foot, on the cold asphalt at the edge of the parking lot. I willed myself to change.

Nothing happened.

Last time the change had come when I'd been afraid.

Change. Change. Change.

A car's engine revved as it came into the parking lot, not slowing. The lights turned as the driver sought their spot. For now, I was hidden by a transformer box, but that wouldn't last.

Change.

C'mon.

I looked up at the sky; the damned falcon still circled.

I hopped into the air.

Change.

I landed, wincing at the impact, and stamped my feet against the cold. Huddled with my arms across my torso. The cold wasn't helping either.

There was a sound like rain slamming on a tin roof, and I looked up. Three horses, complete with riders, ran on the air, as if hurtling down the side of a mountain toward my building. The horses stopped next to my balcony, and their riders—all women in white—hopped off. Glass shattered and they entered my apartment.

Holy shit. The valkyries. I looked at the horses tied off to my balcony as if it were a hitching post. I was going to die.

Or worse.

I thought I heard someone call my name. I could barely hear from the pounding in my temples.

"Michelle?"

Shit. The driver was Veronica. My nosy neighbour across the hall.

"Are you okay, Michelle? Should I call—Oh my God!"

I hadn't felt the change, same as the first time, one moment I was a woman, the next I was a horse. My hooves rang off the asphalt. She backed away, hands up as if trying to ward off attack and she ran. She'd seen me turn into a horse. There was no going back from that. My life, as I'd known it, was *definitely* over.

I heard crashes from my apartment. The valkyries must be upset I wasn't home. My "I don't want to die" instincts fought with my "I *just* got my kitchen the way I liked it" anger.

"Time to go," Loki said.

I ran into the air, and into the night.

I think every kid grows up wanting a magic horse, but how many kids want to *be* a magic horse?

This "gift" wasn't something I'd asked for, but it was all I wanted anymore.

To run. To fly.

Nothing compared to this.

Not work. Not food. Not sex.

I could fly.

It's hard to describe the exhilaration of flying. High in the sky, north wind slapping against my body, I didn't feel its chill, only the rush, as I ducked, and dived, and climbed and plummeted.

In that tiny moment, all my troubles were forgotten.

We landed in the Assiniboine Forest, a popular hikers' destination, right inside the city, but fortunately not so popular at this time of night.

"They won't look for us here," Loki said.

"Why not?"

He twirled around, fingers pointing at nothing. "Because it's lousy with elves."

"*Right*," I said. "Because of the *elves*."

I sighed. Elves being real would be the least weird thing about tonight, so I shut up and dressed. Loki was in clothes the moment he landed. Not the dark jeans and dress shirt he'd been wearing as "Ted" but a rumpled suit that looked tailored for a much larger man.

I stared at Loki. "How come your clothes don't get shredded when you change shape?"

He shrugged, and smiled. "I'm more magic than you, I guess."

"Typical," I muttered.

Loki motioned for me to follow him deeper into the trees.

I lost track of how long we walked in the stillness of wood, dead leaves crunching under our feet, and misted breath drifting to join the clouds.

Loki broke the silence. "So … are you freaked out?"

A little. I didn't want to admit it, and ultimately, what I felt above all, was *awesome.* "I'm great," I said. And I meant it.

"You should keep practising," Loki said, out of nowhere. "'Til the change is second nature."

There was room on the foot path, and the cool night air didn't bother me. It was the in-between step that was the problem.

"You just want to see me strip, you perv."

"It is our third date," he said, winking.

I gave him a shove, and he staggered. "Give it a rest. It's not going to happen. It's never going to happen. *Grandma.*"

"I was kidding," he said, and I chose to believe him. But at the very least, he did shut up.

For a while.

"How could you *not* suspect you're at least part horse?" Loki asked.

My eyes narrowed. "You need to tread very carefully, god or no."

Loki's voice was shiny as a new penny. "You're long of limb. Long of face. You don't eat meat. Like shoes."

"Oh yeah, *so* obvious now that you point it out."

He shrugged. "It was all there."

I hurled my side bag at him and made the change.

Changing shape was exhausting. My stomach growled, and my body was slick with sweat. I made the change standing in place, I made it running. I made it jumping, and I made it backing up. Learning to speak in my horse body had been the biggest challenge. My mouth and tongue didn't want to form the human words. By the time Loki was satisfied, I felt as if I'd been running all night.

"You'll need to eat to keep up your strength," Loki said, reaching into my bag and passing me an apple.

I bit into it gratefully. It tasted amazing. Juicy, fresh. I'd been so worried about having enough clothing to survive any accidental transformations, I hadn't thought about food. I had been full from dinner, and flushed with the excitement and terror of my new crazy life.

"Eat," Loki said, passing me a protein bar.

I took it in hand and unwrapped it. I wondered where he was getting the food, because it sure hadn't come from my kitchen.

"You need to eat more," he said.

My eyes narrowed. I felt like he was leading up to something ...

"Like a horse!" he hollered, slapping his thigh.

I should've slapped him, but it only reminded me of our—my—predicament. "They'll never stop, will they?"

"No."

My eyes fell. That single simple word felt so damned defeating. Loki nudged my chin up. I didn't see any mischief in his eyes. No sass. Nothing but the truth when he said, "But I'll never stop, either."

"Shit." I didn't know if I found Loki's promise comforting.

"We'll get you trained up, and keep you on the run. I'll run interference for you when I can. You'll be fine. You're a sharp little filly."

I bristled at the "compliment." All that was missing was him patting me on the head, like a pet. Maybe that's all I was to him. "If you were so good at interference, those flying bitches would be shy three horses."

His eyes dropped. I wasn't sure if it was embarrassment, or if I'd hurt his feelings. I didn't feel great about either result. Regardless of what had gotten me in this scenario, Loki was my only ally, my only way out of it. And he was *trying* to help. But I also needed to help myself. I couldn't run forever.

"I'm sorry," I said. "What I said … it was cruel, and unnecessary."

"But true," he said. "I do mourn the loss of any of my children. No matter the time or generations between us."

"We've got to teach the valkyries not to come at me," I said.

"That means fighting, not running," Loki said. "You up for that?"

"I'll have to be."

"Look," I hissed. "They're up there."

Backlit against clouds, glowing with moonlight, were the valkyries. At least, I assumed it was them. Unless I was suddenly in a Johnny Cash song, who else could it be? Riding horses. In the air.

"Are you out of your damned mind?" Loki jerked me under a branch.

"You think they see us?"

"I wouldn't put it past them." He shook his head. "I wouldn't put anything past them."

"How can we—"

"Kill them?"

It sounded so permanent when he said it, but I was glad he did. To be able to say the words out loud made them real. Made it a real thing that I believed I could do. I didn't like to think I could actually kill.

I asked, "Can we bribe them?"

Loki shook his head. "You're the only thing they want."

I ground my teeth. He wasn't helping. "Can I outrun them?"

"Probably in a straight shot, but their horses are more used to being horses than you, so they'll be able to out-manoeuvre you, whether they have armed ladies on them or not."

When I turned around, a tall, muscular woman stood in Loki's place. The woman wore a white-feathered cloak, white leathers. With her pale skin and white-gold hair, she looked like an apparition more than a real lady. I jumped back, stifling a scream. She glowered, holding a spear across her thighs with both hands. Then she winked.

Bloody Loki.

"This is what they'll look like," said the woman, in Loki's voice. "The cloaks will allow them to glide. Their spears will kill anything they scratch, and let me tell you, it's not a fun way to go."

"Seriously?"

"Ayup."

"How do they control their …" what to say? Horses? Mounts? Slaves?"

"How will they control you?" Loki asked. "Is that what you mean?"

"Yeah."

"They have bridles woven from the hair of my son," he said. "Like a lasso. If they get that around your neck, you're done. And worse, while you're bound, you won't care."

There was something we could use … "Without the bridles?"

"You'll still be you."

I breathed a sigh of relief, so, naturally, Loki had to ruin things. "Assuming they haven't broken you."

"If we lose the bridles, the horses will lose them," I said.

"I'm listening."

"If they don't have … air superiority, they can't out-run me. The cloaks let them glide, not fly, and I run on air. Get the horses away from them, and they can't catch me. And if their captured …" I needed to know what to call them—what to call *myself*.

"Vindafolöld?" he offered. "It means wind-foals."

More poetic than I expected from the likes of him. "If we scatter the … vindafolöld, they'll never get all of us. With luck, the valkyries leave with nothing."

Loki smiled. "I'm glad to be a part of this plan."

"What plan?"

Loki laughed maniacally. "Exactly."

The ground whizzed by below us. If I concentrated on the movement of the ground, and not that I had a mythical god riding my back, I could pretend I was looking out the window of an airplane.

The moment never lasted.

I *did* have a god riding me.

"Tally-ho!" Loki yelled.

I shook my head. The salvation he promised couldn't be worth the irritation.

"There they are," Loki called, gesturing with his spear.

The valkyries circled the forest, lingering over the river. Moonlight cast their shadows over the water, making it seem as if there were more of them. As if they had shadowy followers waiting to help bring me down.

I wanted to turn back. I wanted to run forever. Loki must've felt my hesitation. He uttered a yipping war cry that would've put Xena to shame and could've been heard in Saskatoon.

The valkyries stopped circling and swung around to face us. It was mildly interesting to note how they did so—they didn't turn in a wide arc like flying birds would have; instead they wheeled as if the air were solid, and charged in a v-shape, straight at us.

"I really don't like this plan anymore," I said.

"It's *your* plan," said Loki.

I had nothing to say to that. I hated that he was correct. I hated being in this situation. But the only way out was through. Through three murderous goddesses who could kill me with a scratch. The only things stopping them were that they'd prefer to enslave me, my ultimate-great-grandmother, and a horse body I was still learning to use.

Loki patted my neck, and offered me a knife by the blade. I bit down on the hilt, trying not to think of how ridiculous I must look.

The valkyries were silent, other than the clatter of their steeds' hooves against the sky. Silent. Grim. Implacable. We barrelled toward one another. The timing would be hard to judge.

"Almost … almost … almost …" Loki whispered.

Now.

Loki leapt from my back, screaming, "This one is *mine!*"

I barely heard him. I changed. It came, not effortlessly, but immediately.

My galloping hooves lost their purchase on the air. My legs ran against nothing and my arms pinwheeled as I struggled for balance I didn't have time to retain. The knife that'd felt so tiny and delicate a moment before suddenly felt huge, and the handle pained my jaw to contain.

I grabbed the valkyrie's bridle. My shoulder wrenched as my fingers closed around the braided horse hair. My momentum swung me against the horse's flank. I almost dropped the knife getting it in hand, but I held on.

"What in Hel?" the valkyrie cried.

She raised her spear. I had no time to cut. No time to think. I was going to die. Just a scratch, Loki had warned. Only a scratch.

The valkyrie looked a lot more stabby than scratchy.

I raised my knife, and she laughed. She didn't stab. *She laughed.*

The valkyrie's laugh ended when I slid the knife blade behind the bridle and slashed outward. I fell, taking the bridle with me. She had enough time to reach for the horse's mane before my momentum dragged her off its back and into the air.

Her feathered cloak unfurled, and her descent slowed as her horse galloped away. She stared death at me and reeled me in by wrapping the braid around the wrist of her free arm. Christ, she was strong. It felt like she could pull my arm clean off. The spear, she kept levelled.

I raised my knife and she laughed again. Until I severed the braid and dropped.

I bit the knife handle again, willing myself to change.

The transformation came more easily now, as if each time I did it, this unnatural thing became a more natural part of my body. Which concerned me. What if it meant someday I'd transform and forget what it meant to be human? Loki never forgot to be an asshole, regardless of his form, so hopefully I'd be okay.

I ran as the valkyrie drifted to the ground, and I scanned the air for the rest of them. The freed horse ran in the opposite direction of me as fast as possible. Which probably made it the smartest horse in this race.

Two valkyries fought atop the back of a second flying horse. I had to assume one of them was Loki. At least he was still on plan. The third ... where was the third?

I felt a shudder. A sensation you'd describe as someone stepping on your grave. But I wasn't in the grave. Yet. A shadow passed over a cloud beneath me. I looked up and saw a horse flying away.

An explosion hit my back. I'd spotted the third horse. But not the valkyrie, and now she was on my back.

"Not so clever now, are you, beastie?" she hissed.

Her fingers tightened in my mane. She jerked my head back. Instinctively, I stopped running. I didn't want to, I wanted to bolt. But I couldn't. I reared as the valkyrie's heels dug into my flanks.

I cried out, and as the neigh of protest escaped, so did my knife.

"I should kill you," she said. "But we're already down two steeds. I will settle for breaking you."

"Go ahead and try."

The loop of a bridle passed over my neck. Shit. That was a good try. Without hands I couldn't get it off. With hands, I'd start falling, and hang myself.

Loki hadn't said I could turn into anything other than a horse, but he was a shapeshifter, and assuming the god of lies had told the truth this time, his blood was in my veins as much as my horse-grandfather's. Maybe I *could* do something.

I changed. I fell.

My hands came back first. I slipped them under the loop just before it choked me.

The valkyrie laughed as I swung at the end of her line. My human feet kicked feebly as I gasped and danced on the air.

"Michelle!" Loki cried from somewhere. Somewhere distant, and growing more so.

My vision greyed, and tunnelled. My world shrank. I needed my hooves back. If I changed, would my front legs get caught in the noose? Would it kill me? Or break the bridle? It was magic. My heart thudded in my ears as grey turned black.

My first change had come when I was afraid.

I was plenty afraid now.

Afraid to change.

But I needed to.

My feet hit purchase. I stepped up as if climbing a ladder, and felt the braid go slack. Slack enough to loop it over my head and turn around to face the valkyrie. Human arms tugged and jerked. My torso hadn't changed, just my lower body. The valkyrie was much stronger than me. Without the added mass of being a horse there was no way I could overpower her. I dug my hoofed feet in. It slowed the process, but didn't stop it.

The first valkyrie we'd kicked off her horse glided toward us, spear arm cocked back. She threw.

I looped the braid around one arm and changed to a horse again. I ran down, jerking the valkyrie into the path of the spear.

She cried out and the line went slack. When I whirled around, the valkyrie was gone. Her foggy afterimage glared at me before the wind caught it and dissipated her to nothing.

The valkyrie who'd thrown the spear screamed in protest. She scanned the sky for her last sister. I looked too. I saw Loki—I assumed it was Loki—flying as a hawk beside one of the horses.

"You're outnumbered, lady," he said. "Go back to Hel."

"I'll be back for you, trickster," the valkyrie snarled. "And your little horse, too."

The valkyrie faded into the clouds the same way her shish-kebabbed sister had, and was gone.

"Wow," Loki said. "I can't believe that worked."

I shook my head, panting. "I think you're *exactly* the man my mother warned me about."

Far Gone and Out

The first thing Tilda Eilífsdóttir did was get the hell out of Winnipeg.

She invoked the travel rune, Mannaz, and called the remnants of Bifröst. The rainbow bridge had once connected the realm of men to Asgard, home of the gods. Only an aurora remained of its brilliance, which flared, intensifying, and enveloped Tilda. Each step she took carried her further. Feet. Yards. Blocks. Kilometres. Tilda stepped town to town as the travel-rune enveloped her. To a casual observer, or to the car whose headlights grew ever closer, the shimmering light almost touched the highway. A door rested on the road. From the past, she heard tires squeal on asphalt, and the echo of a dying horn.

Tilda stepped through the door.

Tilda wanted to run away.

Again.

Only this time, she'd make sure she got away. She was fifteen and sick of having visions. Tired of knowing people's actions before they took them. Tired of writing her visions in a journal for her amma to pore over and dissect, looking for anything the Norns could use to their advantage.

Tilda was exhausted from the future, the one she imagined and could never have, and the certainty she saw in the visions that slammed her without warning. The Nine Worlds may have been lost to Ragnarök, Yggdrasill may have burned away and its connections to those worlds severed, but she wanted to have experiences—adventures—of her own. She wanted to leave the lakeside town of Gimli behind and see *this* world. Before it was too late. Once she did as her amma desired, and brought life to the Norns' next generation, there was no adventure Tilda could imagine. Only diapers, and feedings, and worse, managing their stupid teahouse that no one ever came into in the first place. She'd avoided it once already. Mom and Amma had freaked when she'd taken a morning-after pill and delayed Amma's "retirement." As if she'd ever stop bossing them around, visions or no. Now Tilda purposefully avoided looking in that future's direction, but glimpses still came unbidden.

The future seemed a burden at times, but her mom's present, baking scones, making tea, and tallying the books wasn't enough, either. Mom seemed happy enough, but Tilda suspected Vera Eilífsdóttir also wanted more than her lot in life.

Her mom, Vera, hadn't had the same buffer Tilda had growing up. Vera's mother and grandmother had died shortly after Vera was born, leaving Urd, her langamma, to raise the girl. There were technically so many years between them that ancestor might feel more appropriate, but Tilda still thought of Urd as "amma," the guise they'd used to hide their family from mortal scrutiny her entire life. The false title become true with time, in the same way the other Norns' truer names of Urð and Verðandi wore thin becoming Urd and Verdandi. Tilda loved Amma, but she knew her too well. Hard. Unforgiving. A stone ready to tip over and crush you if you didn't watch where and how you stepped. Tilda couldn't imagine life without her mom as a buffer.

She'd packed a bag, squirrelling things away a bit at a time, to not set off her mother's visions. She didn't need much. It wasn't so much Tilda feared her mom would stop her, but that she wouldn't go if confronted by her mom's tears. She briefly considered taking the runes of power with her. Their magic would come in handy, even if Tilda hadn't mastered them yet. But if she stole them, she wouldn't be dodging the enemies the Norns had cultivated, she'd be dodging the Norns themselves. Amma would never let the runes leave the house with an "untested girl."

Not again.

The runes sat in their leather pouch in the centre of a round, heavy table, waiting to be taken. The room was still cold from Amma's last reading, despite the burning fireplace. The attic was immense, larger than the tea house's main floor. Remnants of Asgard's walls and ash salvaged from the fallen World Tree allowed it to be so. The disorientation the room created opened their supplicants to the readings, and their dooms. Bookshelves lined the walls, filled with an odd mixture of musty-smelling leather tomes and modern coil-bound notebooks. Every vision the Norns had ever had, every secret they'd ever uncovered, waited there to be exploited. Events Tilda wished to be true, and dreaded arriving. She'd studied the future visions the other Norns had left behind too.

A flash of the future: wolves of flame, a grudge still burning hot after centuries, runes swirling around them joining past to future.

No, the future was what she wanted to avoid.

Tilda pulled open the thick curtains letting moonlight break through the darkness. The cold drifted away, and the fire warmed the room. The vertigo effect faded as the room ceased to be connected to Ginnungagap, the space between worlds.

Her hands hovered over the runes, fingers twitching with anticipation. She'd never get away with taking them. She'd never get away, period, if she tried. Which didn't stop Tilda from considering the stones, jumbled together in their leather pouch, destiny waiting to be spilled out, an answer to any question, waiting only to be asked.

She whispered, "Where should I go?"

Urd's voice, rough and sharp, steel on stone, rasped from behind her. "So. You still wish to go."

Tilda started.

Before she could answer, her grandmother said, "Of course you do."

"You can't keep me here," Tilda said. "I'll die."

Urd's eyebrows perked. "You have seen this?"

"Yes," Tilda said, too quickly.

"Lies," Urd hissed, "do not suit you. Truth is a far superior means to deceive. There are many futures. What we see is influenced by who we are, but the threads remain true, even if our interpretation of them proves less so. Be careful of what you wish to become true, or what you fear will be; those emotions will only make the truth worse.

"Don't try to stop me," Tilda said, not knowing what she'd do if Urd intended to keep her home. Not quite believing Amma was ever going to be ready to "retire," when—if—Tilda did have a child to gift her visions to.

"I wouldn't dream of it."

Tilda blinked. "Why not?"

"You desire to go. You will not be happy here. You will not accept your doom when this—" she gestured broadly around the rune reading chamber "—is all you have known. You are restless. Reckless. You are *young*. I could not allow your mother this luxury, but you have time. Come home to us."

"Thanks, Amma."

Urd clasped Tilda's hands in a tight, cold grip. "You *must* return."

"I will." After a moment, Tilda asked, "Didn't you ever want more than this?"

"*Of course I did,*" Urd snapped, each word a whip-crack of rebuke. "But my decision was made for me. I was the last of my line, and our work wasn't done. I did not have the choices offered to you, or your mother, slim as they may seem to you. And so I did what I must."

Tilda bit back a retort. Until this moment, she'd never been privy to any choices not pre-approved by the eldest of the Norns.

There used to be many norns, before Ragnarök, at least. Any witch, elf, or giant with a touch of the Sight called themselves a norn in those days. Tilda had never met anyone else who'd claimed the title, but Amma always said there were only three Norns who mattered. Only three to speak the truth of what was, will be, and what is. Since Amma had come over from the old country they'd revealed the basic thread of fate to their supplicants, whether they'd have a good, bad, or exceptional life. One lot drawn for every man, woman, and child on the planet, and no escaping it. Fate was fate, and the Norns were the last who could make it. Tilda knew her eventual fate, but knew if she tried, she could make a new one, for a while.

Another smile that could bend steel. "Then you must do as *needs* be done." Tilda imagined her reciting her mantra, *and the mantle of Skuld is all about need, the fire that burns in the darkness, the light that shows us the way.* Urd's eyes glanced at the table, and the runes. "Those remain here."

Tilda looked away from the runes and sighed. "Yes, Amma."

"Have you spoken to Verdandi?"

Urd almost never used their mortal names. "No, Amma."

"You would have me speak to her?"

"If you wish it, Amma," Tilda said. "*After* I am gone."

Urd's mouth twitched, not a smile, but a hint of humour, at Tilda testing her boundaries again.

"How will you protect yourself?" Urd asked.

"I'll wrap myself in my mortal name," Tilda said. "Mathilda Eilífsdóttir in truth, not Skuld the Norn."

"You will not have your visions, then. Nor any gifts of our blood."

"I know." Tilda smiled. "I'm stronger than you think."

Urd nodded, accepting a truth she didn't want to bear. "If you will not be using it, perhaps you will lend me your Sight."

Amma held ages of grudges, and if she saw an opportunity in the future to settle them … she would. And the visions wouldn't be recorded the in a journal to exploit later, either. Tilda knew her amma. Her secrets remained hers.

"How else will I know when to call you home?" Urd laughed then, and it took Tilda aback, as if she'd never heard the sound.

Tilda blinked as a stray snowflake drifted onto her staring eye and melted there.

The winter that'd fully swallowed Winnipeg hadn't hit here. Cold. Wind. Nothing on the ground but a dusting of snow, snaking over the highway in the wind. The thread of her past was strong here, on the same spot where she saw Ted Callan—Ófriður—for the first time. The place where she'd first seen the world burning. The headlights of Ted's GTO had burned like Muspelheim's fires, locking her in place, and she'd seen the end ... or rather, *an* end.

Something else had happened here. A choice. A beginning. The forking of her doom's road. No, something *would* happen here. She knelt, and brushed the cold, bare asphalt. Scattered bits of paper the wind didn't touch. Each held a hand-drawn rune. Runes she'd drawn when she'd performed an ad hoc reading in a then-stranger's car. A whim had entwined and changed both their fates. What where they doing here? They should've been littering the road closer to Winnipeg, long gone under rain and snow.

She heard a laugh from her past. From her future. From now.

The memory was wrong. Tilda had snuck out of Gimli in the night. Never confronted Urd. She'd left a note and was gone by morning.

The moment, and the wrongness, melted away as fast as snow on Tilda's skin.

Tilda didn't have many close friends in Gimli—most people avoided her family—but she'd managed to catch a ride into the city with an acquaintance from school. From there, she'd find a path.

Without her visions, Tilda might not be able to control her magic to *see* the future, but she *was* the Norn of the future. Powers or not, hers was the need-rune. She'd get by. She remembered a few big events to come, events that would allow her to build a nest egg. She bought scratchers and played Proline prior to abandoning her visions. She never won enough to make anyone notice her, and she'd cash them in from place to place to help avoid notice. She always won more than she spent.

She hitched her way from Winnipeg to Vancouver and made her way south into the United States. The U.S. had its own problems, but its massive population allowed her to get lost and would keep her mom from finding her immediately. Devotion to the Christian God had scoured monsters from even the outskirts. There were human monsters there, as there were everywhere, in plenty. They didn't worry Tilda. She could handle monsters of any sort.

She'd been raised by one.

Her twenty-third birthday, and the calling of the Icelandic Festival back home, came and went. It'd been years since she'd had a homemade birthday cake. Her first year gone, Mom had sent a care package to where she'd been staying. Showing she could find her, and respecting her decision to leave enough not to follow through further. Her only other contact with home had been hooking up with her some-time girlfriend Mel, who had been in Chicago on a school trip. Tilda ran out of money in North Dakota and she'd needed to pause for a while, too near home for her liking. North Dakota and Minnesota—anywhere—where Norse names were too comfortable on mortal lips could be dangerous for her, but that was where the winds had blown her. She'd had many close calls, but had avoided calling her gifts home.

Long before Ragnarök, Odin had placed a fence around Midgard—Earth—to keep the giants and monsters out. Maybe if he hadn't built his fence from the progenitor giant he and his brothers had murdered, they wouldn't have needed one. Fences make good neighbours, but no fence is perfect and things always slip under, over, and through. Ignorance kept Midgard safe from magical predation, but the moment people were exposed to the Nine Worlds, any protection was gone.

Odin had been a bit of a prick.

Tilda's shift at the diner was quiet, and the time dragged. It was a local chain, this one near an interchange on I-94 in a travel centre with a gas station. Not much to look at while she was there, and not much to see when she left, but it was money. When there were people to leave tips, anyway. No tips meant no cigarettes. No booze. No birthday treat at the end of the night. If things didn't turn around soon … no place to live, and no way out of Bismark but home.

Maybe it *was* time to go home. Without her visions,

dooms still leapt out at her, freight trains, so fast, so bright, she could do nothing but stand there, caught in the path, and be swept along on the rails of another's destiny. The man who would die in a motorcycle crash; the roar of the engine, the scream of metal and the stink of smoke, strong as if she'd been clutching her arms around his waist. The smiling woman, glowing with power—not magic, civic—a chic pantsuit imposed over the T-shirt and shorts she wore tending bar. It was all Tilda could do to not to grasp Naudiz, to clutch the need-fire and reclaim her identity.

It was an uncomfortable sensation. She was supposed to control fate. To know and manipulate the future to the Norns' benefit. She wondered if her family was setting these people in her path in order to subtly guide her home. The longer she stayed in any one place, the more she encountered such destinies. The fated found her, one way or another.

The wind whistled through Tilda's hair, buffeting it behind her. Clouds sped across the moon. There was no wind in Hel. No moonlight. No light at all. No cars— well, *one* car, full of memories she didn't want to consider. Only those same memories had brought Tilda here. Memories were all one had in Hel, until hunger ate them, and only despair was left.

Memories.

Moments.

It was a cold night, not as cold as Hel, but she didn't feel it. Still, the chill cast her mind back to a fateful walk through the underworld.

The mist surrounded her.

Cold.

Cold enough to kill.

Shadows in the mist, memories frozen in time, revealed themselves in no discernible order. Too many memories. Most not her own. Too many had happened long before she was born. So many yet to come. Her mom's life. Urd's. A patchwork jumble of past, future and present. She knew every moment as if they'd happened to her.

Three figures stumbled though snow, all women of a similar age, hunched and bundled against the cold. A distant fire luring them further into a storm toward a village in the shadow of a volcano.

One by one, the sisters fell in the snow, until only one, the youngest, remained. She dragged her sisters as far as she could, to within sight of the closest sod home. She pushed further and further, until even a *jötunn* couldn't force her on. Even iron will couldn't drag her the final paces to knock on the door. Before she faded, the door opened. A woman who looked a lot like Tilda, a lot like her mom, and was neither, hair like a halo of flame, regarded them. And smiled. Tilda recognized Urd, not as she'd known her amma, but as Urd had seen herself in the time before she settled in Manitoba's Interlake.

Tilda waded through the experiences to get to something *hers*, but everything recent brought pain. She knew why Urd had come from Iceland to help build a new Icelandic settlement in Canada. She knew what happened to her true amma, a woman she'd never met, a woman who only existed as pictures and vague impressions to Tilda's own mother, but she couldn't find herself.

Walking through Niflheim to confront Hel had made many things clearer to Tilda, about the coming future and her role there, but she didn't see how that would come to be after her miscarriage. Not when Ófriður—she wouldn't call him Ted—had chosen Loki and the trickster's half-dead brood over her and the child they lost. The child that could have been. *Should* have been. She'd seen it. Her visions weren't wrong. The future had always been hers. How could she have been so wrong? The memory faded in the mist, and Tilda felt relief. Melancholy wasn't her purpose. She'd go no further down the roads of the past.

Tilda knew the true reason why Urd hated Loki, and it had nothing to do with Ragnarök. It was far more personal. Far more prosaic than she'd expected. Too far, she'd gone too far. The memory was gone, lost in fog of time, among other memories hers, and not hers. She knew, too, why she'd never met a norn who wasn't of her blood. Urd had made certain there was no one left to claim the title.

No matter how many recollections crossed her brain, no matter what she wished would be drawn into clearer focus, she couldn't control of the flow. She needed freedom. She needed to feel the last time the world's weight didn't rest on her brow. Tilda's mind retreated to her powerless past.

"That guy's been sitting in the booth all night," Kat said. Kat Olson was a single mom, getting by, who looked older than her actual late twenties, and still cute in a way she didn't take the time to exploit. She'd acted as both a surrogate mom and big sister to Tilda, which wasn't necessarily what Tilda wanted from her, but she hadn't wanted to ruin their working relationship.

"So?" Tilda asked. It wasn't her section, and it wasn't her restaurant, so if the guy in the Enslaved T-shirt and motorcycle boots wanted to milk the free-refill policy, it was no skin off her ass.

"Can you check on him, darlin'?" When buttering the request didn't budge her, she countered Tilda's scowl with, "C'mon, I really need a smoke."

Tilda rolled her eyes but acquiesced with a sigh. Kat was a sweetheart. "Fine. Enjoy your break."

"Thanks!" Kat chirped, and walked away, a little extra swagger in her steps and a toss of her red ponytail.

Tilda headed to the booth with a fresh pot of coffee and the customer's posture stiffened. She topped up his cup. He said nothing.

"Anything else?" she asked, already knowing the answer.

He beamed a smile at her, and Tilda didn't like its thousand-watt intensity. White makeup stained his dyed-black hairline. His shadowed eyes weren't from being strung out; more like a raccoon had gone heavy on the eyeshadow. Bottom lip split from a fight. Full tattoo sleeves on both arms, mostly demons and shit, but she didn't want to stare. Cigarette burn scars on his exposed forearms were the focus point of the demons—eyes and mouths.

"Maybe," he said. Tilda turned. A Magic 8-Ball thudded on top of the table. "I was trying to get an answer I liked," he said, smile still too wide.

"Answers are good," she said, warily. She felt responsibility to help those looking for answers. She shouldn't. Not now. But her nature was hard to resist. She wouldn't do a proper reading—couldn't—but she could help without using her magic. Fate was weird. She wouldn't be going back to Gimli. Not yet. Besides, the guy was cute, in a dirtbag way. Whenever she was attracted to a man, they usually turned out to be dirtbags, or thugs. Or both. "More importantly, what's your question?"

Tilda wasn't sure why she wanted to help. Who was he to her? And yet, there was something in the request's simplicity, and the earnestness with which he'd approached it. Urd would take her to task for providing answers without cost. But Tilda wasn't a Norn—at the moment—and he might leave her a tip.

And in truth, she'd always had a fondness for the Magic 8-Ball, regardless of what Amma had said. Tilda could still hear the disdain in her voice. "*Ridiculous.*" Not "magic" at all. Those who came to Grey Ladies looking for their dooms wanted *traditional* readings. They wanted *the old ways*.

"Will I get what I'm asking for?" he asked.

Tilda turned over the Magic 8-Ball and set it on the table, saying the answer before it appeared. "All signs point to yes."

He smiled. She smiled back. She might get something she wanted, too.

The diner closed. Kat went home. Tilda's cleanup was done and it was time to meet with 8-Ball. The cooks were already drinking.

Then it was past time. Well past time. Tractor trailers rumbled down the highway. When Tilda checked her watch, it was a quarter past this-guy-is-never-going-to-fucking-show. She had a bad feeling about this. He'd been determined to get her attention with his Magic 8-Ball gag. She couldn't believe he'd blown her off.

Tilda ground out a cigarette under her shoe. "All signs point to yes, my ass."

"Going somewhere?" A voice from behind her made her stop short. It didn't belong to 8-Ball and held an edge she didn't like. "Skuld?"

Shit.

"Never heard of her," Tilda turned to face a huge, round-faced man. Tilda was tall, near six feet, and he towered over her, but it was hard to take him seriously with the baby face no amount of greasepaint could hide.

"I don't think so, Norn. We know what you are."

She didn't like the sound of that "we." They came from the shadows, two men, two women, trying to be dramatic. Mr. 8-Ball among them, skulking behind the big guy with an embarrassed look on his face. They were dressed in black leather with fur and chainmail accents; studs and nails jutted from shoulders, elbows, knees, and wrists. Hobnailed motorcycle boots. They stank as if they'd been born in that leather and never changed it. Sweat-slick hair clung to white greasepaint faces accented by black animalistic shapes drawn in runic script. They looked like a metal band. Worse, a black metal band. The kind who were *too* into Norse myth. Exactly the sort Tilda wanted to avoid.

They knew who she was, and they weren't afraid. How much did they know? And *that* made Tilda shudder. With Skuld locked away there wasn't much *Tilda* could do. There was no way she could avoid being hurt. She straightened her back and tried to conjure her best Amma voice.

"If you know who I am, then you should know better."

Her family had *álfur* blood. *Jötunn* blood. Back home, she was tougher, faster, stronger than a human woman her age should be. But blood hidden under her mortal name's protection wasn't protection at all.

"But you're *not* her." Round-face smiled. "Not now. Not yet."

Well, shit.

If this was a band, he was probably the singer. Frontmen tended to be in control, at least publicly, because they were already the group's voice. She kept focused on him. The others spread out, surrounding her. Round-face rushed her first. Fire flashed in his footsteps. Tilda dodged, trying to stay away. She'd had close scrapes since she'd been on the road, but she'd never felt so vulnerable.

Something scythed through the air. She dived to the side a fraction too late. An explosion of pain at the base of her neck and her knees buckled. Tilda dropped to the ground, barely able to get her hands out to brace her fall. Gravel and debris cut and pebbled her palms.

Dimly, she felt the jarring impact up her forearms. Her face scraped over asphalt as her head bounced off the ground. She groaned, trying to push herself back to her feet. She felt hot. Burning.

A heavy strike to the ribs drove all breath from her body and hurled her over onto her back. The white greasepaint faces had a spectral cast in the streetlight.

They snarled and spat as they kicked her, chanting, "Surtsúlfar, Surtsúlfar, Surtsúlfar," together in time.

She covered her head to avoid being knocked out. She knew the words, though she'd never heard them combined together. A name. Their name. She couldn't concentrate. A kick loosened her jaw. Another kick cracked a rib. Tilda bit her tongue to keep from crying out. Desperation flooded her. She *had* to fight or they'd kill her. If she fought, they'd kill her too, but they wouldn't enjoy their victory if she could help it.

Amma had taught her to fight. Which sounds funny until you've gone a round with Urd. Urd had taught Tilda to see the eddies of time as she fought. Size, power, speed—they all mean nothing when you know how your opponent will act before they do. While Tilda's grandmother could no longer see the future, a glance at the past told her all she needed to know about how her opponent would fight. In a moment, Urd would know how you'd acted in every fight you'd ever had. She didn't need the future to predict a person's actions anymore.

Tilda tensed her muscles, took another boot to the

stomach, and curled around it, grasping the leg. Wrapping it tight kept him from kicking her again. As he struggled in her grasp her Sight flashed. Saw how his knee had been damaged before. Saw his worry she'd disable him for real.

She also saw that happen.

She shouldn't be seeing the future. She had no powers. She hadn't called them back. She could escape if she kept fighting. It wasn't time to go home. Not yet. She'd been in worse scraps. She *would* be in worse scraps. It wasn't time to die. Not yet.

Not yet.

Tilda twisted hard, and cartilage snapped, the sound almost lost in 8-Ball's wail. She smiled, satisfied, as the potential future became certainty. She kicked the only ankle not in heavy shit-kicker boots. A woman yelped and fell on top of her. A fist thudded into her temple, and cracked her head back into the cement. Tilda's vision greyed at the corners and they dragged her toward a bright light. Her future was here, and it was over.

She shouldn't be seeing this.

This wasn't what happened.

On the shoulder of the road, Tilda murmured, "That wasn't what happened … Is it?"

A voice, hers? Someone else's? She was alone, lost in the past, it must be hers.

"You can only run so far, or so fast. You'll pay for what she did to us."

She? Who was she?

"You know who I'm talking about. You know what she did."

Deeper into the past. She sat around a hearth warming herself with the three she'd pulled from the snow. They shared her meat and mead.

The names came unbidden, not thought of in decades, if not centuries. Katla, Hekla, and Askla. Sisters. Thralls. Taken for their visions to serve, slaves to fate, as she had been. It was after Ragnarök and she was the last of the "true" line of the Norns. She didn't trust her children would inherit her power, or that she would still have her Sight if they did.

The sisters' eyes fluttered. Urd's welcoming laugh became cruel.

Fire in the distance. Coming closer. The end of the world. The fire to consume all. A cackle, a whisper. Hot breath in her ear. Another laugh, deeper, like explosions in time. Tilda's feet were locked to the asphalt, straddling a double yellow line; fingers clenched her shoulders and whispers filled her ears.

Tilda woke to screeching sounds—Ragnarök all over again. The goddamned band was practising. She must be in their rehearsal space, an old garage, or metal shop. Tools abounded. The windows had been papered over with concert posters for a band named Surtsúlfar. Wolves of Surtur, or Surtur's wolves. Whoever they were, no good came from anyone who wanted to align themselves with a world-ender. It was also hard to care about the eventual end of the world when they were trying to end her, in the here and now.

They'd thrown her in an old oil change pit, a metal grate trapped her within. She smelled old oil, grease, sweat and ... fire. Bloody fingerprints scored the cement walls. She wasn't the first person dumped here, but she was alone now.

She pressed her back against a wall and peered up. Beyond the lip of the pit blackened skeletons were displayed like tapestries. Fire-seared metal framed as art. Shadow casters displaying wolves on the hunt flickered with primal fire. In addition to the aggressive guitar and duelling drummers, punctuating the singer's guttural howls, were samples of screaming, shouts of "Fehu!" and the whooshing of flame. Even in rehearsal they were pyros. *Definitely* Surtur-followers. Fire erupted from the stage. From the shadow casters. Tilda heard the skeletons' echoing last screams.

She didn't want them to know she was awake. Through half-lidded eyes, Tilda scanned the room. They were an odd outfit, this five-piece metal band. Guitar, bass, two godsdamned drummers, and the singer who didn't hold an instrument she could see other than his bone-clad microphone stand. 8-Ball was on bass, one woman was on guitar, and the other was a drummer. Tilda's head pounded in time with the drums. She ached all over. Her ears rang. She blinked, trying to focus, to keep her bile down.

She needed to draw the need-rune. Bring her gifts home. See a way out. The grease and oil might work, but she needed a stronger connection to her true self. She cut her wrist on the rough edge of the grating, letting the blood drip to her fingers. She couldn't choke down her groan.

Before she'd drawn the first line of the rune, as one, the band stopped playing. Sustained notes hung in the air. The singer smiled.

There was no way they should've heard her small cry over their amps. But they had.

"Good," he said, putting his microphone back its stand. "You're awake."

"You've really screwed up," Tilda said. "Doom is coming."

They laughed and sauntered closer, looking down

on her. The singer had an oversized rune pendant hung around his neck. The others followed behind him. They each had their own runic trinket too.

The singer fingered the rune, licking his chapped lips. "We've been looking to change our fates."

Tilda glared at them.

"You're going to make it happen."

"I don't see how."

"We will give you to Katla, and she will give you to Surtur. And after she has ripped every possibility from you, *we* will have our power."

"We're gonna be strong," 8-Ball said. "Strong enough to crush any who stand before us."

"Hard," snarled the female drummer. "Hard enough the entire world breaks against us."

"No one's ever gonna fuck with us again," the singer said.

"Strong," Tilda whispered. She was stronger than this. She knew she was.

"Strong," Tilda murmured to herself, as the lights on the road grew closer.

Strong and hard were different, and while her journey through Niflheim had brought clarity to her jumbled vision, the memories that belonged to her mother and grandmother had made her harder, more brittle, more unbending. Less herself. More alone.

All alone.

Only she wasn't alone. A finger brushed her hair away from her ear. A familiar voice—she'd heard it in Amma's memories, and her own—whispered, "I knew you'd return here. I knew I'd see you again. And here you are. With *all* the visions, not just the future. After I take back what was stolen from us, what other secrets might I wrangle from your weave, Skuld?"

A halo of runes swirled around Tilda's head, then circled her body, stretching off into the night.

Katla was achingly familiar to Tilda. She was Kat. Or the woman who'd pretended to be Kat. Tilda wasn't certain which. She hoped the later. She hoped there was a real Kat Olson out there, baking for her kid, and that their friendship wasn't only a trap. Her face didn't change much; rather, it relaxed. A few more lines, a couple stray grey hairs emerged and became streaks. What had been a pretty and welcoming face lost all pretense, turning hard, and predatory. A shawl of mixed raven feathers and wolf pelts, with no shirt underneath, and tattered jeans replaced her diner uniform. Where the whites of her eyes should've been, orange, red, and yellow flickered and swirled like a campfire.

She watched Tilda like a tired groupie protecting her territory. Kat to Katla's stance changed more than her face. Anything resembling the accommodating posture of a life in the service industry evaporated, replaced by a towering anger within, barely contained by flesh. One who expected not to serve, but to *be* served. Implacable. Immovable.

"Keep practising, kids," she said dismissively. "The adults need to have a chat."

The band grumbled, but headed back to the stage. Dissonant notes filled the garage. Katla raised a wand etched with runes in her fist. No, not a wand, an arrow. The shaft had fletching, and a flint-knapped arrowhead of obsidian.

She spoke, "Ansuz," a rune of breath, and communication, and the music warped around them, both there and not there, they could speak easily, and in turn, not be heard.

"You don't deserve the gifts you inherited, let alone the ones you *will* inherit. You will falter and break. My sisters and I had the Sight too, until we crossed Urd. Odin was dead, there was no longer any fear of mistreating one's guests. After today, I will have it back. All of it." She stroked Tilda's cheek. "So powerful. So alone."

"All the visions." Tilda didn't know what she meant.

She didn't have *any* visions right now. Didn't have any powers. Her visions were locked away. Amma and Mom were as protected in Gimli as if they were behind Asgard's walls.

"I looked deeply into the future. That was my gift once, too. Until your progenitor stole it. My Sight *burned* with possibility. With *certainty*. I witnessed what's coming. What *you* fail to stop."

"I don't think you saw clearly."

"I've seen how badly you and your line have failed."

"You don't know a damn thing about us."

"I know your 'Amma' killed my sisters. Threw them into the fire like offal and stole their visions as they screamed and burned. I begged her to leave me my Sight, she had no need for it, but she took it anyway. She hurled me into the fire, too. My flesh burned and my bones cracked as the fire took them, but before I died, I heard the voice that lives in the flame."

"Surtur." Saying the name aloud burned Tilda's tongue.

Katla smiled. "He pulled me from the flames, and I healed. I taught myself to read the Now, with the future denied me." She gestured toward the band. "My children will wear the skins of giants. They will *be* giants in the coming world."

"Funny," Tilda said. "I've never heard of them."

"They will shake the world. You will make it so. We will use his power, and yours, we will make a new world."

No question who he was. The King of Muspelheim. "You can't harness his flame. No one can."

She knew them.

Or, rather she *had* known them. She *would* know them. Tilda would see them again. But they weren't the fire she feared. A flicker of the future, of her future. The whispers dragged her back to her past.

Surtsúlfar left at least one person watching her at all times when they weren't practising. Their practice itself was ritual. In those times, Katla watched her with burning eyes. They'd break from time to time, argue about song choices, Icelandic pronunciation, or to go on a beer run. For the first time 8-Ball had been left alone to keep tabs on her. He wore a metal brace on his leg now, protecting the knee Tilda had ruined. It had runes scratched onto its surface, either to aid his healing, or to return his mobility while the knee healed naturally.

8-Ball ground out a freshly lit cigarette on his forearm, a breath hissing past his teeth as the cherry sizzled against his skin. He lit another. Took a deep drag, pressed it to his forearm into an old scar.

"Why?" Tilda asked.

"Don't wanna scream when I die," he answered, after a sip of his beer.

The walls between Matilda and Skuld were weakening. Intent mattered as much as action, sometimes, and in trying to draw the need-rune, she had called herself back. It was just taking its sweet time to happen. She looked back. "You will."

Another smoke. Another hiss. Another burn.

He was wrong. He could prepare all he wanted, but he'd scream long after he died. There was no gain in serving Surtur. No promise withstood Muspelheim's fires. He met her gaze, coughed, and went back to playing with his Magic 8-Ball.

He asked, "Is the Norn correct?"

He stared at the toy and Tilda knew what it read: "YES" or some variation of the affirmative. She knew before his eyebrows rose, and he choked on an inhale of smoke, coughing. She grabbed his boot and jerked. He squealed, and fell onto the grating, knocking it loose.

The 8-ball tumbled from his hand. And into Tilda's.

In the distance, Katla the would-be Norn screamed, "No!"

But with an element of fate, a tool of forecasting, Tilda had an out. Her future cascaded past her mind. Without runes, her visions had always been limited, uncontrolled. There were times, however, times when stress, or fear, or desperation, jacked her right into the electric heart of her power. She rode the raging torrent as rivers of possibility flowed through her.

Her mortal disguise fell away, and Mathilda became Skuld. She saw the fight before it happened. She would lose. She saw that now. Surtsúlfar rushed her. She fought.

Katla wanted her visions. Amma had wanted them too, and she hadn't given in then. Tilda had set her future aside, but she wouldn't let it be taken.

Tilda blinked, eyes tearing from the cold. Snow had settled upon her shoulders. That wasn't what had happened. She'd escaped them without ever calling on her powers. Hadn't she? Her closest call in eight years of close calls. She'd walked past a discarded cellphone, it rang, and Tilda knew it was for her. Her mother had found her. Urd had called. Tilda stopped and answered.

"Hello, Skuld," Amma said. "You have accepted your doom. It is time to come home."

That was how she remembered it. Had her time in Niflheim revealed a hidden truth, or distorted her memory?

A cackle. A whisper.

"Not so fast."

She blinked. The memory replayed. And replayed. She fought 8-Ball. She lost. She escaped. Was caught. But she never called the Need-Rune. Never cast off her mortal name. She never went home. She had no home. Urd had killed her daughter and her daughter's daughter, and she would do the same to Tilda. Just as she'd killed Katla and her sisters.

That wasn't how it happened. The memory rewound without Tilda's bidding. The phone rang and rang but Tilda couldn't find it.

No one was coming. No one would help her.

Tilda was alone.

A familiar voice, "You're trapped in the past. In your *powerless* past. There will be no escaping this time. When your visions are mine, your powers will be mine. The mantle of all three Norns will pass to me, through *my* line. As it should've been."

As the visions passed through Tilda to somewhere else—some*one* else—she could view some, not all. Not events. Not stories. Just moments. Feelings.

Visions, from all over her life, from before, from after. Hliðskjálf, Odin's high seat beckoned. Not the All-Father's throne, safely hidden back home at Grey Ladies, in Gimli. And yet, the carved wooden throne rested at the base of the high seat, with Thor's next to it. Somewhere in frozen Canadian north, the seat waited, deep within a mountain. A sliver of Asgard bonded to that cold, cold place. Waiting. Waiting for Tilda.

Future became present. Time unmoored. Tilda flickered between now, then, and beyond.

Katla laughed. "*You* will burn this time."

"… What do the bones tell you …"

"… Your fate here—today—is not what you think it is …"

"… the need-rune. My rune …"

"… Does your mother see you now, *Norn* …"

"… I don't want this …"

"… I want to run away and never come back …"

"… It would be easier …"

"… after he lost you …"

"… What do the bones tell you …"

"… You *know* doom. And you seek to dodge it. One of you may today, but not forever …"

"… Destiny and fate can get … confused where wishes abound …"

"… cast off the shackles the Norns have spun …"

"… The rules were set. Only if everyone in the Nine Worlds wept …"

"… Well, shit …"

"… tie your nuts to a goat …"

"… Harlot of fortune …"

"… I've escaped a lot of fates. You'll have to be more specific …"

"… this is my rune …"

"… Fucking magic …"

"… Seethe …"

Different futures than the ones she'd seen before, different pasts than she'd lived through—had they ever been possible?—cascaded in a torrent. Were they ever possible, or was it only Tilda's desire that prompted them? A child quickened in her belly. A child who could be, *children* who could be, who could have been. Children yet to come. If there was a yet to come. That hadn't been decided. Tilda saw the life she would have, and the life her daughter would have, and she didn't want it. The life. The daughter. But which was it? The one she had given up when she'd taken that morning-after pill? Or the one who would be taken by a mara? She didn't know. She couldn't decide.

"Fucking magic."

Ófriður, A tattooed man striding the water like a god. Flaming wreckage behind him, clutching her lifeless body. Around him the Nine Worlds burned. He said her name, and the utterance was a lightning bolt from blue sky. He'd been saying it a lot, lately. She hadn't wanted to listen. She still didn't want to listen. She wasn't done. Wasn't alone. She repeated the last words she'd spoken to him: "I'll see you at the end of the world."

Then, headlights.

A car approached. Back at the beginning. In the past. In the now.

Tilda had been walking for too long in the rain and

was soaked to the skin. She readied her thumb, stepped slightly onto the shoulder of the road to visible in the headlights, and extended her arm. Her boot touched asphalt. She opened her mind to see whether this would be the person to stop for her, and whether she need worry if they did. The light kissed her. Dazzling in the rain.

No. Not the car.

Her visions.

The future was here. Her past was here. Her doom was here. What she'd seen when a GTO had pulled over to give her a ride in the rain.

Doom.

Headlights.

Fate. Destiny. Doom. Running her down. As always. For good or for ill. It was here. No more running.

"This … is … *my* rune."

Her past was here. The future was here. Her doom was here. If she never saw Ted again she wasn't alone. Not while the Norn visions were within her. Her mother was here. Everything she'd ever seen. Her amma was here. Her line's beginning. Tilda could never be alone, even when their mortal forms were dust. There was more. Visions Tilda had never seen. Not even in Urd's memories. She saw Katla and her sisters doing as they'd claimed Urd had done. Killing other norns. Devouring their visions. Trying to usurp her family's place and power.

What Katla wanted, Tilda wouldn't give up. She hadn't asked to hold all the Norns' visions. Katla had pushed too hard. Pulled at threads tied to memories too dear, too new, too raw. Tilda didn't trust her story of Amma betraying the norn sisters, even though she knew Urd was capable of it. Tilda also wasn't the first person Katla had waylaid in search of power. She couldn't give the future to Surtur.

Katla stepped away. Watching the valkyrie spear Tilda carried. The runes circled between Norn and norn. The fire in her eyes dimmed to smouldering coals. Her rune arrow snapped, an end held in each hand, but otherwise, she appeared as she had when she'd first met Tilda.

Her cheeks puffed as she snorted angry breaths, in and out. "The future is vast, Tilda Eilífsdóttir. And it will be mine again."

Tilda looked through her, into the future, and smiled. "You wanted my power," Tilda said.

Katla paused; stared at her hands, clenching and unclenching them into fists. She took in a deep breath through her nose, releasing a prolonged, exhaled, "*Yesssssss*" as fate flowed through her.

"You like that feeling?"

Another, "*Yessssss.*"

Katla couldn't see Tilda's smile as the wind whipped the hair in front of her face, the smile Amma had before she fucked with someone. Tilda reached past her name, to Skuld—the needful fire. The light of the future. A brand burning in the dark. She changed fate. Being a Norn, a true Norn, was more than having the Sight. She cut Katla off from the runes. From their power. From possibility itself.

Katla screamed. Rage. Regret. Despair.

"This isn't over. I'll see you again, Skuld. I'll end your line."

Tilda raised her spear. "No. No, you won't."

Golden Goose

linking lights at the tips of the Cessna's wings flashed like tiny lightning in the night sky. The dick in front of Ted Callan had called shotgun, which left Ted's knees crammed into his chin. Despite the dragon-scale invulnerability his tattoos provided him, his legs were numb. Former football players weren't meant for small planes.

The dick in question was Loki. God of mischief, Loki. He'd dressed like a glam-rock star today, sporting bright purple hair, oversized sunglasses that made him look like a bug and a significant number of tattoos. He'd said he wanted them to match, to help Ted "blend." Ted was covered head-to-toe in tattoos, but Loki's disco-ball shirt and leather pants didn't really match Ted's jeans and black T-shirt. At least Loki hadn't said "trust me." Those two magic words always meant Ted's life was about to go to shit.

"Trust me," Loki said. "This is a much safer way to travel."

Unsaid was Loki's original reasoning he didn't bother to share with the pilot: "They'll be expecting us on the highway."

Today was the first time Ted had flown in an airplane since he'd been tattooed by a trio of Norse dwarves in a grotty motel room in Winnipeg. Those dwarves had wanted to use him to bring back the good old days of myth and magic. They'd given him nine gifts—and made Ted a lightning rod for trouble.

An inky storm-cloud tattoo—like his dragon scales, a gift from the dwarves—moved just under the skin of Ted's chest, matching the clouds outside the plane. That tattoo responded to the weather. The weather responded to his mood. Which meant a lot of unexpected thunderstorms. Truth was, the tattoo might be recent, but the storm had always been in Ted's chest. It was only the damage that got flashier with the dwarves' handiwork.

It was almost two years to the day since Ted had received his nine legendary gifts—and since Loki had introduced himself. He'd lost a few gifts, and traded a sun for the sword along the way. But he still had the storm. The hammer. The sword. The horn. The horseshoes.

Ted had expected something to pop up to mark the anniversary, but not that someone would steal his car. Granted, Loki had stolen the car first, but Ted still wanted his ride back.

He'd spent the last two years fighting monsters. Protecting people from the rising tide of mythological bullshit. One thing he'd learned: if you let a monster take something from you, you have to fight to take it back. If you didn't, they'd keep taking. It was just a car. But it was Ted's. It'd been a gift. And he'd get it back.

He took a deep breath. Flying had been enough of a pain in the ass, between the cramped accommodations and increasingly Orwellian security theatre. A death by inches. Ted hadn't been looking forward to the flight even before Loki had booked the smallest plane he could find with a pilot trading an opportunity to build hours for gas money.

Ted grunted, shifting toward the window again.

"Want to switch seats?" the trickster asked.

"Yes."

"Lots of room on the wing, buddy." Loki pointed a cocked finger at Ted, and mock-fired with a wink.

Ted snorted a laugh. Loki hadn't said switch seats with *him*.

He still wasn't sure the flight was a good idea. Takeoff went okay. Now they just needed to land safely. Except, like Ted, trouble followed the trickster like the running of the bulls.

He wished he could smoke. The growing twitch of nicotine withdrawal did nothing for his bad mood.

Ted pinched the bridge of his nose.

The pilot, a young woman named Amy, turned to face him. Her headset looked like Princess-Leia buns on the side of her head. "Nervous flyer?" she asked.

"No, ma'am, I'm not," Ted said. He tried to smile. "Just need a smoke."

"We should be landing in a couple hours."

"Ted has many gifts," Loki said. "But patience isn't one of them."

Amy didn't get the pun. "Why are you two heading to Flin Flon?"

Ted had no idea what to tell the pilot. He sure as shit couldn't tell her the truth. Loki saved him. In a manner of speaking.

"Kind of an anniversary for us."

"Congratulations!" the pilot chimed, her smile as bright as Loki's sequined shirt.

The drone of the engine was lulling, coupled with Loki chatting up the pilot, but out there, something in the air was following them. He could feel it.

And it held a grudge.

Which could be goddamned anybody.

Rain pattered the windscreen. The clouds could be hiding anything. Wind tossed the small plane, cracking Ted's head into the window.

"Whoa. You okay?" Amy asked.

"All good." Ted smiled as he rubbed his head to sell it.

Loki gave Ted a long look as the pilot turned back to her instruments, muttering at the storm, and scanning the sky. Ted couldn't do anything but worry. Which made the weather worse. More rain. More wind. And that made the flight bumpier, and Ted more worried. And the storm grew.

"Relax," Loki said, as if forgetting that few things riled Ted up faster than being told to relax.

"I'm. Trying."

Loki mimicked Ted's clipped tone. "Try. Harder."

The stars went out and the sky lit up with lightning. They were surrounded by thunderheads. Rain blew past the plane too fast for Ted to see.

Amy whistled, "Nothing like this in the forecast."

"Crazy, right?" Loki said. "Weather's as unpredictable as a redhead."

He knew what Loki was getting at. He also *knew* there was something out there, but he couldn't see it. And it had nothing to do with his red hair. He tapped his boots on the floor of the plane and drummed his fingers to a Zeppelin song no one else could hear, trying to calm down.

Ted would've felt better with his feet on the ground. Something about having his toes in the dirt and calling to the sky felt entirely different. Hippy-dippy bullshit. But it was one thing to bring the lightning to him, and an entirely different one to be up among it. In the sky, trapped in a fragile winged tube, the storm felt vaster somehow.

He nudged the thunderheads. He didn't know what

effect bold action would have on their plane. Even his "gentle" attempts seemed problematic. The pilot's grimace intensified, and she twitched with every flash of lightning; but she kept them in the air.

It wasn't something following the plane, but many somethings. Ted caught silhouettes in the lightning flashes. A flying "V" on either side, and one behind them; their honking cries audible over the engine and rain. It wasn't the dragon Ted had been looking for, but it might be worse.

Geese.

So. Many. Fucking. Geese.

Even with a brisk tailwind a goose shouldn't be able catch a plane, but no one had told these geese that. Ted had seen a Canada goose drive off an angry bull. Geese didn't give a shit. They were the Canadian honey badger. Maybe they could fly over two hundred klicks an hour just out of spite.

"I'm diverting around this storm. We're gonna land in Dauphin and ride this out on the ground." Amy sounded to Ted liked she was trying to hide her nervousness, but wasn't quite there.

Once they were on the ground, he'd bet bourbon to

beer he could take whatever came at them. But they had to get there first. He felt the storm's motion, the roiling clouds, the flashing lightning, the buffeting winds and his tattoo moving to match. Ted felt like he was drowning. Being so close to the storm, so far from earth, Ted swam against that storm. It wanted to lash out as fiercely as possible. It wanted to destroy.

He wanted to destroy.

But he couldn't.

He wouldn't.

If he gave in to the flash of the lightning and the peal of the thunder, Amy would definitely die. Ted would be fine; the horseshoes tattooed on the soles of his feet allowed him to walk on the air. Loki would be fine. Loki would always be fine, no matter what Ted did.

He caught flashes in the lightning and the rain. In every flash of light, the flying wedge grew closer, and larger. And their honking cries louder. It filled the sky as much as the storm. They surrounded the plane, pacing it. Their tightening proximity nudged them directly toward the centre of the storm.

Ted did better with threats he could hit. The hammer tattooed on Ted's right forearm gave him the strength to go toe-to-toe with monsters. It also drew giants to Ted like flies to shit.

It wasn't fucking fair. Those geese probably weren't even geese. Loki was a shape-changer. Lots of giants were. And since the dwarves had given Ted the power of

Thor's hammer, Mjölnir, along with his storm, the giants had carried over their grudge from the god to Ted.

He looked out the window. The geese were closer.

Motherfucker.

One goose turned its head and stared. Right. At. Ted.

"Can't you outrun them?" Loki asked.

"You'd think so." Amy didn't seem happy that it hadn't already happened. "But apparently not. They can climb higher than our service ceiling. If they want to catch us, they will."

Ted took off his boots. "I guess I better fight them."

Amy turned, shocked. "You better *what*?"

Wind buffeted the plane side to side, up and down. They hit an air pocket and dropped like a rock. The greasy burger Ted had eaten before getting on the plane wanted out. He choked it down. The geese were back on them in a moment.

Lightning traced across the sky and Ted bent a bolt toward the furthest goose he could see. Missed. Another bolt was building. He could feel it.

Trying to nail a single goose an indeterminate distance away was different than hitting a giant. The more bolts he called, the bigger the storm got, the more likely the plane would get hit by stray lightning. Ted couldn't direct them all. He hit one. He was sure he hit one.

"Stop it!" Amy yelled. "Whatever you're doing, stop! You're going to get us killed!"

"Point of order," Loki said. "He's gonna get *you* killed. *We'll* probably be fine."

"*Not* better."

Amy banked the plane away from a wedge of geese, but one broke from the formation and landed on the wing with a thud, forcing it back to true. Its neck craned toward the window, black eyes glittering, white chin straps electric in the storm. It was huge. Fucking ostrich-huge. It slammed its beak into Ted's window, spittle streaking across the cracking glass until it was lost in the rain.

Amy asked, "What do they want?"

"To kill Ted," Loki answered. "Maybe me, too?"

"Oh, that's all? I should let them have you."

"Maybe they want *you*?" Loki jumped as a second goose slammed into his door. "It's hard to tell who's pissed off whom sometimes. Hit any geese with your plane lately?"

Amy stared gawp-mouthed at the trickster, but said nothing.

A thud above, a second goose on the wing. They banked sharply, Ted cracked into the window. Amy rocked the plane, trying to shake the geese. A third goose landed on the nose and the plane dropped into a dive. The pilot side door tore off and a goose darted in, hissing and honking. Ted punched it in its stupid goose face and knocked it off the plane. But there were more. Lots more. And they were driving the plane into the ground.

Ted released his seatbelt buckle and put his hand on the pilot's shoulder. "Time to bail."

Loki nodded and turned into a harpy eagle. He screamed at the goose trying to bite him. Amy screamed at Loki.

Ted didn't have time to answer or reassure her. He tore her seatbelt free from the airframe and jumped out of the plane taking Amy—still in her seat—with him. Loki followed Ted out the gaping pilot's side of the plane.

The geese swarmed the trickster as Ted and Amy tumbled, ass-over-teakettle. Loki disappeared in the clouds. The spinning was getting disorienting. Ted held Amy tight to him and let her seat fall. He unclenched his curled toes, his bare feet touched the air with intent, and they stopped dead.

They stood, suspended in the air. Amy checked to see if he wore a parachute. Double-checked the sky for the telltale silk, and a reason why their plummet had stopped.

A wedge of geese dived at Ted, and he changed direction. The horseshoe tattoos allowed him to pivot as if he were a running back on a football field instead of in the clouds.

"Hang on," Ted said.

A skein of geese, moving together like starlings, chased another flying shape backlit against the flashing clouds. More came after Ted. Loki would be fine. After all that Loki had survived, including the end of the world, he wouldn't be taken out by some fucking geese. Ted needed to keep Amy alive. She hadn't asked for any of this shit.

Her hair stood on end as he gathered the storm. No plane to worry about anymore, but he still had to be careful. A lightning strike wouldn't hurt him, but Amy would take the full brunt of any stray bolts. Lightning flashed from cloud to cloud. The lightning followed the same path across the storm tattooed on this chest, in time, arcing from there to his tattoo of Mjölnir.

In the brightness of a flash, he bent the lightning to the geese.

They were too close. The thunderclap that followed was loud enough to scare shit from a wolverine. Lightning bisected several of the geese like they were meat on a spit. Their afterimage burned on Ted's retinas through closed eyelids and in the moment it took for his vision to clear, more geese were on them.

They hovered as they flapped, snapping at him and Amy. Ted dropped. The geese collided in a thunder of honks and meaty thuds. As Ted fell, he spotted a goose he'd struck with lightning, gliding roughly towards the earth, still smoking, but alive.

"Tough fuckers," he muttered, but he was long past believing these geese were local.

Ted kept the geese away. Drop. Dodge. Light 'em up.

A simple plan, but effective, and eventually the geese flew off.

Ted and Amy landed amid some jack pines and rocks. There was no sign of Loki.

Ted and Loki had come a long way since the first time they'd met, and Ted had wanted to beat the shit-eating grin off the god's face. Now Loki was more like a brother. And sister. And sometimes a weird aunt who kept trying to help him get laid. In a way, the god of mischief was the only family Ted had left.

Amy slapped Ted's hand away. "So, remind me why you needed a plane?"

"I can't fly."

The pilot looked at the sky, still flashing, and blinked away a fat drop of rain. "Coulda fooled me."

Ted waited for Loki to spring out from the bushes. When the trickster didn't appear, Ted asked Amy, "You okay?"

"I'm not hurt." She paused and shuddered at the distant honking of geese. "But I'm pretty far from okay. And you owe me a plane."

Ted didn't want to antagonize her by pointing out— as Loki surely would have, had he been here—that *technically* they owed her uncle a plane. Or diminish her statement by saying she'd get used to it. He didn't know that. Maybe she would, maybe she wouldn't. Getting used to magic was a fucking lie, anyway. He'd been balls-deep in magic for years now, and there was always something that came up to make him shake his head, and go, "Why? Why the fuck would anyone … Just. Fucking. Why?"

"Smoke?" Ted offered Amy the first unbroken cigarette he'd tapped out of his pack.

"No thanks. I don't smoke."

"Mind if I do?"

"Knock yourself out."

Ted lit the cigarette, savouring the butane, the crackle of the paper catching, and the peace of the first drag. He inhaled deeply, exhaling the stream of smoke away from Amy. "I should probably quit." He snorted a bitter laugh. "Loki says it would be the end of the world if I tried. Again."

"This usual for you?"

Ted nodded. "Usual in the unusual. Giant-geese problems are new."

Amy asked, as if afraid of the answer, "What … what are you?"

"I'm Ted," He didn't have a clever answer for what the dwarves had done. Ófriður, they'd named him. Weapon. Troublemaker. Un-peace. "I'm just a guy."

"Just a guy," Amy threw his words back at him.

"Never seen another guy do what you just did, outside of a movie."

Ted braced himself for the "but they were better-looking" dig that Loki might've provided, but it never came. "Loki is, well, Loki. He's a god. Small 'g.' Mythological motherfucker of mischief."

"Wait. Loki is *Loki*-Loki?"

"Last time I checked."

Her eyes narrowed. "Wait, if he's Loki, does that make you—?"

Ted cut her off with a laugh. It would piss off Big Red and Dead to no end to hear that. "Nope. Similar portfolio. I fight monsters."

"What monsters are there in Flin Flon?"

"The kind that stole my car."

"I'm in this mess, because of *your car*?"

"It's a magic car."

Amy groaned. "I wish I'd never met you."

Ted heard that a lot. His dad always said: wish in one hand, and shit in the other, and see which one fills up first. He didn't repeat that to Amy. The advice hadn't helped him growing up, and wouldn't help Amy now.

Something rustled in the bushes and deeper in the trees. Ted's first thought was Loki had found them. But that didn't seem right. Ted and Amy weren't in the middle of anything embarrassing, so there was no need for Loki to show up now, of all times. And Loki didn't give warning to his arrival.

Ted hopped to his feet, and got in a boxing stance. Lightning crackled from his storm-cloud tattoo up his right arm to Mjölnir.

Amy called out, "Who's there?"

Ted put a finger to his lips and mouthed, "They've found us."

"Who?" she mouthed back.

"Geese."

The air seemed to go out of the clearing as the honking and screaming began.

It wasn't geese that came tearing out of the woods first. It was campers dressed in filthy jeans, flannel, and down jackets that seemed a bit heavy for early September. They were drenched. From rain, from sweat—Ted wasn't sure.

"Run!" the lead camper yelled. "They're right behind us!"

Geese burst out after them, hissing and honking. They flapped their wings as they ran, and few took to the air in great leaps, landing between the campers, separating them.

"Get behind me!" Ted called. He dug his toes into the

sodden earth and felt for the storm. "Get out of here! *Git!*"

The geese didn't listen. Instead, they advanced in a semicircle.

Amy yelled a warning. "The campers—!"

Ted spun to see the campers grinning at him with far too many—and too sharp—teeth. Their eyes had gone all black. Two of them pulled a sleeping bag over Amy's head and two others scrambled to get the drawstring at the bottom tight as she kicked them.

"Oh, fuck me." Ted didn't see where the first bolt of lightning hit. Two campers he'd turned his back on threw a sleeping bag over his head, too.

Ted fought to break out of the bag. But the fabric wouldn't budge. It stretched with his every punch and kick. He stepped into the air. Something hit him from behind. Several somethings. A baseball-bat-heavy goose kick. He shook off the strikes until one caught him behind the knees. He tipped backward, and the geese piled onto him.

The air inside the bag reeked of stale farts and wet marsh. Their rasping bills sawed at his pant legs as they clasped his ankles and tried to stuff him fully inside. He kicked and hit something solid. It squawked as the beatings continued. Dragon-scale invulnerability was great and all, but he still felt things that couldn't kill him. And the rocking and rolling from all the goose onslaught left him dizzy. He couldn't focus on where to call the storm.

Rainwater seeped into the sleeping bag. Distant thunder rolled. He could still feel the storm, but he couldn't use it.

The sword. It had stopped the biggest, baddest giant Ted had ever fought. It would cut through a fucking sleeping bag. The sword formed in Ted's left hand. It was too long to swing in the tight confines of the sleeping bag—it was damn near Ted's size—but the brilliant white-blue blade slid tip-first through the sack. Ted could see.

He spun the Bright Sword in a wide arc. The geese danced away. Avoiding the light, or the sword's edge, Ted wasn't sure. But now he could see where Amy was, and that the geese surrounding her were running at him, bellowing in anger.

"Goddammit." He hated his part. But it wouldn't be the first time he'd called a bolt from the sky right on top of himself. He paired his storm tattoo with the sky. Small lightning danced over his body, bright as his sword. Instinctively, Ted reached for the sky with his hammer hand, and brought the lightning home to Mjölnir.

The stink of ozone filled his nose, then fire. Feathers burst aflame. The water drenching his body boiled away. All in an instant. Then, honking cries of pain were drowned by a thunderclap. Ted had a feeling of weightlessness as he was blown off his feet. He hit the ground before he could set his feet under him.

He hurled the rags of the sleeping bag off his body. A

ring of geese lay on the ground. Stunned or dead, Ted couldn't say. He took a moment to confirm. Their chests pumped like a slow bellows. The geese were alive. Bully for them. A couple of down jackets were left in a smoking pile, their owners disappearing into the woods.

Ted recalled the sword into his arm and braced his hands on his knees, catching his breath as Amy wriggled out of her sleeping bag. He stood and cracked his back, digging a fingernail into his ear. It did little to stop the ringing.

Where the hell was Loki?

Ted helped Amy to her feet as the stunned geese stood. Ted groaned and readied for round three. It didn't come. The geese took flight, honking with laughter.

Honking, at least. But it sure as shit felt like they were laughing at him.

Ted couldn't help but feel they'd been travelling in circles. He'd hoped to salvage some supplies from the wreckage, maybe even his fucking boots, but no luck.

Whatever the goose things were, they reminded him of a story he'd heard about swan maidens. Shapechangers who could take a swan form thanks to a feathered cloak. He'd seen Freyja's falcon cloak in action before.

This type of magic wasn't new to him. Although why the hell anyone would want to turn into a fucking goose, he had no clue.

Of course, swan-maiden cloaks were a *gift*. Goose cloaks seemed like a curse.

There was an old joke about Canada geese being where Canadians deposited their hate and ill-tempers. Ted didn't know about that—he'd seen plenty of shit that couldn't be blamed on geese. Maybe whatever was affecting these campers had made that saying literal. Ted didn't know how it might or might not spread.

Ted lost track of how long they'd slogged through the muck. His watch was toast. In the distance, where the trees started to thin, he saw something. A wall, maybe? They crept closer.

It wasn't a wall. It was a nest. An island-sized nest. Impossibly big. See-it-from-fucking-space big. Instead of being woven from grass, entire trees were crammed together and glued in place with mud, stacked to the clouds.

"I do *not* want to meet the goose that lives there," Amy said.

"You and me both."

A handful of geese landed, almost disappearing against the nest. They preened their chests and Ted thought he heard a zipper sound. A human stepped out of one big goose, then the next, until all the flock appeared human. They shook their coats of feathers, turned them inside out, and put them back on. They were quite the crew, wearing matching red down parkas.

They carried sacks, presumably offerings, or prisoners. None seemed large enough to hold Loki, but Loki being Loki, any, or none, of them could be the trickster's prison.

The nest shuddered, shaken as if by a tornado-wind. A dragon-sized neck snaked up and over the nest's edge. The humans climbed up the black bill and scrambled up the neck. Ted held his breath, waiting for the titanic goose to spot and devour them. It didn't. When all of its campers were aboard, it lifted its head and brought them into its nest, and out of sight.

"Welp," he said to Amy. "I'm going in."

"You're *what*?"

"Loki's got to be in there. I'm getting him out."

"In. There."

"He'd do the same for me."

"Really?"

"He'd probably be the reason I needed rescuing, but he'd show."

Amy considered that. "Okay. Let's save him."

"'Let's'?"

"You two owe me a plane. I'm not letting you out of my sight until I get it back."

Ted held out his hand. "Okay, partner."

This time she didn't slap it away and nodded. "Let's go."

"Put this on."

Ted handed Amy one of the trashed parkas from the ambush. He'd put the fire out before they'd been completely consumed. Both still had feathers sticking out of it and were more rips and tears than coat.

Amy wrinkled her nose at the parka. "I don't want to turn into one of them."

"You won't." She didn't look convinced. Ted sighed.

He put his coat on first, then walked out of the trees and toward the nest. When he didn't change, Amy followed. She still looked dubious. Beyond dubious. Incredulous. Shit's sakes. Ted had turned into Loki. He hadn't said, "Trust me," but he might as well have.

"You didn't ask for this," he said. "You weren't meant to get caught up in this. And I'm sorry. I'm doing my best."

"Your best."

"I'll try to keep you safe."

"'Try.' No promises?"

"This is the real world, and magic is just as real. Shit happens. I've learned not to make promises I can't keep."

"Thanks for being honest. I guess." Amy took another long look at the nest. "What do I do if one of them comes at me?"

"Grab it behind the head and snap its neck."

"Won't that kill whoever is inside?"

"The people inside seem to be entirely in the body of the goose."

"How does that even work?"

Ted shrugged. "Fucking magic."

He joked, but he needed to remember, there *were* people in those goose bodies. Maybe they were innocent. Maybe not. He'd been lucky not to kill any of them with his lightning. Once he'd dealt with the big fucker, they'd see what happened. But Ted didn't kill people. Didn't even like killing monsters, if he could avoid it.

Big Goose lowered its head for them, honked loud enough to shatter the windows of a truck, and spread its bill wide. Its tongue warbled from the cry, thorny spines pointing back towards its throat. Each of those spines was big enough to impale a person. Shit. They were bigger than most people. If it got Ted in its mouth, he'd have to fight his way out through the stuffing chute.

Its heartbeat was audible as it regarded them, eyes black as slough water at night. It closed its bill. Ted waited a moment before clambering on. Stinking, marshy exhales wafted over him from the goose's nares. Ted climbed between the eyes to the neck. He checked over his shoulder. Amy was still following him. So far, so good.

Big Goose lowered them into the nest. At its centre seemed to be a clutch of eggs. The goose things carried their prizes toward it. Ted and Amy followed. If Big Goose had captured Loki, that's where he'd be. After ten minutes of walking, they didn't seem any closer. It was kind of like trying to walk across the High Level Bridge in Edmonton while drunk, though there was more goose shit to dodge here.

"Nothing good about goose shit," Ted grumbled.

Ted really wished he'd been able to find his boots. His feet would never feel clean again. Another ten minutes walking and Ted wanted to burn what remained of his jeans. When they finally reached the "eggs" Ted saw they weren't eggs at all. They were camper trailers.

"The fuck?"

"Greetings, Ófriður."

The voice was loud. Loud as the thunderclap when Ted had dropped lightning on himself. He spun around and Big Goose's head was *right there* behind him. Grinning. It knew who Ted was. Knew the name the dwarves had given him. It had to know one more thing.

"Where's Loki?"

"My golden goose?" The big black-and-tan prick honked a laugh. "If you can find him, you can keep him."

The goose-things flipped their parkas, and changed.

"Ted—"

"Amy, get in one of those trailers. Now. Lock the door."

She nodded and ran. Something about this fight didn't smell right, and it wasn't the goose shit. Ted couldn't put his finger on it. It smelled … cold. Like the time he'd been too impatient to defrost his old freezer and took a screwdriver to the ice, puncturing the Freon canister. He didn't have any time to consider it further. The geese were on him.

Ted grabbed one by the neck with each hand and spun, swinging them to clear a path for Amy to get to the nearest trailer. The geese didn't make as good weapons as Ted had hoped. He snapped one's neck like he was flicking someone with a wet towel. The goose went limp in his grasp and he hurled it at the growing crowd. He did the same with the second goose. It barely delayed them. The geese were back on him in no time, slamming him with their bony wings, and knocking him into the slimy ground.

Ted heard the click of the trailer door closing behind him. These geese could probably tear through its walls like they were paper, but Amy was as safe as he could make her. Time to cut loose.

He pointed at Big Goose. "Give my friend back, fucker."

"Friend?" the goose howled with laughter. "*Loki* is your *friend*? Loki has no friends. The only thing he has of value is his name."

The sky rumbled as Ted cocked a finger at Big Goose. "Guess again."

Big Goose laughed as the first bolt hit home. And kept laughing as Ted peppered it with lightning. The goose was bigger than anything Ted had ever fought. Too big. None of Ted's bolts had any effect. Ted gave up on the lightning and ran up into the air and out of the goose shit. Big Goose's neck moved too fast for Ted to grab, and flattened him into the mud with its bill. But he caught a foot as the enormous goose took to the air, tipping the camper trailers in the downdraft.

The goose felt real. Hit like it was real. But it couldn't be. If there was anything out there this big, Ted would've heard noise. Ted called lightning. *All* the lightning. Enough to strike any and every bit of the giant goose's body. He knew why he'd recognized the cold smell. Illusion. None of this was real.

Big Goose rippled under the lightning strikes. And disappeared. A second, smaller goose appeared, leg still clutched in Ted's hand. Smaller, but still pretty fucking big. Over twenty feet tall. Ted knew this shape was real.

Big Goose slapped at Ted with its heavy wings, buffeting him into the now much closer edge of the nest. It turned its head to the sky and honked as it took a giant greasy green dump on one of the trailers. It noticed Amy peering out of the roof of one of the overturned trailers and ran, wings spread, toward her.

Sweet musical Christ.

Ted jerked Big Goose's hind leg until he heard something pop. He dug in his heels and hauled against the bird's immense weight. There was no traction in the muck, and the goose dragged him along. Ted stepped up into the air, and his horseshoe tattoos bit in. Big Goose stopped dragging him, and Ted hauled it back.

It honked its displeasure and whipped its head around, slamming into Ted. Its rasping teeth shredded what remained of the already damaged down jacket. Ted released the goose's foot and grabbed it by the neck, suplexing it onto its back. Mud and shit splashed, coating the trailers. Ted scrambled on its belly and punched. He kept the goose's neck vise-locked in his left hand while he punched with his hammer hand. Every time Big Goose got too bite-y, Ted punched it in its stupid goose face instead.

He punched until it stopped honking. And he kept punching, punctuating every hit with curse. "Fucking … goddamned … geese … where … the … fuck … is … Loki?"

"Ted! Stop!" Amy called.

He stood, sweating and panting on top of its unconscious breast. He really needed to quit smoking. The feathered cloak shrouding Big Goose had torn, and Ted recognized the face he'd been hitting. It was Loki's giant form. The trickster's face was mangled and bloody, but he was alive. He might not've been if Amy hadn't stopped him.

Ted cradled Loki's head. "I'm so sorry."

A booming laugh filled the nest, but this time, there was no nasally honking. Ted looked up, way up. Standing by the cluster of trailers was a giant, better-dressed than most. Looked like he'd actually had a suit tailored to his hundred-foot size, and kept his beard groomed with something other than mud and blood. "Pity. Would've been lovely for him to die at the hands of his adopted family. Again."

"Giants," Ted muttered. "Why is it always fucking giants?"

"What, you don't know me?"

Ted didn't recognize the giant, but he knew the look. He had the glow of a man who'd just taken a twenty-minute shit on company time. "Should I?"

The giant smirked. "Útgarða-Loki. You *will* learn it, Ófriður."

Útgarða-Loki. Ted didn't need to learn it. He knew it. Loki of the Outyards. The giant who'd tricked Loki (no mean feat) and Thor (a considerably easier feat) for shits and giggles back in the days before Ragnarök.

"Motherfucker, I'm ready for you right now."

"No, thank you. But we'll meet again. Soon."

The giant smirked and everything was gone. The nest. The giant himself. Everything but the vehicular "treasures". They were standing in a campground littered with cars and trailers, a crumpled Cessna, and some very confused campers standing in piles of rotting feathers. A gleaming metal cube rested in a fire pit. Ted's magic car.

Ted had no doubt Útgarða-Loki would turn up again. He wasn't looking forward to it. He was fucking exhausted with fighting old grudges from another world. But he'd keep at it. There was no other choice.

Loki looked up. "What happened to you?" He rubbed his jaw and groaned. "What happened to me?"

"Long story."

"That wannabe's always wanted my name for his own. Made me think you were him. Thought I finally had him down. Until you started hitting me for real." Loki's form shifted to the one he'd worn on the flight, hiding his injuries. "Did we win?"

"We're alive." Ted said, bouncing the cube on his palm. "I got my car back. I'd call it a win."

"A win?" Amy said. "What am I gonna tell my uncle?"

"The truth?" Loki said.

"The truth?"

"You hit a bird. A big one."

She groaned.

"Or," the trickster said with a smile. "You landed to get out of the storm. And you let me fix it."

"How?"

"Trust me."

"It'll buy you some time for us to fix this," Ted said.

"Fix it?" Amy gestured at the wreckage. "You're a certified aircraft mechanic? How can you fix this?"

"That Outyard wannabe isn't the only one who can play with illusion." The trees swallowed the wreckage. "I'm not a mechanic, but I know someone who is."

"They won't want to help," Ted said.

"I'm charming as hell, and if that doesn't work ..."
Loki rubbed his jaw. "Ted can be *very* convincing."

No Sunshine in Hel

There's no sunshine in Hel.

They didn't call it Hel anymore. It was Nornheim now. Icy grey fog roiled at the realm's boundary with Niflheim. Her mother, Tilda, once Skuld the Norn, Mathilda Eilífsdóttir in the living world, had said never to refer to home by its old ruler and namesake, but "Hel" felt more apt to Erin Eilífsdóttir than the name her mother had given it.

Tilda had been able to conjure her daughters from the void, but only within her domain. The sun had never lit Erin's face, nor wind tousled her hair. She'd had companions—men, women, among the dead—not love. Sometimes she felt like a fire ready to ignite, but one couldn't build a new life in a dead world.

Erin fiddled with the small pendant at her neck—a worn, grey stone with a hollow centre plucked from a beach she'd never visit. She looked past the giant-bone gates and muttered a curse into the mists. No sound came from the fog; either it, or the falling ash, smothered what little sound the dead's steps made. Their bodies had no weight, and gave little warning. It was as if all Niflheim's grey had settled upon her. The *gloom* wanted to infect a mind. Erin tightened her grip on her axe, the hand-etched runes on its haft glowing in response. If something didn't change soon, they were fucked.

She repeated her worry aloud. "If the dead don't come soon—"

"They'll come," Erin's sister Hilde said. Reassuring, as always. Easy to do when one could see the future. Erin could only see the Now. Hilde's arrival hadn't surprised Erin; she'd been looking into the Now. It was a game, who could surprise whom. The sister who saw the future or the sister who saw the present. Hilde's cloak fluttered despite the lack of wind, and her staff scratched over the stones.

"No travellers since Mom went Upworld."

"Time flows as it needs here."

Erin rolled her eyes at her sister repeating the axiom to her. But Hilde wasn't wrong. There'd been long stretches with no new arrivals; this span only *felt* longer because they'd been left in charge. Tilda hadn't given them much notice when she'd left. She was still used to being a vagabond at heart, and Hel's mantle weighed heavily at times.

"All come to Hel in their own time," Hilde said.

Another axiom. The unsaid bit: "and they never leave it." Which *wasn't* true. The dead escaped—ghosts and *draugar* who tormented the living. Baldur had gotten his life back (eventually); Hel herself had seen her half-life replaced with a living body. Hilde wanted to comfort, not annoy; but still, Erin was antsy. A distant roar cut through the mist—the only sound that *ever* pierced the mist. Níðhöggur hungered, and it wasn't wise to keep a dragon waiting. Especially *this* dragon.

Hilde offered, "We could send her some dead from the hall?"

Erin shook her head. "They've already been judged, Mom wouldn't allow it."

"Mom's not here."

"What do we do, then?"

"We could ask Langamma."

"Mom said never to ask Langamma's advice."

"She was a Norn almost as long as Niflheim has existed. Longer than Nornheim. Longer than Hel. She could help."

"Mom said no."

"Again, Mom's not here." Hilde chuckled. "Since when do *you* do what Mom says?"

Erin bristled. "The dead can't be trusted. They're governed by their loss and by their desires."

"*We* are dead."

"We never lived. That's different."

"We are dead. The sooner you accept our place here, the better."

Hilde pulled back her cloak hood and shook out her poker-straight, white-blonde hair. Sometimes Erin resented how Hilde took after their mother's appearance: tall and willowy versus her short and stacked.

Erin ran her fingers through her short red hair. There were no barbers in Hel, so it was typically shaggy and unkempt. The freckles over her nose and under her eyes made her look younger than she was. She had to fight to be taken seriously among the often-warlike spirits who found their way here.

Erin's fierce red hair, Hilde's blonde, and their matching blue eyes, were the only colours in Nornheim. Otherwise the sisters looked much the same as the spirits in the hall: greyscale. Muted. Even their clothing. Tilda brought them new clothing from Midgard, but Niflheim's mist leached their wardrobe's life the way it stole warmth from the living.

"Not dead. Not completely."

Hilde acknowledged the point with a wan smile. "Too dead to be alive."

All the dead touched by the Nine Worlds came to Nornheim, no matter how heroic or monstrous, since there was no Valhalla, and no one obliged to choose their death for them. They were drawn to a thin spot in Winnipeg, where Erin's father, Ted "Ófriður" Callan, had battered his way into Niflheim, and then to Hel. Some refused the call, and lingered where they fell as *draugar* or spirits. Before the former queen, Hel, had been thrown into Niflheim by Odin, there had been no realm for the dead, no road, no bridge—only grey fog. Hel had carved out her hall to mock the Aesir and to have her own seat of power. She'd been evicted. After Ragnarök. After Ted. Then Tyr had ruled in her absence, then Tilda after Tyr's second—and final—death. The realm of Hel became Nornheim. A renaming to give comfort to the only living being residing here.

The dead that came faced their final judgement at the hands of the three Norns who now ruled this realm. Hilde saw the future. She knew which dead might be problematic and where they might best serve. Tilda's mastery of the past allowed her to look into the dead and determine who stayed in Nornheim—and who filled Níðhöggur's belly. Erin saw the Now, when the dead reached the underworld, and greeted them at Nornheim's gates; it was a lonely walk down the last road, they needed to see their end didn't need to be full of terrors. And if terrors lurked within them, Erin was also the first line keeping back wolves at the gate.

There were no dead in Erin's visions of the Now, only dead Yggdrasill's long roots dangling from an unseen ceiling, lost in the mist. Mingled among those blackened roots were new living growths, from a second world tree planted after Hel's ouster. The dead roots had been carved into stories of days long gone, her parents' adventures. When Erin first woke, the roots had whispered nightmares to her. A horror unseen. It came to her sometimes when she slept: as Tilda, or Hilde, or an old woman, sometimes Langamma, sometimes not. Laughing over a world aflame, laughing at a world without her. Almost always, it came for Erin. And when it did, it killed her. Every time. The visions had been mostly silent since she'd come into her power.

Beyond Nornheim's fence, resting on a grey hill: the Nornhall. A reconstruction of the Norns' Gimli home, though without the colour her mother had described. The house shouldn't have been able to contain the vastness of the Hall, and yet it did. It needed to be, to hold all those who came to Nornheim, and no matter how many arrived, the Norns found them a seat at the table.

More time passed, or the seeming of time passed, and with it, still no dead came to their walls.

Níðhöggur's growls grew closer, and more frequent. Erin could wait no longer.

They were in Erin's room. The sisters each had their own quarters on the second floor of the Nornhall, but were rarely apart. Erin had no memory of a time without Hilde next to her. Hilde claimed the same. Neither wanted to take orders from the other, but they were a good complement to one another. Most days.

What passed for days in Hel.

Erin opened herself to the Now as she drew runes from their leather bag, concentrating on an answer to why the dead wouldn't come.

Tilda had—until she'd brought her daughters back—held all three visions: past, present, and future. Before that, she'd been Skuld, Norn of the future. She hadn't controlled dispensing the visions to her daughters, something Erin suspected irked her mother. She'd expected Erin to inherit the future as the youngest. Fate had counted the sisters' ages differently.

The sisters joked (and argued) about who was older. Erin, because she'd been further along before Tilda miscarried. Hilde, because she'd been conceived first. Erin, because fucking magic, she didn't know.

Erin placed seven stones down, two side by side, until the last stone, her answer, should be revealed. All Erin saw was herself. She tried a rune reading to find the dead. She saw nothing new, no matter which spreads she chose. Even drawing a single stone guided her visions to one solution. Herself. Urd, their langamma, watched them impassively from across the room.

The sisters used to do readings for each other but it'd ceased being fun when Hilde knew the answers before Erin could say them. Much as Hilde had never wanted to learn how to fight, Erin hadn't been the best student of the runes. She didn't have the patience to draw the threads of meaning between the stones. Erin could rarely see beyond their existence's eternal sameness. Especially lately.

"Allow me." Hilde held out her hand, and Erin dropped the bag of runes into her palm.

Hilde drew one simple spread. The Three Norns: one rune for past, future, and present; what has been, what is to come, and the choice that must be made. She looked intently at the stones, and grew quiet, and distant.

Hilde's eyes flickered behind half-closed lids. She gasped.

Erin looked at Hilde's draw. Naudhiz was Tilda's rune, the need-rune; Ehwaz a journey rune, representing Sleipnir, Odin's eight-legged horse, symbolic of the soul travelling between worlds; Hagalaz was Langamma's rune, or Hel's rune, depending upon who you asked. Erin knew their meanings, and could guess at what they implied, but not what Hilde had seen. She hadn't been the one to cast the stones, and so she'd had no vision. She reached out with the Now, but Hilde veiled herself with her cloak hood, keeping her thoughts, and the vision within, hidden.

"*What did you see?*"

No answer.

"What did you see?"

There. A backwash of probability, of certainty, whether it was the Now, or the dregs of Hilde's vision, Erin wasn't sure.

At the edge where Niflheim brushed Midgard, something stirred. Tilda had said Norns never gave readings without payment.

"Why won't you tell me? What is your price?"

"I want you to promise you won't leave Nornheim. *That's* my price."

Erin bored into the Now, but the vision slipped away. She felt as if she were being tricked. Goaded into a choice she couldn't see. "No."

Níðhöggur's roar grew closer. Erin hefted her axe. "I'm going. I'll cross the Gjöll and drag Midgard's restless dead in myself, if I have to."

"Don't." Hilde put a hand on her shoulder. "Please, Erin. Listen to me. There's nothing there for you."

"There's nothing for me *here*, either!"

Hilde jerked her hand away as if Erin had struck her. The runic trim around Hilde's cloak hood flashed bright. She vanished from sight, her pained expression lingering in Erin's mind.

"Tell me what you saw!" Erin screamed after her.

Urd, former Norn of the past, cleared her throat, disappointedly. She'd been Hilde and Erin's first babysitter, and tutor, until Tilda had stopped trusting her. Not a word, but she was right. Erin needed to apologize. What she'd said, that there was nothing here for her in Hel, poison in her secret heart, while true, had been unconscionable to say to her sister, a cold chunk of Niflheim puked up and hurled at Hilde.

Tilda had tried—and failed—to give true life to her daughters. She hadn't been able to convince the Nine Worlds they were worth the effort. Erin had always wondered who'd laughed in Tilda's face and survived. Who hadn't wept?

Frigg had set the precedent in her bargain with Hel: if everyone in the world wept for Baldur, he could come back to life. It had worked about as well as Tilda's attempt, but at least Frigg and Odin had someone to blame for holding back on that last tear. Erin had nothing, no one to hate. Her lucky stone pendant, impregnated with almost all the tears of the Nine Worlds, was a constant reminder of what could have been. Erin and Hilde had never been alive. Had never drawn breath. No Norn had ever laid out their fates. They'd been a possibility, and then … nothing. Instead of true life, Tilda had conjured her daughters from her dreams of what might've been, what could've been, and what she'd wanted to be. She gave them form from Niflheim's mist, bound together in the golden threads of discarded fate from lives lost to the Nine Worlds before their assigned time.

And yet, despite all their mother had given her, Erin resented it. All Tilda had done in her life—travelled, loved, saved the world. Erin had done nothing. Tilda had seen the sun, had memories of a life, a time before. She was still alive.

And she certainly hadn't conjured her daughters for

their own benefit, trapped as they were in Hel. Erin sometimes wished she hadn't bothered.

"No desire for my advice?" Urd gathered her knitting. She was forever knitting the girls sweaters. "You think me simple because I no longer have any visions. I'm no longer a Norn. I foresaw Asgard's end, and the Nine Worlds' second rise. I saw Yggdrasill burn and its child rooting. I saw my family end and yours rise."

"You *are* family, Langamma."

"I am a ghost." Her stern glare bored through Erin. "My family listened to me."

Then she walked away, too, leaving a new sweater behind. An intricate weave of grey, black, and white yarn.

"For your journey."

Erin stormed out of the Nornhall. She hacked dead roots with her axe until there was a pile of kindling surrounding her. Her temper would've gotten her killed by now, if she weren't already dead—an inherited trait, she'd been told.

Tilda hadn't tried to hide her father's identity, though she rarely spoke of him. Erin figured they were too different—or too alike—to get along. She couldn't know for sure, she'd never met the guy. In her charitable moments, she wished he was dead, as that was the least hurtful reason for his absence. At those times, she'd looked for him in the Now, and failed to see him, but never asked Hilde to use her gift. Most times, she just didn't care.

Erin's thoughts went back to Hilde, and she felt her shoulders sag with the weight of her guilt. It didn't matter what she wanted, it was terrible to suggest that her sister, who'd been with her through everything, meant so little to her.

At Nornheim's gate, she again cast the Now into the mists.

Hilde might've followed. Her cloak could hide her even from the Now. Each sister had forged something imbued with runes to prove their understanding to their mother, and take their place at her side. Erin, the axe, Hilde, the cloak.

"Hilde …" No answer. "Sorry?"

Nothing.

The mists quivered at the edge of the gate. The Now screamed alarm, threatening to split Erin's skull. A black, serpentine form breached the fog. Spines tore rents in the fabric of Niflheim itself. After each wound, the mists flowed back together, never showing Erin more than a glimpse of the dragon's immensity. Black scales darkened the fog all around them. Nornheim was enveloped.

Níðhöggur had come to Nornheim.

She dwelt in Niflheim's deepest depths, swaddled

in the icy mists. Níðhöggur. Nightbringer. Root-eater. Death's End. A voracious dragon who'd gnawed Yggdrasill's roots and glutted herself on the corpses of criminals. Since Tilda had taken Hel's mantle, it had fallen to the Norns to hold Níðhöggur in check.

To keep the dragon from the still-growing new World Tree, the Norns offered certain spirits to the dragon. Rapists, murderers, the neo-Nazis often drawn to Norse stories, those who abused the runes, and their gifts were given to Níðhöggur. They were unrepentant, and even in death, unwanted. Tilda didn't want "those assholes" at her table, said she knew from her time above they couldn't be trusted with a second—with any—chance.

The dragon's house-sized head stopped at the gate. "Where is the Queen of the Dead?" she demanded, imperious as any god. "*Where is my due?*"

Erin didn't want to say Tilda was gone. Not the right tactic for dealing with the dragon. Her mother's power was the only bond holding Níðhöggur's hunger at bay. She also didn't want to lie.

"She's busy."

"*Busy.*" Mist snorted from the dragon's nostrils. "She's *gone.*"

Shit.

"Your mother sent me her discards. Where is *she* now?" Níðhöggur asked. "Have *you* been discarded?"

"You wish."

"It falls to you to fulfill our treaty. I. Hunger."

"No souls have come to Nornheim. We have nothing to give to you."

"Liessssss." The dragon's word hissed through the mist, reverberating in the fog until it seemed Niflheim would collapse. Ash dusted from the ceiling. A dead root cracked and tumbled between them. She eyed the dead streaming from the hall, ready for battle. "Your hall is fuller than my belly."

"Back to the hall," Erin ordered the dead. "This doesn't concern you."

The dead couldn't stop Níðhöggur, but Tilda's protections on the Nornhall would keep them safe for a while. Maybe long enough for her to find out her daughters had died well.

Erin set her feet wide. Trying to claim space in a staring contest with a dragon was ridiculous, but she wouldn't let Níðhöggur intimidate her. That would be her destruction. Then Hilde's. And Nornheim's end. She could set the full hall against the dragon and it would be the same result.

"Not a lie," she said through gritted teeth. "Nothing's crossed the Gjöll. They were judged, and they are not for you."

"If I must subsist on dead roots," Níðhöggur said, snatching the fallen root with a clawed hand, "I will start with your home. And the spirits within."

"You will touch no one beyond this gate. They. Are. Not. For. You."

Níðhöggur clawed at Erin. Erin's axe screamed through the mist, its edge whistling like hawk's keen, ringing off the dragon's scaled claw. The dragon didn't cry out. Showed no hurt.

"Wait!" cried a voice. Hilde's.

She *had* followed. Or, the dragon had drawn her here.

Erin swung again. It was too late to wonder why Hilde had come to her rescue. She didn't know whether her sister was speaking to her, or the dragon. Níðhöggur batted Erin away, a cat playing with a mouse, and another leg burst from the mist, pinning Erin to Nornheim's fence.

She gasped at the pressure. *It hurt.* But she was made of mist. Erin's body joined Niflheim's fog. An arm slipped from Níðhöggur's grasp. She wrenched her axe free and swung, trying to declaw the dragon—literally. The dragon laughed, buffeting Erin with her tail.

With strength came resilience. Erin didn't need to worry about breaking her hand by punching someone full out, which also made her good at taking a punch.

Hilde entreated the dragon to wait again. Invisible, but nearby. Níðhöggur's claws tightened as she sniffed for the voice. She stopped a moment from crushing Erin.

Níðhöggur asked Hilde, "What offer will top this morsel? Almost alive."

Hilde pulled back her hood, leaned on her staff—tired, or resigned—and said, "Me."

"Hilde, no!" Erin struggled to free her axe. She growled to the dragon, "You'll not touch her."

Níðhöggur's sinuous neck made a small island of the space between Erin and Hilde, enveloping them.

"*I* will get you your due," Erin said. "I'll bring you what you're owed."

"Eat now, or eat later," Níðhöggur mused. "Eat now, *and* eat later."

Despite their fight, Hilde had to go and do something stupidly noble. Or she wanted to do it because of their fight. To prove once and for all who was the big sister. In the shittiest way possible. This couldn't be the end. Wouldn't. Erin hadn't apologized yet.

The dragon's claws tightened. Níðhöggur viewed her struggle impassively, then reared back and sucked mist into her maw. She vomited the concentrated mist of Niflheim over Erin, a rank admixture of jagged ice and corpse breath. Erin didn't need to breathe, but the fog filled her. Choked her. Until only nightmares long buried remained.

Hooves.

All around her.

A stampede.

Too dark to see.

Screaming. Is it hers?

Pain, so much pain. She can't see. Can't feel her way out of the dark. They've taken her hands. Can't run, they've taken her feet. Can't even scream. And who would hear? Her clothes stripped. Her body hurled onto a bed of damp, rotting hay in a bone pen. The darkness bleeds away, revealing a hag's face. For a moment the pain stops. For a moment. She knows this because it's happened before. The pain stops so it will hurt more when it resumes.

Erin's fingers brushed the carved runes of her axe's haft. The darkness receded. Níðhöggur set Erin beside Hilde, but she still couldn't meet her sister's eye.

"Oh, no." Hilde brushed ice from Erin's hair. "You saw her, didn't you? The mara. The one who's been stealing the dead."

Níðhöggur released her. "I assumed she worked for you, circumventing our bargain."

"No. Never." Erin's words came out as ragged breaths.

The dragon cocked her head. "She worked for Hel in the past."

"This isn't Hel," Erin said, without believing it. She turned to Níðhöggur. "She isn't ours. Hilde is a hostage, a hostage only, until I return."

Hilde whispered harshly, "What are you doing?"

"My duty. It's *my* job to find the dead and lead them into Nornheim. And …" The nightmare replayed itself in her mind's eye. Erin made a point not to talk about her nightmares with Hilde—her sister had her own visions that kept her screaming—and she wasn't about to let Hilde track down a mara to face them first-hand. "I can't let her take you."

Hilde brushed her cheek. "Why do you think I'd want you to trade yourself for me?"

Erin eyed the dragon, watching them impassively with its cold, reptilian eyes. "Don't be stupid. Mom needs you more than she needs me."

Hilde didn't argue the point. "You don't come home, Erin."

Erin sighed. There it was, Hilde's vision revealed. "Then tell Mom goodbye."

Resigned, Hilde said, "The mara won't come for me while Níðhöggur's here."

She was safe, but not safe. A snake in a cleft stick, only instead of two bad choices, there were no choices at all. Not for Erin. Not for Hilde.

"I'm …" Erin began. The word "sorry" caught in her throat.

"If you have something to say to me, say it when you come home." Hilde turned her back. "Just … come home. Fix this."

"Yes. Fix this," Níðhöggur said. "Or I'll feed you to *my* children, eat your mother, your home, the tree, her grief, whatever I choose. I will eat you all."

The dragon's mention of grief reminded Erin of how she'd earned her half-life. She asked, "Did you weep for me?"

"I know what it is like to lose a child." An answer fit for Loki, saying much and saying nothing. Reptilian eyes bored into her. "You meant nothing to me, girl. Not your death. Not your life. Your mother bargained my tears for peace, but there is one yet who hasn't wept for you. *One.*"

There was weight to that small word. Erin knew what else Hilde's reading had revealed. "You saw her. You knew."

Hilde nodded.

Erin turned back to the dragon. "Do you know her?"

"I do." Níðhöggur chuckled, a dry sound, like a dying man's cough, and curled around Nornheim's walls, her maw blocking the gate, watching Erin. "But not as well as *you*. She feeds upon your fears. Your hopes. Still, and always."

Erin wasn't just facing *a* mara. This was *the* mara. The reason Erin hadn't been born.

"Where is she?"

"Where the Gjöll nears Midgard," Hilde said with a sigh. "There is a black road. She's carved it for herself, and waits for the dead before they can cross the bridge. Nothing comes back from the end of that road." Hilde touched her forehead to Erin's. The cords of their lucky necklaces wrapped around each other, stones clinking together. "But you *must*."

Erin left.

She didn't look back. She didn't need to, wrapped in the Now, Hilde's tears were a flood. One of them wouldn't survive this. Erin didn't know if their mother could bring her back a second time. She kept her feet on the road, and her eyes ahead. Uncertainty *was* living.

A hard lesson for a Norn, even a dead one. The dragon wouldn't see her tears.

And she wouldn't see Hilde's.

She'd do her duty.

Erin stayed in the Now as she stalked the road through Niflheim to the bridge over the Gjöll. Mist gorged on the path, swallowing the way home behind her. Tilda had widened the path during her rule; more dead than ever were finding their way to Nornheim. Until now.

The further Erin left home behind, the more tangled Yggdrasill's roots became above her. She couldn't see any new growth, and the whispers, quiet in Nornheim, called her name with every step she took. Urd's sweater, with its World Tree design, offered no warmth. There was no warmth in Niflheim, and no comfort in Hel. Erin had never felt warm—no sweater could change that.

Hilde was safe in the Now's far edge. Safe. If you could call being a dragon's hostage *safe*. Her sister's fore-sight was no good in a fight. Fights were for the Now. Especially since Hilde hadn't inherited any gifts of the martial persuasion. She was stronger and tougher than a mortal woman her size—their mother's daughter—but despite Erin's urging, Hilde had never learned to throw a punch. And still she'd bested Níðhöggur in a way Erin couldn't. She'd made the dragon pause. And bargain.

Erin reached the Gjöll, and soon after, the golden bridge spanning it, a bridge only the dead could travel. If no one living could cross the bridge *into* Niflheim, could nothing dead cross the other way? Could Erin keep walking? What would happen to her if she could? Would she melt away, like fog in the sun? Ted had crossed it. Tilda had crossed it, and long ago, before Ragnarök, Odin's steed Sleipnir had borne the god Hermod safely across to beg Hel for Baldur's life. She hesitated at the foot of the bridge, her raised shoe dangling over the ash-covered gold.

Asgard's ashes fell still, and perhaps would forever, trying to bury the golden bridge. Golden glints showed through across the entire span except its edge closest to Nornheim. Despite the dearth of dead arriving in Nornheim, the bridge had been well trodden. Nothing had made it across.

Erin's boot touched the ash. It puffed up under her foot as she set her full weight upon the golden span. Her body didn't unravel into the mist. She didn't feel the weight of Hel dragging her back. Another step. Nothing happened. Pressure grew as she forged ahead. If Erin could step onto the bridge, could she cross it? Keep going to Midgard? No, it would mean abandoning Hilde and Nornheim.

Midway across the bridge, Erin sensed another path.

The black road, like a parasitic tributary of the Gjöll. It pressed on all sides of the Now, collapsing her vision. Something was out there. Something *alive.*

From the mist, walked a cat. A *live* cat. The presence she'd felt at the edges of Hilde's vision. It regarded her with mismatched eyes. The cat gave the road the barest touch possible, as if it couldn't bear more contact with the thing.

Erin knelt to greet it. Tortoiseshell cats were almost exclusively female; a weird bit of trivia she'd picked up. "How'd you end up here, girl?"

"So, Erin, we meet at last."

She talked. Not a cat, then. Erin knew her, now. Without ever having met her, she knew her. She'd been warned about her. "Loki."

The cat tapped its nose with a paw. "In one."

Everybody loved Loki.

Until they didn't.

The trickster was a notorious outlaw, despite having helped save the world. Pretty much anyone with power in the Nine Worlds wanted Loki dead.

"I *knew* if they disappeared while you were looking, you'd come running."

Erin pinched the bridge of her nose. "What's your fucking game?"

The trickster's feline features appeared … wistful. "Shit, you're so much like him. I miss my friend. I miss him so damn much. I imagine you do, too."

Ted. Loki was talking about Ted. "Can't miss what you've never known."

"Maybe, but you feel the lack."

Erin hadn't thought much of Ted. Or Loki. Maybe why Tilda had never expanded on her time with them. She hadn't asked, and had been—to be fair—a bit of a shit whenever Ted's name came up.

Erin didn't want to talk about Ted. "I need to get the dead back."

"I can help you."

"Prove it."

"I can show you the way."

"I already know the way."

"I know who's responsible—"

"So do I."

The cat looked crestfallen.

"You won't have to face her alone."

She had Erin there. She couldn't see how the cat could possibly help, but the only thing worse than being Loki's ally was being Loki's enemy.

"C'mon, then."

"Just like your dad."

Her grip tightened on her axe. She bit her bottom lip to keep from snarling. "I don't want to talk about him."

And then the trickster shut up. *That* was odd. She'd expected Loki to keep hammering her about the good old days. But she didn't. The cat just watched her with those queer mismatched eyes. She could sense Loki reading her, it reminded her of how Tilda looked at the runes.

"I can trust you?"

"Search your feelings, you know it to be true."

The trickster's words had the feel of a private joke. Erin didn't care if it was at her expense, or Ted's. Loki could argue in circles for hours, twisting words and intent. Eventually she'd get what she wanted. *Erin* wanted to find the dead and didn't have time to argue. Or to ask if Loki knew why Ted had abandoned her. Maybe when this was done. She thought on Hilde's reading. Probably not even then.

"Your dad trusted me."

Erin scoffed. Like she could trust the opinion of someone she'd never met. Someone who, as far as she knew, hadn't ever tried to visit her. But confronted with the trickster, for the first time in ages, Erin wondered what'd happened to her father.

"If you want to help me, you can start by leaving *him* out of it."

The cat stared at her intently, as if waiting for an apology.

"What? What feelings am I supposed to have for somebody I've never met?"

"He wanted to know you so much."

The cat walked the black road, away from her, tail raised, showing Erin her asshole.

The black road grew tighter. Smothering. Fever-hot, and still freezing cold. Erin felt she had to inch forward sideways to avoid touching the mist.

"Why are you a cat?"

"I pissed off the wrong nightmare. She remembered me from a different role. Locked me into it and here we are." Loki shook her head. "Freyja would fucking love this."

"I never heard of your being a cat."

"Never told anyone. My nature is protean. I try not to repeat myself, but she has me stuck good. Can't even turn into a *different* cat. Always this tortoiseshell, always these mismatched eyes. She's used my power to hide in the mist. Nightmares never die."

A nightmare. A mara.

The Now's insistence grew, pulling her away. She didn't want to leave. Not while she travelled with Loki. She didn't trust the trickster. Not yet. Maybe never. Her visions took her elsewhere.

The dead. She saw them now, huddled in a shadowy hall. All human, aside from their grey skins. A seemingly endless tide extended behind them. How many souls had been stolen from Nornheim?

The hall was home to every nightmare, anything one

could dread glinted, just out of sight in the torches' twilight red glow. The tattoos the dead had borne in life—runes, and other familiar icons—remained, like darker scars against their ashen skin. Some gleefully cut upon the newly dead, not to kill, but to watch the mist bleed from their bodies. They swallowed that mist before it could mend the dead, and grew larger, firmer, while their victims diminished. Erin was certain her mother would've fed the aggressors to Níðhöggur. The floor opened beneath the weakened dead, the walls took others, as if the shadowy hall hungered, a thing alive. But nothing lived here.

Laughing at the scene, an ancient woman, crouched low, knobbed knees above broad shoulders. A face that looked to have been hewn into stone with hammer and chisel. She tapped a wrinkled knuckle against a cracked tooth, her bloody fingernails scratched the stone floor, scouring lines into it. Each tap promising more pain to come. The mara turned and looked, as if directly at Erin. She smiled and laughed.

"I. See. You."

The Now shattered. Erin swam back in fear. Tears trickled down her cheeks, cutting tracks through the ash. She gasped as her knees buckled and she fell to the black road. She pushed at her temples with her palms hoping to push the image from her mind. She sat, head in hands, trying to compose herself.

"I saw … her …" She shook as the vision faded. She could still hear the mara's laugh in the mist.

She'd never seen the mara's face so clearly before, and still it stained her spirit. She lurked in Erin's dreams, at the edges of her awareness. The old woman, the shapeshifter, who came for her time and again in nightmares. When she did, Erin would wake in Hel, not Nornheim; Erin couldn't shake feeling her nightmare had never ended, that she'd never leave Hel's mists.

Erin shook, fists balled at her side with nothing to punch. You couldn't punch a nightmare. She punched the road anyway. It accomplished nothing but dust her face in ash.

Loki snaked under her arms and patted her face with a paw. "In some ways, I'm responsible for the predicament you're in."

Erin snorted. "An admission you should make far more often than you do."

The cat's mismatched eyes bored into her, glittering, then seemed to roll with familiar annoyance.

"The mara … I'm not the reason she chose to go after your folks. They already had targets on them, but she wouldn't have been the one to get to them if not for me. It could've been all different. Once, long ago, she was locked away, and I let her out."

"She did what she did, not you."

Loki cocked her head to the side. "You're more charitable than I'd be in your place."

Erin wasn't feeling charitable. "I can't believe Mom didn't deal with her already."

"She would've if she'd found her."

Of that, Erin had little doubt, "How'd she get you? Steal your power."

"Caught me sacked out. Sun's gotta shine on a dog's ass someday. I got away. Well, most of me. I keep trying to get myself back. So far, no dice." The cat looked away. "Your dad and I had split, working an angle from both sides. I didn't like the divide-and-conquer idea ... That was the last time I saw him. I guess he found something he couldn't punch his way out of."

Loki looked like she wanted to say more, but didn't.

For someone like Loki, being locked into one shape and not being able to shift and switch at whim *would* be a horror. A reminder of her binding in the time before Ragnarök, well-deserved or no. Erin had heard she'd softened, although the trickster's reputation as a troublemaker hadn't diminished since she'd helped end the Nine Worlds, or since she'd helped save this one in particular.

Erin sighed. The mara had stolen the Now. The black road took her back into the void. The home of nightmares and whispers. The mara just under her skin, waiting to claw out and unmake her. Again.

The cat looked away. "You don't want to face her. You don't have to. Not for me."

"I'm not facing her for you. I faced Níðhöggur, I'll face anyone."

She didn't tell Loki how that fight had gone. They walked down the black road in silence. The mist pressed in on them, there was no sign of where they were going, or how to get back.

"We're here."

The mist thickened. A black spot, as if Níðhöggur lurked, unseen. The black road became a hungry maw. Something was there. Old. Familiar. Beyond a fence of snakes—a mockery of Nornheim, or an homage to Hel—the hall undulated, moving closer to her, as if it were alive. It wasn't. Nothing was. Tilda had chased Hel's serpents out into Niflheim, but apparently they hadn't died in the mists. The mara had claimed them for her new realm. She'd rebuilt Hel's hall, woven from snakes and dripping with venom.

The only thing lacking from the replica was a rooster on its roof. No cock to crow another world's ending here.

Wordlessly, Erin and Loki strode toward to the hall. Its doors were gone, if there had ever been any here. The mara would want to encourage intruders. Erin used her axe as a shield, sheltering under the blade as the serpents above the door hissed at her. Loki scrambled onto her back and hid in the axe's shadow. Venom fell like rain, spattering over her axe's blade, but it didn't touch them. Inside, broken dead lingered, barely any substance left to them. Beyond them, stacked bones were piled like retaining walls and impaled bodies had turned to bones. Bodies stolen from Níðhöggur's barrow or dead heroes who'd tried to beard the mara in her lair? Erin wasn't sure.

Torches lined the walls; their flickering light did little to dispel the darkness. They only accentuated it. Erin's eyes were drawn away from the darkness, as if there were something there she didn't want to see. She ground her teeth, focused, and turned her head back. At the end of the hall, on a throne carved from Yggdrasill's charred roots, sat the mara.

Her dirty, cracked nails dripped blood. Matted grey hair hung past her waist, parting over a belly bloated with gobbled fears. Her body gaunt, yet unnaturally strong. Erin knew her grip well. Feral eyes, sweat slicked, and greasy. She had a corruption you could *feel*. Fouler than Hel, but different. Fear. Death. For her they were one. The mara glided forward, toenails barely touching the floor, and yet they were thunder.

"I've missssssssed you," she hissed in Erin's face, drawing out the word until Erin wanted to scream. "Such delicious fears you have."

The mara's bloody fingernails were impossibly long—longer than the hag's body was tall. She raised her hand effortlessly, and her arms stretched across the distance between them.

Erin snarled and swung her axe. The blade passed harmlessly through the mara's arms. "You stole my life."

"You got better," she replied with a cackle. "Mostly. I saw to *that*."

Loki had crept halfway across the hall. She yowled as the shadow of the mara's claws fell upon her, piercing her shadow. She stood, frozen, hair on end, a drawn-out hiss scratching past her muzzle.

"You won't find your waking there. You cheated me once, trickster. Never. Again." The mara clenched her fist. Bloody talons scratched over themselves, and Loki screamed. Then, gone, except for her cries. Nowhere to be seen, swallowed by the shadows. "Your nightmares have been waiting. So. Long. Remember your time under the earth, that seeming eternity? It will be as nothing. There will be no one to give you succour. Not for a moment. Not in *my* prison."

Erin rushed to Loki, but the shadows were solid as a wall. She battered them anyway. It was like striking dragon-scale. Hissing buried the cat's cries. "What are you doing to her?"

The hag smiled, cracked teeth like shards of broken glass. "What. I'll. Do. To. You."

From the shadows beneath every torch, the dead came to the mara's call. Erin gripped her axe tightly to keep from covering her ears. She couldn't show fear.

Maras fed off fear. They drank anguish. For all the brave face Erin put on, the axe trembled.

Grey-skinned dead, some men, some women, all nude, rushed her. Rune tattoos marred their bodies, other symbols—symbols of hate—were given equal pride of place, fouling the magic her family was meant to hold and protect. They shrieked, inchoate screaming, a beast in pain, dying. No sound that should've ever been uttered by living mouths.

Their wails cut through Erin's brain.

The dead had her surrounded.

Erin swung her axe in wide, scything strokes to keep them at bay. Her ability to shift through the mist worked against her. There were too many of them. Even wielding her rune axe one-handed, she'd be overrun. The mara's hall shrank around her, tightening like Níðhöggur's black claws. Any she cut, their smoking wounds mended almost instantly.

The axe's runes protected her from them, which they also sensed. Instead of battering her torso and legs, they targeted her arms, trying to force her to drop it. Erin swung her axe. She stumbled against one of the fallen dead, still reconstituting. One of the dead caught her on her backswing. Then another, and another. They draped on her forearms, slowing her swings. They bit and scratched her hands. Erin's fingers went numb and her axe flew from her grasp, engulfed by the serpent floor. Her screams were lost in the hissing of snakes.

The mara's shadow swallowed the hall. Tightened around Erin. The mara cackled. This was the *Now*. Nothing existed but this moment. It was inevitable. She was a nightmare. You can't punch out a nightmare. Erin had tried. They're smoke and stink. Heart attacks and strokes. A cancer. They aren't there until they are. Her whole existence had been a nightmare. Erin's fear for her future, her fears from her past, shattered the present before it could form a way out.

The hag dragged her to the hissing floor with a long, bloody talon. She stepped onto Erin's chest, the weight as if a giant perched there. The pressure grew. Stone upon stone piled atop her chest. A fist on her heart. Weight beyond bearing. The weight of expectation. The world's weight. The sum of her fears.

Crushing her.

The pain should've made her cry. She couldn't. She did.

"You are mine now," rasped the crone's voice, hollow and hungry. Then she laughed. Her eyes flashed red. "Again. *Always. Mine.*"

A strand of hair fell across Erin's eyes, the vibrant red now a muddy grey. Vision tunnelled at the edges. The Now collapsed. Shadows enveloped her. The darkness was everything.

In Nornheim with Hilde. Fighting Níðhöggur. Again. Still. Erin couldn't remember which. The fight was familiar. She couldn't grab Hilde before the darkness swallowed her. Níðhöggur laughed from the darkness.

Ted Callan covered miles with every step. A giant. A void. Swallowing her expectations, dreams, and nightmares. She'd never met him, but it was Ted. Ravens picked over the dead and dying he left in a trail of smoking cities.

He didn't look at her as he passed by her.

Not. A. Glance.

Erin would never match her parents. Would never be free from Hel.

No axe. The Now was a prison, not a gift. A transparent, grey spirit, dining from an empty bowl and drinking from an empty cup in a snake-walled hall.

She wasn't left in charge. Her mom didn't trust her. She'd abandoned her.

Upworld.

Free, but she couldn't find her way home.

North and down. North and down. To the gates of her mother's hall.

The gates were barred and the hall was shut.

"The way home is north and down. North and down. North and down."

Erin repeated her mother's words as a mantra, as if she feared, should she stop, she'd lose her way home. As if she feared she'd lost herself. She'd been proud when they'd been left in charge. To have a *mission*, but it'd all gone to shit. What if this place, this fear, was all there was? What if it unmade her? Worse, what if the mara wouldn't give her an end?

Shadows crushed her brain. Wrung out her soul. Distilled everything she feared, hated, loved, and turned it against her.

Every moment of triumph turned on its head. Every failure magnified. They'd taken her axe. *Her axe.* For a moment, anger pricked her fear's edge, scratching holes in the shadows.

She whispered a rune, "Kenaz."

A spark from the hearth rune. Its fire was nothing against the vast dark. The black crushed in.

Erin felt herself unravelling. Un-becoming. Her substance turning into mist. Even as the mara flayed her to her core, that golden thread fate—her possibility—remained. The mist was everywhere. It *was* her. The axe should protect her from the mara. If she could reach it. The nightmares hadn't started until they'd knocked it from her hands. She couldn't reach the axe, couldn't find it. The mara had hurt her. Hurt her worse than any punch. Any kick, or bite.

The hurt.

The hurt was the key.

Erin stopped fighting the pain. Stopped fighting her nature. She was the mist. Made of it, tempered by it. She took in more.

She focused on the pain, to reach the Now. Accepted the pain to see beyond it. Beyond the Now had never been Erin's strong suit. Her axe writhed with snakes, a void in the pain. The mara was real. The fear she'd inflicted wasn't. A dream. A nightmare. Bad enough it felt real. She saw events as they were, not as they had been, or would be, or as she wanted them to be. Not alive, more than dead. Hilde's vision be damned. She was still in the fight.

Erin couldn't punch her way out, but she wasn't only her father's daughter. She was a Norn. Fate answered to *her*. She had to believe that. The Now was undecided. Not the stone of the past, or the chains of the future. The stronger she was, the stronger her runes would manifest. North and down. She could always find her way home. The Now was clear. The hurt Erin had experienced in the nightmare, as the dead had swollen with power for cutting the new arrivals, had allowed her to draw enough of the mist to her that she could touch her axe. Its runes would protect her from the mara's magic. *Her* magic would do the rest.

Dwelling within the Now also meant fully accepting the nightmares. She would never be her father. She'd never be her mother. Hilde might never forgive her. She might never get home. But Erin wouldn't let fears rule her. Hilde waited for her. For now. Her mother was coming back. Erin had found the dead. Ted had wanted to see her.

She was in the mist. She *was* the mist. She shifted what remained of her body. Her fingers brushed the haft of her axe. Serpents struck. Their venom burned, more pain to focus beyond. The shadows shrank. The mara shrieked. Her weight lessened. Snakes hissed as Erin grasped the axe. As Erin's nightmares assaulted her, she saw the mara for who she was: a pitiful thing with no dreams of her own. A jealous, spiteful shade who reflected the worst of her victims.

The mara screamed, "No!"

Erin wrenched her axe free from the serpent floor. She smashed the axe butt against the floor and the runes on the haft glowed bright blue. They swirled around her body, until they ringed her head in a halo. Runes knifed through the mara's greasy darkness. Erin tossed her off, and the hag skidded to a stop before her throne.

The mara turned to run, but Erin was there. She brought her axe down, and this time, it connected. Her runic halo wound tightly over the hag, binding her. Imprisoning her. She struggled. Wild eyes darted past Erin to the dead, who'd retreated to the darkness, only faces peering from the shadows.

In a low voice, Erin asked the mara, "What do *you* fear?"

The mara didn't answer.

"Bring back Loki." The shadows receded. A trembling cat appeared. "Release the dead."

"No. They're *mine*."

Erin tightened the runes. Cut off from the mara's power, the dead stopped screaming. They weren't the ones who needed to be scared. They weren't who needed to cry. Erin turned her focus to the mara.

"Weep."

"I. Will. *Not.*"

Kenaz provided little light in the underworld, but it wasn't the only rune tied to fire.

"Fehu!" Erin yelled, naming the rune of primal fire. Torches flared, the mara's hall became bright as Erin imagined the sun. Brighter. The newer dead, the ones the mara hadn't poisoned yet, burst out of the darkness and into the light. They fell to their knees. The others, the ones Erin knew Níðhöggur would take, cowered at the edge of the diminishing shadows, hiding their eyes from the fire of life. The mara hissed, smoking away under the light. "Weep, for what you took from me. Weep, or I burn you to nothing."

The mara blanched at Erin's implacable face. The mara would never have a hold on her again. She'd fear again. She'd hurt. But *this* beast wouldn't crush her breast again.

"*Weep!*" She screamed the word so loud the serpents forming the mara's hall unknotted themselves. The hall collapsed. Its snakes fled into the mist.

A tear, and the barest whisper of a breath, escaped the mara. Niflheim's cold froze the tear solid. Another came. It froze too. Gingerly, she plucked them from the mara's face, holding them in her palm like jewels.

Life waited in the tears. She need only put one into the lucky stone around her neck. But Niflheim was no place for the living. She'd waited this long, she could wait a bit longer. She placed both frozen tears in her pocket.

"Níðhöggur hungers." Erin wanted the mara dead. Beyond dead. *Destroyed.* But vengeance didn't belong only to Erin. It was her mother's responsibility. Tilda had been hunting the mara for a long time, and there were appearances to maintain. Nornheim was Tilda's realm, not Erin's. Judgement belonged to the goddess of death. To act now would undermine her mother's rule. No matter how much she might approve, no matter how much Erin wanted vengeance.

She'd settle for victory. Life. In her grasp.

Erin smiled and the hag paled. She crumpled within the ribbon of runes as if the symbols were all holding her upright.

With the mara defeated, Loki's old abilities returned. A middle-aged man with pinprick scars surrounding his lips appeared where the cat had vanished. Loki's human form was short, though still taller than Erin. Rat-faced, with a winning smile. Erin had no idea where his clothes had come from, but he *was* dressed, thankfully. Loki dusted himself off, and for the first time, Erin saw Loki as her father might've. He didn't impress at a glance, hadn't taken a form to impress her, and *that* impressed.

"I bet Mom's been waiting for you for a long time." Erin flashed a grin at the mara. "She's not as forgiving as I am."

Erin took the dead back to the bridge and over the Gjöll. She wouldn't chance them escaping again. Each was bound with the rune chain holding the mara, for their protection as much as Erin's. Judging the dead wasn't her duty; she saw what was, not what had been—but Níðhöggur had a taste for criminals and cowards. Erin knew who'd sided with the mara. *They* had no place in Nornheim. At the gates, these murderers, rapists, and white supremacists who poisoned the runes with their hate, all became food for the Root-eater. Erin watched the dragon eat—she felt it her duty, as the one who'd led them here. If the dragon took more than her due, she'd answer to Tilda's judgement.

Níðhöggur nodded, sated—for now—and sank back into the mist, revealing Hilde.

Erin embraced her sister. "I came back."

"You did." Hilde's gaze drifted down. To the pocket holding the mara's tears. "But not to stay."

"No, not to stay."

Hilde smiled. "I'm glad *you* beat her. She'd have always lurked in your nightmares otherwise. But I'm always here for you. *We're* always here for you."

Erin wasn't sure if Hilde's "we" meant her and their mom, Nornheim, or both. She *could* leave. She didn't have to. "You always have a place here" is different than "Your place is always here." Home could be a funny thing. Nornheim had never felt like home, the outside world mightn't either, but she was going to find out.

Erin held her lucky stone and looked at Loki.

"I *love* what you girls have done with the place," he said. "But I'd prefer not to stay."

"He's alive," Erin said. "He doesn't belong here." And Erin didn't trust him to find his way out. Or that Tilda would leave the outlaw alive if she caught him here. And she *would* catch him.

Hilde glanced knowingly at Erin's necklace. "You're correct about one thing: our hall is no place for the living."

"Will I be able to come home?"

"Of course you can return, you know the way."

"North and down."

Instinctively, Erin could tell the tears apart, knew which was shed for her, and which for Hilde. She placed one frozen tear into the hole in her lucky stone, and it sank into the stone's protective magic. The stone danced in her palm, joining her mother's labours, Nine Worlds' worth of weeping. The blush of life filled Erin's flesh for the first time, her heart beat, her lungs filled. The air stank and it was beautiful. She shivered with cold. Breath passed her lips. She had weight to her steps. Nornheim seemed to creak under her feet.

"Time flows at it needs, Hil." Erin smiled as she tossed the axiom back to her sister. "You'll hardly miss me."

"You can't see the future coming," Hilde said, sadly.

"*You* can," Erin said.

She smiled like Erin had answered her question.

Erin offered the second frozen tear to Hilde. "You could come with me."

"But I don't want to leave."

"I'm sorry I'm not happier here. Hilde, I'm … I'm so sorry for what I said."

"I'm sorry, too. I was selfish and couldn't bear the thought of losing you. My place is here, with Mom. You *need* to leave. You were never satisfied here. But I only wanted to protect you."

Erin closed Hilde's hand over her tear. "I'll probably be back before Mom gets home."

"You'd better be. *I'm* not taking the blame for *you* leaving."

"C'mon," Loki called from down the road. "I've got such sights to show you!"

Erin embraced her sister, and turned her back on Nornheim—not on her fellow Norns, not on her family. She watched Hilde in the Now, and walked with the trickster at her side toward daylight. Her steps grew louder with every boot that fell upon the path to Midgard.

To see the sun.

Afterword

You may have noticed there's no "Loki's Guide to Norse Mythology" in this book. Give a god a break, maybe he's too tired from appearing in so many of the stories in this collection to write one up. It was nice of Loki to leave me holding the bag, so to speak, to come up with something to say to close out the collection. (Is it bad form to blame your own characters for decisions you, the author, made well ahead of deadline?)

In reality, after discussion with my editor, and because this collection was something different in the series, we decided to treat the book's back matter a bit differently too. So welcome to some behind-the-scenes information on the origins and drafting of each of the stories in the collection.

Hope you don't mind—and if Loki were here writing this, he'd point out: it's too late now, isn't it?

All Cats Go to Valhalla

Originally published in *Swashbuckling Cats: Nine Lives on the Seven Seas,* Tyche Books, Rhonda Parrish, editor, May 2020.

Confession the first: I am not a cat person. I used to be. Before I had to live with one. I loved cats until I had a roommate with one. Then things changed. Now I guess you could say I admire the little jerks as impressive murder machines I'm glad I don't have to share my home with.

Why the hell would I write a cat story, then?

I was there at the beginning of a Twitter joke that became an anthology (this is neither a huge surprise or coincidence, I am ... often on Twitter). Editor Rhonda Parrish and her publisher, Margret Curelas, at Tyche Books, started joking about this pirate cat anthology, and so I joined in the fun along with many other writers and readers, tweeting silly cat GIFs, pirate GIFs, and puns, not really thinking an actual open call would happen. But when it *did*, since I'd been egging it on, I felt obliged to offer up my metaphorical axe via viking cat GIF.

The first thing that came to me for "All Cats Go to Valhalla" was my protagonist's name. I'd had a note about a character named Kills-the-Sky in my miscellaneous writing folder for ages, but hadn't found the right personality to attach it to, or the right story to use it in. (Fun side note: Kills-the-Sky was also the name of my Tabaxi Ranger in an online game of Dungeons & Dragons Curse of Strahd with some Calgary writing pals; so, thanks, Adam Cole, David Fortier, Erika Holt, and Simon Larter.) I couldn't shake the image of that axe-wielding viking kitty GIF, though, so I knew I'd make the story Norse-mythology-based, and if I was writing a Norse myths story, why not make it a Thunder Road story?

The next part of the story to arrive was the title, which was unusual for two reasons. Hey, did I mention I don't typically care for pun titles? Second, the final title is usually the last thing I type in a story, watching the end of submission window growing closer while I mutter, "fuckfuckfuckfuckfuck." It was kind of refreshing to have it locked from the near the start of writing.

The plot spun out from a line in *Tombstone Blues* about vikings coming to North America to bury their nightmares, which had been my attempt to tie stories of Newfoundland Old Hag sleep-paralysis to the myths of maras. Having the first spur of the plot, I took some historical elements, such as an article I'd read about vikings travelling with cats on their ships, and I set the story in the far beginning of the Thunder Road mythos, and went for it, figuring if I tried to plan too much that the cats would just have their way, anyway.

I decided not to make my viking cats anthropomorphic because I figured real cats, stuck at sea, would have its own tension even before I started throwing monsters and gods at them, and, as an added bonus, I'd be able to fit the story more neatly into my existing universe. Years and years ago, I'd really enjoyed *Tailchaser's Song* by Tad Williams, so that probably influenced me, too. Finally,

I pulled up lots of images of Norwegian forest cats to cast my characters, and started following Black Metal Cats on Twitter for inspiration. This story ended up a bit darker than I thought Rhonda might want, but it was the story in my head, and anyway, there's some humour in there. And, obviously, things worked out. Rhonda liked "All Cats Go to Valhalla" enough to include it in her anthology and readers enjoyed it enough to nominate it for an Aurora Award for Best Short Story, which it won in 2021.

A Door in the Rock

Originally published in *Those Who Make Us: Canadian Creature, Myth, and Monster Stories*, Exile Editions, Kelsi Morris and Kaitlin Tremblay, editors, November 2016.

"A Door in the Rock" was directly inspired by my research trip to Flin Flon to location scout for the finale of *Thunder Road*. It's also one of the stories that most directly picks up a plot point from the trilogy: the rock troll that Ted fights and injures. For a long while after I'd finished writing that fight, I wondered what'd happened to the rock troll with the broken arm. There was just no room to mention it in the novel.

As I explored Flin Flon, I came across an odd sight. A squarish wooden door carved into an escarpment of rock with the word "fuck" spray-painted upon it. Everyone I asked gave me a different answer for what was behind that door. In that mystery I found a story. What else could be behind that door in the rock other than dwarves?

I really enjoyed filling out a bit more of the *dvergur* culture and it left me with a bit of a path for more of the same when it came time to work on *Too Far Gone*. Bláinn and Brunna were interesting to create, and it was a challenge to write someone "dwarven" but distinct from the better-known Andvari from the series. Brunna was also one of the early female POV characters I wrote, and loved the dynamic between her and Rocky the troll. I've been meaning to get back to those two in a new story. Writing Bláinn let me flex some horror writing muscles, even though this wasn't a horror story.

Blood eagles, whether real or apocryphal, are a powerful image. A vicious punishment; a torturous death; where the ribs were separated from the spine and bones and skin pulled outward to make a set of gruesome wings, and the lungs removed from the chest cavity. My understanding is that there's no archaeological evidence the practice actually existed. However, where magic exists, you could do such a terrible thing to someone and make them live through it.

Thanks to David Jón Fuller for the Icelandic language assist and helping me name Sögusalur, the History Hall of the dwarves.

Murder Mystery

Originally self-published in *Wolf and Wing: A Thunder Road Collection*, October 2017.

Once I started appearing at comic conventions, I wanted to ensure I had something new for readers at my table each year, which is why I started doing some short convention-exclusive pieces in years when I didn't have a new full-length book releasing. "Murder Mystery" originated in one such convention piece. Only fifty were ever printed, so this story is likely new to you.

Even prior to writing about Huginn and Muninn in *Thunder Road*, I was reading about ravens in books like Bernd Heinrich's *Ravens in Winter* and *Mind of the Raven*. They are incredible birds. I saw some up close when I was up in Flin Flon for research and Thompson to teach a workshop, and they are *huge*. I used to wonder when I saw a large crow, "Is that a raven?" If you have to wonder, it's not.

There were always a lot of crows in my old neighbourhood, and while I never went so far as bribing them with food or shiny things, I often said hello as I walked by, like a good neighbour should. Somewhere before writing "Murder Mystery," I came across the concept of crow funerals, which was my initial inspiration for the story, but mostly, I wanted to see what Huginn and Muninn's days off would look like after Ted booted them from his skull. I really enjoyed their bickering camaraderie in the series, and it was a treat to see the world of Thunder Road through their eyes for a change.

Runt of the Litter

Originally published in *On Spec 96*, vol.26 no.1, Susan MacGegor, editor, Spring 2014.

I loved the contradiction of this little big man, a runty giant. "Runt of the Litter" was the first Thunder Road short story I wrote. I was thrilled to have it published in *On Spec,* which also happened to be the venue of my first fiction publication (they were also the first venue I submitted a story to, and my first rejection) so they, and this story, will always have a special place in my heart.

I met Diane Walton from *On Spec* at my first-away-from-home convention, the 2008 World Fantasy Convention in Calgary. After a panel on short fiction, I approached her to chat. I'd recently submitted my first story to them and it'd been rejected, but they'd offered some excellent feedback and advice. I'd subbed that story to a writing contest prior, but this was my first attempt to sell it. In hindsight, I probably should've opened my conversation with something other than, "You rejected my story." I saw Diane stiffen up, and I didn't understand at that time how often editors get confronted at these events by irate authors convinced of their genius.

Fortunately, I quickly followed with my appreciation of them taking time to read my first story, and for offering feedback. Diane encouraged me to send more work, and I did.

Susan MacGregor was my editor on this story at *On Spec*. In addition to being an editor, Susan's a fine author as well, and we shared an Aurora ballot when *Tombstone Blues* was nominated for Best Novel. There's a funny photo out there of us pretending to square off like we're ready to fight in front of the CSFFA (Canadian Science Fiction and Fantasy Association) Prix Aurora banner, but we never had an adversarial author-editor relationship.

I modelled Grim's apartment after the one my wife lived in when we first met. It was a gorgeous space (and such high ceilings!), so I'm glad I still get to spend some time there even if it's only in a story. "Runt of the Litter" became a bit of a blueprint for tales I liked to envision: Loki checking in on his distant offspring, and Loki being … Loki. A new character. An old character. Loki tends to crop up in my Thunder Road stories often because he's fun to write and I've got so many positive comments from readers on my take on the trickster. People get Loki, or the idea of him at least, and he can lead them into my take on Norse myths without as much explanation as Ted or other new characters require. But I still loved writing Grim. Fenrisúlfar, my name for Loki's descendants through Fenrir, was crafted by David Jón Fuller.

Eating of the Tree

Originally published in *Parallel Prairies*, Enfield & Wizenty, Darren Ridgley and Adam Petrash, editors, October 2018.

Inspired by my writing pal Marie Bilodeau and Masters of the Universe toys, I'd started writing "Eating of the Tree" for an anthology of comedy stories, but never finished it. I felt I wrote funny moments but had never tried to write *funny* and that was certainly a roadblock. When editors of *Parallel Prairies*, Adam Petrash and Darren Ridgley, approached me about contributing to their anthology, I dusted off "Eating of the Tree" (still untitled) and was finally able to finish it without the pressure of considering it "comedy." I hope it's still funny. *I* find it funny. A few changes have made their way into this one since its original publication, mostly to strengthen its ties to the novels, and to sneak in bits that relate to some of the stories in this collection.

Marie Belanger has a bit of the personality of her namesake, but is not the real Marie. However, in addition to being an award-winning author, Marie (the real Marie) is also an amazing storyteller, and has a very compelling speaking voice. I heard Marie's voice (the real Marie) in my ear while I was trying to draft the story, and so I just ran with it. But Marie (story Marie) is also full of stories that were shared with me at a Christmas party, by a friend of a friend, who worked a lot of security—so thanks for those, Bernadette. I couldn't fit them all into one short story, but I did what I could to do them justice.

The image of the destruction from the end of *Tombstone Blues* and the new growth coming from it really inspired me to check back into Winnipeg after those events. I've also wanted to get Ratatoskur into a story in a significant way. We don't see Winnipeg much in *Too Far Gone* and so it felt good to pop back in to show the consequences of my stories.

Ballroom Blitz

Original to this collection.

Once, at a family wedding, I was introduced as a writer to another guest who happened to be from Calgary. When they learned Ted was Albertan they got briefly excited, but when I said he was from Edmonton they flatly said, "It would be better if he was from Calgary." (Which reminded me of the certainty with which my younger cousin Tanner had said, "Your books would probably sell better if they had Batman in them." I know, buddy, I know.) I *did* think it was important to give

Calgary some onscreen series time, though, since I have so many pals and readers there. Maybe one day I'll write a story about a city I love to visit without also wrecking up the place, but this is not that story.

"Ballroom Blitz" became the second story I wrote to be set in the post-*Too Far Gone* timeframe. This story sat as a stub of scenes, mostly DD's interactions with Ted and Loki for a few years, without any of the connective tissue coming together. Hell, Megara "DD" McCain didn't even have a name until August 2021. One of the things I love to write in Thunder Road stories, even if it hasn't gotten much page time yet, is Ted from the viewpoint of other characters caught up in his shenanigans.

Scatter the Foals to the Wind

Originally published in *Equus*, World Weaver Press, Rhonda Parrish, editor, August 2017.

Much like with "All Cats Go to Valhalla," I didn't think I had a horse story in me. I'm not a horse person. Never have been. I don't think I've sat on a horse since I was twelve. I've hardly ever used equines of any sort in my writing; even in my sword and sorcery writing, my characters are usually (conveniently for me, and inconveniently for them) between mounts. So when I first saw the open call for *Equus*, I thought, "Cool. Shame I've got nothing for it." However, I'd also just spent time on a myth and folklore panel with editor Rhonda Parrish at the When Words Collide conference in Calgary, so I knew she was awesome and I really wanted to work with her. This ended up being the first story in an ongoing author/editor relationship between us.

At the time of that open call, I was fighting a book that wasn't working, and I needed a distraction to get my creative juices flowing again. Going Norse also meant I'd have a chance to play in the world of Thunder Road again and it would cut down on the amount of world-building I'd need to figure out so I could concentrate on character and plot and meet deadline, while not losing too much time on the book I was avoiding.

I decided on a descendent of Sleipnir, Odin's eight-legged horse, who could run over air and water as fast as over solid ground. In addition to being Odin's mount, Sleipnir was also a son of Loki from when the trickster had disguised himself as a mare to win a bet (Loki gets involved in … interesting bets). The joy of featuring a descendent of Loki was that Loki could play a part in my story, too. Loki is one of my favourite characters to write (even when he leaves me homework like this afterword, *ahem*).

Sleipnir's offspring don't get a lot of mention other than Odin's valkyries using them as mounts. As far as I could find, there wasn't a specific name for the valkyrie's mounts, which, as well as giving me potential antagonists, also allowed a lot of freedom to play around. I wanted my "equine" to be human—or at least, she'd been living a human life, unaware of her heritage, or weird relations—until she, and the reader, enter the story. She would be a shapeshifter (because Loki) and would be able to run on air (because Sleipnir) but I still had no idea what to call her kind.

After toying around with what to call them (long after the draft was done, and almost long enough to miss the submission deadline) I settled on wind foals—which also gave me the elements of my title. Fortunately, David Jón Fuller stepped in again with the Icelandic assist and so the Vindafolöld were properly named.

Far Gone and Out

Original to this collection.

"Far Gone and Out" was inspired by one of my favourite songs by The Jesus and Mary Chain, and shares its title. I've been trying finish this story since 2014 after I finished edits on *Tombstone Blues*. The structure proved tricky (pro-tip: seers as POV characters are a pain in the ass. Especially when they can look into the past, present, *and* future) and I think I spent most of the time between story conception and first draft completion just shifting scenes around. Tilda hasn't had as many short story appearances as Loki, or even Ted. Her power set is part of the reason, but that's also just an excuse. The truth was, I was afraid to get her story wrong.

Which was why it was worth it to try.

I knew I wanted to present a quilt of Tilda's life, her past, present, and future (at least as of *Tombstone Blues*). More than anything, I wanted to do her voice, and being, justice. Maybe that pressure held me back until I actually had a deadline to meet. "Far Gone and Out" was always on the list of possible new stories to complete for the collection, but it was only after we'd largely assembled the book that I bore down to finish this story. Because I had to. I knew with the number of stories Loki touched, and the weight Ted holds over the series and collection, that Tilda's absence would be notable, and unwelcome. She *had* to tell some of her own story.

Tilda's words to Ted at the end of *Tombstone Blues*—"I'll see you at the end of the world"—hung over the story long after the series was complete, but I'm glad this one is finally out into the world, and we didn't have to wait *that* long to read it.

Golden Goose

Originally published in *Air: Sylphs, Spirits, & Swan Maidens*, Tyche Books, Rhonda Parrish, editor, August 2020.

A wise man once told me: "There's nothing good about

goose shit." I still try to laugh about that as I navigate my way through the greasy green minefield the feathered menaces leave all over Winnipeg. "Golden Goose" wasn't supposed to be a Thunder Road story. The only thing I liked about my original run at Rhonda Parrish's *Air* anthology was the idea of people being forcibly transformed into Canada Geese, like a far more aggressive take on the swanmay myths.

I had some material from another abandoned story stub, where Ted and Loki try to take a flight to Iceland with disastrous consequences (which reminds me that I *really* need to get to Iceland so that I can get my characters there too). I was able to cobble the ideas together and make it work. This also became the first glimpse of a post-*Too Far Gone* world (other than that novel's epilogue) and it definitely gave me a taste to write more of the same. Also, Útgarða-Loki (Loki of the Outyards, or Loki of the Outlands, to distinguish him from Loki-Loki) tricking Thor and Loki is one of my favourite tales in Norse mythology, so I was glad to bring him back and introduce him to the Thunder Road world. Much like how I justified Loki being crafty enough to escape Ragnarök, I figured Útgarða-Loki would be smart enough to avoid that fateful battle. Thanks to Timothy Gwyn and Lindsay Kitson, my pilot and writing pals, who helped with the aviation details. Any mistakes are mine (or Loki's), not theirs.

"Golden Goose" wasn't the first story I wrote featuring

Ted, but it was his first that wasn't self-published (nothing wrong with self-publishing, and I'm proud of those stories). This one was a lot of fun to write, and I hope you'll enjoy reading it. I will note, and maybe it's a coincidence, but I've definitely noticed an uptick of geese around me since publishing this story. So far, none have attacked, but they are watching.

Always watching.

No Sunshine in Hel

Original to this collection.

I've been thinking about this story for a while, if not as long as "Far Gone and Out." "No Sunshine in Hel" was shaped by what it isn't. What it almost was. What it could have been. Much like the character of Erin herself. It's set an indeterminate time after *Too Far Gone*, my third post-trilogy story.

The story began with a letter I wrote from Ted to his miscarried daughter, Erin. This letter persisted through many drafts, but in the end, it made the story too much about Ted, and not enough about Erin. While the letter didn't end up in the final draft, either, it still hangs over the story, and it too will find its way out into the world eventually. Tilda once had a larger role in this one, appearing physically at the end, instead just being seen through the eyes of her daughters.

"No Sunshine in Hel" initially had a ton of possible song titles that might've been its name, a veritable mix-tape of its own, in fact. But in the end, I went with a line from the story itself instead. A song title felt too … Ted, and I was trying to distance Erin from her father. Kind of like she was.

So while this story had a lot of elements that didn't stick, it also fulfills one of my earliest desires for the collection: bookending the deep past of "All Cats Go to Valhalla" with the nebulous future set post-trilogy. I knew even before I proposed the collection to Ravenstone that I wanted to open the book with "All Cats Go to Valhalla" and so it made sense to me that the final story should rhyme with it, echo it, or call back to it in some way to tie the collection together. Loki? Check. Mara? Check. Drawn from moments in the trilogy proper? Check.

I think the mara would've played a role in this story regardless of whether "All Cats Go to Valhalla" had ever been written, though. She's the shadow cast over Erin's existence. Her nemesis in a way that Surtur was to Ted. Because I will likely never tire of telling stories in the Thunder Road world, I wanted to show something of its future. Comics have also made me love legacy characters who take up the role of mentor or parent.

I hoped I'd never see swastikas and Confederate flags being waved on Parliament Hill, but while I was revising this story, that's exactly what was happening. Writing with Norse mythology influences feels especially fraught these days. White supremacists have been co-opting Norse myth and other symbols for a long time, but are far more visible today than I ever recall. They also take silence as agreement with them. There's a reason why Tilda doesn't want them at her table in Nornheim, and why their only fate in *Thunder Road* is oblivion in the belly of a dragon. I tried to avoid any of the runes that they are actively using to promote their hate, but if I missed one, I apologize, and I'll continue to be vigilant. There are historians and academics, Ásatrú practitioners, and lovers of the sagas trying to push back against their hate, and not let these stories and symbols be poisoned. Since much of my work is full of musical references, here's another one from Dead Kennedys, "Nazi Punks Fuck Off."

Huge thanks to Melissa Morrow for interrogating the character of Erin deeply to draw out something unique to the post-*Too Far Gone* worldbuilding from me instead of taking the easy road of what might've been an adventure tale in Edmonton that could've just as easily featured Ted. We honed this story in almost every aspect. Writing spooky scenes in Hel were some of my favourite bits of writing *Tombstone Blues*, and my reading of the mara attack in that book allegedly gave one audience member nightmares. Which. Is. Awesome. (Also, sorry.) And that led to something I hadn't even considered yet: the specific dynamics of Hel, now Nornheim, and what the new management of the realm meant for Erin and her relationships with her family. As much as this story changed, Erin's struggle with the mara was one of the few elements that remained across all drafts of the story, and homing in on the best way to tell that story, and direct that conflict was the driving force behind this story.

I'd love to write more about Erin someday—and if you don't believe it, ask my editor; my first draft was twice as long as what got published.

There you have it. A secret eleventh story—or a twelfth story if you count the introduction, thirteen if you count the acknowledgments—a bit of unseen history. Any continuity errors you may find with the novels belong to Loki (yeah, that's the ticket). But congrats on being a careful reader. Hopefully that'll hold you until I have time to publish some new Thunder Road stories, and maybe we can do this all over again.

As always, thank you for reading.

Chadwick Ginther

Acknowledgements

I feel like the more of these acknowledgements I write, the longer they want to grow. So many folks have a hand in a book making it to press, and that was certainly the case with this one.

First off, thanks to team Ravenstone for getting another gorgeous book to press and believing in this series over the last ten years. Melissa Morrow's editorial helped me avoid too many "Norse Crisis Flowchart" repetitions of theme and content in structuring this collection, and making the new stories the best they could be while finding a path from story to story. David Jón Fuller contributed copy edits and Icelandic guidance, and is just generally a great guy. Many of the words unique to Thunder Road came from my consultations with David.

This collection also couldn't exist without the original editors of the stories: Samantha Beiko, Susan MacGregor, Kelsi Morris, Rhonda Parrish, Adam Petrash, Darren Ridgley, Kaitlyn Tremblay, and the venues that first published them: *On Spec*, Enfield & Wizenty, Exile Editions, Worldweaver Press, Tyche Books, thank you for believing in them. Clare C. Marshall made a kick-ass cover for my self-published collection *Wolf & Wing,* which included "Murder Mystery" and designed my convention banner. I love when working with friends can be a positive experience. Wayne Tefs was the editor on *Thunder Road* and *Tombstone Blues,* Michael Matheson editor on *Too Far Gone.* The series was definitely better for your efforts, and I hope those lessons made me a better writer for this book.

To the stories' first readers from across the years: LeeAnne Berkvens, Shen Braun, Karen Dudley, Mike Friesen, Frank Krivak, Chris Smith, thanks for putting some time in with them before they were ready for the world's eyes. A number of writers and professionals answered my questions about story collections during the early stages of assembling this book: Samantha Beiko, Suzanne Church, Sarah Johnson, Stacey Kondla, Derek Künsken, David Nickle, Robert Shearman, and Douglas Smith. Your guidance is appreciated. It was incredibly sweet of Kate Heartfield to mail my winner's envelope to me after she announced "All Cats Go to Valhalla" won the Aurora for best short story. David Fortier offered some Calgary directions for "Ballroom Blitz" and Lindsay Kitson and Timothy Gwyn were incredibly generous with checking and expanding the plane and piloting information in "Golden Goose." Any errors after their guidance are mine. Thanks also Leslie Van Zwol (and Lola!), Marie Bilodeau, and Bernadette

Doyle-Swereda for being good sports with your names and stories. Sandra Wickham has shared so many health and fitness tips (and a love of *Star Wars*) with me, and kept me writing when I didn't want to.

To my convention friends who shared stories and drinks before COVID-19, and gaming friends who shared adventures and dice (and drinks) in person and online, I miss you all. Friday night Forbidden Lands crew and Saturday afternoon Greyhawk, you've helped keep me going through the pandemic.

The Manitoba Arts Council has supported *Thunder Road* since its early days with a travel grant to Flin Flon and an emerging writer grant to complete *Thunder Road*, and a grant to complete *Too Far Gone*. The stories in this collection spun out from that early support, and it has always been appreciated. It's wonderful to have an organization helping uplift Manitoban artistic voices.

My heartfelt thanks to all the readers who nominated and voted for "All Cats Go to Valhalla" at the Aurora Awards. I never expected to be on that ballot, let alone win. Thanks also to all the fine authors I shared that ballot and TOC with, and the booksellers and librarians who have helped get these words into the hands of readers like you.

My parents and friends and family who believe in me, even when I don't.

Wendy, always Wendy.